FINDING PURPOSE

Book 1 of the Mylin Valley Series
by
Angela E. Powell

Let's Connect!

I love hearing from readers! The best way to tell me you've enjoyed my book is to leave a review or rating.

You can find my other books, my blog, or drop me a note on my website: www.angelaepowell.com.

Editing by Doreen Martens & Kelly Messier
Front cover image by 100Covers

Paperback ISBN 978-0-9991594-4-6
Hardback ISBN 978-0-9991594-5-3
Publisher Name: Angela E. Powell
Publisher Address:
PO Box 513
Huntsville, Utah 84317
www.angelaepowell.com

Dedication

I dedicate this book to my son, Israel. It is because of him, and the life he experienced before I became his mother, that my own journey into the study of neuroscience came about. If we hadn't become a family, this series very likely wouldn't exist.

Chapter 1

"That doesn't sound good," said Scott.

"No, it doesn't," said Heather as she watched Dad guide Ed Burton's horse trailer into the barn. The truck's diesel engine couldn't drown out the distressed whinnying, snorting, and stomping coming from inside the trailer. Considering that this horse had been in a terrible accident that took the life of his owner, she'd expected him to be easily spooked. But the high-pitched squeals and kicks that rattled the trailer spoke of something far worse.

"I think we better create a chute before we let him out," Heather said. "He's really worked up, and I don't want anyone injured. Zeke, you and Scott grab the fence panels from the ring outside. Let's move quick. I don't want him in there any longer than necessary."

Scott, Heather's older brother, and their fifteen-year-old cousin Zeke ran out to bring the panels into the barn, creating a short path to the horse trailer.

"Dad, can you get the door to the stall closed after Littlefoot is inside?"

"You betcha, sweetheart."

She peered around the side of the trailer to see if the driver, Ed Burton, planned to help them. His spectacled eyes met hers in the side mirror, and he lifted his arm from the open window in greeting. But he made no move to exit the vehicle or even turn off the engine. Once Littlefoot was secure, she and Ed would need to have a serious conversation.

She watched Littlefoot through the trailer's windows. His eyes were wild as he moved about in the small space. In her mind, she went over the steps needed to get him out: *Open the door, then the divider, then get out of the way, fast.* Another deep breath and she unbolted the door. The horse hadn't stopped kicking, and at the sight of the open door, his agitation increased. He attempted to rear up and kicked hard at the back of the trailer.

"Okay, boy, okay. You're all right." Heather spoke calmly but firmly and tried to make eye contact with him. She wouldn't approach the divider and release Littlefoot until she could do so safely. He kicked again, hard enough she wondered if he'd cracked his hooves. After another minute, he calmed down a little, seeming to understand that she wouldn't come any closer if he didn't. But he still shifted his weight from foot to foot and whinnied. Moving quickly, Heather unlatched the divider, turned, and ran out of the trailer, pulling the divider open as she went. She grabbed the fence panel and swung herself over to safety.

Littlefoot bolted from the trailer and reared up on his hind legs when he found himself penned in by the temporary fence panels inside the barn. He kicked, reared, and ran back and forth along the short route from the trailer to the stall.

"What do we now?" asked Zeke.

"You do nothing but watch and stay calm. Your mother would kill me if she found out I let you help with this," Heather said before swinging herself back over the fence panel and positioning herself between the trailer and the horse. She raised her arms and moved toward Littlefoot, speaking to him in a commanding voice. He paced and whinnied, but he'd calmed down a little and no longer kicked at everything. Littlefoot backed away from her, his head down. A couple of times he looked as though he might charge but then thought better of it. There was nowhere for him to go. Behind her, Heather heard the truck's engine rev. She glanced over her shoulder and saw the trailer pulling away.

"Scott, can you close the gap behind me?" Littlefoot's agitation increased again. He reared, snorted, and pawed at the ground.

Scott rushed to move a fence panel.

"Heather, get out of there," Dad said warningly.

"I've got this, Dad."

Littlefoot lowered his head. Heather waved her hands and

shouted, but the horse, seeing the daylight behind her, galloped toward his last chance at escape. Heather blocked him, waving her arms, shouting, and moving confidently toward him so he would know she intended to be the boss in this relationship. Littlefoot reared, shook his head, and stopped only a yard in front of her, pawing the ground. Heather didn't stop or hesitate, and the horse reluctantly began moving backward. As soon as his entire body was inside the stall, Dad swung the door closed. Heather followed the movement of the door with her step, keeping eye contact with the horse in case he made a rush toward the dwindling opening. Thankfully, he didn't, and Dad latched the door.

Heather immediately turned and jogged out of the barn hoping that Ed had parked outside. No luck. All that remained of him was a cloud of dust trailing down the driveway. She wondered if he'd even bothered to stop and latch the door on his trailer.

What had he omitted from his story? When Ed first called her, she'd done her research. She knew Littlefoot's owner had been killed when a semi crossed into oncoming traffic, striking the truck and trailer. The newspaper had reported on the accident, but the story had focused more on the humans involved and the traffic backup it caused. There wasn't anything in the article to suggest Littlefoot's injuries were severe. Obviously, he had unresolved trauma. She'd expected that. She hadn't suspected anything unusual when Ed wanted to send a scanned copy of the signed surrender papers over to her rather than deliver them in person. Most people preferred that method these days. But not helping with the delivery and taking off even before Littlefoot was secure? That screamed of something not right. It was possible he simply wanted to get rid of his dead neighbor's nuisance of a horse, but wouldn't the best method for accomplishing that be to help them?

Heather blew out a frustrated breath and walked back to the barn, where Dad, Scott, and Zeke stood watching Littlefoot from the gate of his stall.

Heather joined them, resting her arms on the top of the stall door, watching Littlefoot pace the confines of his new home.

"Do you really think you can fix him?" asked Zeke.

Littlefoot's eyes were dark brown pools of fear. Even though his body looked calmer now, the terror in his eyes hadn't disappeared. Her gut told her things were much worse than they looked on the surface, but she hoped his fear would lessen as he got used to his new home. After a while, she'd be able to assess the horse and his needs better.

"Yes, I do," she told Zeke, hoping she sounded more confident than she felt.

Dad sighed and raised his eyebrows. "I don't like the look of this one."

Heather attempted a smile. "Yeah, he'll be a challenge."

"It's not just that. He's dangerous. In a moment of panic, he'll charge."

"He's terrified and wanted to escape. In a few days he could be a totally different horse. And I'm always careful, Dad. Besides, you and Mom aren't far away if I need help."

"I can ask my mom if I can sleep here in the barn tonight and keep an eye on Littlefoot," Zeke offered.

Heather reached up and tousled Zeke's brown hair. He was almost taller than her now. "I think you and I both know your mom would never agree to that. You know how hard it was just talking her into letting you take riding lessons. I'm not sure she's going to be thrilled knowing you helped with this little operation, either."

Zeke rolled his eyes. "I didn't help that much. Just with the fencing."

"How's it going?" Mom's voice came from the front of the barn. Everyone turned in that direction.

"Mom, you should have seen it," said Scott, heading toward her.

"I don't know about that," said Dad, following Scott. "I suspect if you had seen it, you'd be piping mad right now. But we got him in the stall, and now Heather can work her magic."

Heather gave Littlefoot another long look before joining the rest of her family.

"I've never seen a horse so hell-bent on getting out of a trailer before," said Scott.

Mom's eyebrows shot up, and she folded her arms. "Sounds like quite an ordeal. No one got hurt?"

"Nah," said Scott, rubbing a hand through his wavy sand-colored hair. "Heather made sure we were all cool."

"Good. Anyone want a ride back to the house? Dinner's ready and everyone's waiting. I'm sure they'll be happy to hear the entire story, too. Zeke, your mom was pulling up as I headed over."

Scott gave Heather a playful shove. "Making us late for dinner because of a horse, just like when we were kids."

"Uh, excuse me? What about all the nights you were out doing stunts on your mountain bike?" she said climbing into the back of the truck with Scott and Zeke. Dad chose to ride in the cab with Mom.

"Hey, it's not my fault Mom and Dad wouldn't let me build my ramps closer to the house so I could hear when they yelled for me."

Mom glanced at them before climbing behind the wheel, grinned, and rolled her eyes. "You both had your fair share of delaying dinner while Harry Jr. was slaving in the kitchen, with Parker underfoot, driving him crazy."

Harry Jr., the oldest of her siblings and their dad's namesake, had found a passion for cooking at a young age. All four of them had been required to help with meals after they turned five, but Harry Jr. loved it so much he'd taken over most of that chore by the time he was in high school. As the baby of the family, Parker had idolized Harry Jr. and followed him around wherever he went, leaving Scott and Heather free to pursue their outdoor passions.

"Aunt Amy, do you think you can convince my mom to let me spend the night in the barn to keep an eye on Littlefoot?" Zeke asked through the open back window of the truck.

"Michelle is my baby sister, and I can talk her into a lot of things, but letting her precious son sleep in a dirty barn with a traumatized horse is not one of them. She's never been too comfortable with the riding lessons. I don't think she'd like this idea."

Zeke's shoulders sagged, and he nodded.

"Hey, my barn isn't dirty," Heather protested.

Everyone laughed.

"Hay is for horses," said Scott.

"Cows eat it too," Dad finished the old joke.

Back at the house they said goodbye to Zeke and Michelle before heading in to join the rest of the family around the dining room table. Grandpa Sam, their dad's uncle and adoptive father, sat at one end of the table. Dad took the seat at the other end. Parker, Heather, Scott, Harry Jr. and his wife, Lisa, filled the other seats.

"It's about time," said Parker. "I'm starving."

"Sorry, it was more challenging than I expected to get the new horse into his stall."

"Is this the horse that was in the accident?" asked Grandpa. Heather nodded.

"Sam, do you want to pray over our meal tonight?" asked Mom. "Oh, sure."

The hum of conversation ceased as Grandpa cleared his throat and said a prayer of thanks. Heather claimed a roll from the basket in front of her before passing the basket to Parker, who took a roll for himself and one for Grandpa.

"Harry told me a little about this horse," said Lisa. "Is the trauma from the accident all that's wrong with him?"

Heather shrugged as she let a spoonful of spaghetti plop onto her plate. "I thought so, but the way Mr. Burton acted tonight, I think I'm missing part of the story." She handed the bowl of spaghetti to Parker and took the salad bowl from Scott. "He took off before Littlefoot was secure, so I'm going to track him down and try to get the full story."

"That's too bad. Is there anything you can legally do if the owner doesn't give you all the details?" asked Harry Jr.

Heather shook her head. "It's pretty much the same as an animal shelter, except people can't just drop a horse on the doorstep and leave. I need *some* paperwork, but technically they're only required to give me basic information. If they choose to leave out details, there's nothing I can do except try to talk to them. But if Mr. Burton won't talk to me, and my gut is right about Littlefoot, I might be forced to put him down."

"Goodness, that must be so hard," Lisa said. "These horses have such unique experiences. I imagine figuring out how to help each one must be quite a challenge."

"Yeah, it can be. But it's so worth it after you've worked with a horse for a while and you see them gain confidence and trust. That's a good feeling."

"How's the fundraiser planning going?" asked Mom.

"Great! I've had so many people call and ask if they can have a booth that I've doubled the space I'm using, and I'm still having to turn people away. It's stressful, but I'm on track so far."

When Heather started the horse rescue four years ago, she'd come up with the idea for a fundraiser as a fun way to educate people about horses, find homes for the ones she rehabilitated, and bring in enough money to keep the rescue afloat for another year. The event itself was free to attend, but the vendors paid a fee to participate and were asked to consider donating items or services to be auctioned or raffled off, or donating a small portion of the proceeds they earned at the event to the rescue. So far, the fundraiser had kept her rescue going, but barely. Every rehabilitated horse Heather had presented at the fundraiser found a new home, though.

"Scott, are you okay?" asked Mom. Scott's leg had been bouncing nonstop.

"Yeah, fine. Why?"

"You're vibrating," said Heather.

"What?" Scott looked down at his legs. "Oh, sorry. It must be leftover adrenaline from helping unload Littlefoot and, uh, nerves over my upcoming race." His leg didn't stop.

Heather tilted her head and looked questioningly at him. The adrenaline junkie of the family who rode mountain bikes down steep, narrow mountain trails, skied black diamonds, and had jumped out of a perfectly good airplane, twice, just because it was fun—that guy got a rush from unloading Littlefoot? Doubt at Scott's explanation appeared on more than one face around the table.

Parker changed the subject. "I know it's three months off, but I was thinking we should have a birthday party for Grandpa. A big one, not a family meal like we usually do, but something special. I was thinking we could have it at The Gathering Place." Parker looked expectantly at Harry Jr. and Lisa.

The Gathering Place was their restaurant. They'd met and fallen in love while attending culinary school. When they got engaged, they'd debated about where to start their restaurant. Harry Jr. wanted to be close to his family, and Lisa wanted a thriving city. When they came for a visit, Lisa found that Ogden, Utah, satisfied her requirements for an urban setting. It was the closest city to the family homestead in the small town of Mylin Valley and only a thirty-minute drive away.

Harry and Lisa looked at each other. "We can make it work," said Harry.

"What do you think, Dad? Are you up for a big birthday party to celebrate your ninety-sixth birthday?" asked Harry Sr.

"Oh, boy," said Grandpa. "I haven't had a party for my birthday since I was in grade school. I suppose a party would be all right, just so long as it doesn't get too wild and you don't keep me out too late."

Everyone chuckled.

"Don't worry, Grandpa, we'll make it an early birthday party," said Parker.

Grandpa tugged on Parker's sleeve. "Don't let it interfere with your studies either, young man."

"I won't. I'm almost done with my bachelor's degree anyway. Finals are coming up in the next two weeks, and I'll only have one more class to take next semester and then I can graduate."

"Only one class? What will you do with all your free time?" joked Scott.

Parker rolled his eyes. In his last two years of high school, he'd done concurrent enrollment with the University in Ogden. After graduation two and half years ago, he'd immediately signed up for six college classes and had continued to take six courses each fall and spring semester and five in the summer. In the evenings he worked for Harry and Lisa part-time in exchange for room and board in their house in order to maintain his crazy school schedule.

Mom and Dad had set aside money for college for each of their kids, but so far Parker was the only one who'd taken advantage of the money. Harry Jr. had allowed them to pay for his first semester of culinary school, while he got settled, but insisted on paying his way from then on, and Scott had shown no interest in college.

Heather had always known she wanted to open a horse rescue ranch and didn't need a degree to train horses. She'd asked for ten acres of the family's forty-acre plot instead of the college money.

"Maybe you'll actually learn to live a little, loosen up. Or even find a girlfriend," Scott said to Parker.

"Scott, be nice," scolded Mom.

"Actually, I'll be busy looking for a place to live." He bit his lower lip and glanced down the table at their parents. "I have some news."

Everyone quieted and looked at him expectantly.

"I've gotten a job offer from a company in Washington State as an information security analyst. They get a lot of government and military contracts, so it's really high-security stuff. As soon as I graduate, they want me to start."

"That's wonderful news," said Mom, grinning.

"That is great news, son," said Dad.

"I hope you're not disappointed. I know you like having us all nearby.

"Oh, honey," Mom said. "We aren't disappointed. A little sad, maybe, but never disappointed." She got up from her seat and moved over to Parker to wrap her arms around him. Parker visibly relaxed. "I know you've always felt a little different because no one else in the family shares your passion for technology, but I promise, your father and I will always get you back home for a visit. Technology changes so fast, we can't keep up. We're going to need your help whenever we have to buy a new VCR or television."

Everyone laughed.

"Mom, hardly anyone even knows what a VCR is anymore," said Parker, shaking his head and grinning.

"See, you'll have to come home and keep us updated with all the new stuff." She kissed the top of his head before returning to her seat.

"That's cool, bro, congratulations," said Scott.

Parker's news seemed to dim Scott's adrenaline high, and he was quiet throughout the rest of dinner. Even his leg stopped shaking.

After dinner, Heather helped Scott clean up the dishes, then said goodbye to her other siblings before heading back out to her barn, which stood next to Grandpa's house. It used to be Grandpa's barn when the whole forty-acre plot belonged to him and Grandma Edna.

The story of how Grandpa Sam had come to be the patriarch of the Fletcher clan had always intrigued her. She remembered sitting cross-legged on the floor in her grandparents' house, listening to

Finding Purpose

Grandma Edna tell all kinds of stories about the old days.

Dad's mom had died while giving birth to him, and his father, Joe, couldn't raise a baby alone and continue working. So they moved in with Joe's brother, Sam, and his wife, Edna. The pair had married a few years after the Great Depression ended and were never able to have children of their own. They welcomed little Harry with open arms.

A couple of years later, Dad's father got sick and died. Grandpa Sam and Grandma Edna continued to care for their nephew, whom they legally adopted as their own son.

When Dad turned eighteen, Grandpa gave the land and the small herd of Jersey cows, which they bred and sold as milking cows, to him to take care of. Several years later, when Dad married Mom, they built their house a half mile down the road. Far enough to give each couple privacy, but close enough that they could care for the aging Sam and Edna when they needed to.

When Heather asked for the ten acres in trade for college money, they'd included Grandpa in the discussion and settled on the section around his house, and the old barn was part of it.

She'd had to make some minor repairs to the walls and roof, but the barn was the perfect size for her small operation, and she loved its history. It had two large doors on opposite sides and a wide-enough thruway to drive her truck through. The gambrel-style roof created a lot of space in the loft. She stored some feed and supplies there, but mostly it contained old boxes and keepsakes the family had stashed there over the years. Inside were seven stalls, five on the left wall and two centered on the right wall. Each stall could hold two horses if needed. In the empty corner at the front, right of the barn was a long workbench and storage for tools, and space where she stored items she didn't use often. Along the back wall, Grandpa used to have a desk and file cabinets. Heather enclosed that space and turned it into an office where she could work and take phone calls without the noise of the horses interfering. She enjoyed stopping in to visit with Grandpa for lunch several times a week whenever she happened to be working in the barn at that time.

As she walked, Parker passed her in a golf cart, with Grandpa in the passenger seat. They slowed down.

"Can you believe that sunset?" asked Grandpa.

"It's beautiful." The sun hovered just above the mountain peaks at the far end of the valley, shooting golden rays of light across the fields all around them and casting long shadows from the giant cottonwoods that Grandpa had planted long ago along the edges of the property, for privacy and as a wind break.

"Don't work yourself too hard, young lady," said Grandpa.

She smiled. "I won't." Heather waved as Parker sped the cart up.

Ever since Grandma Edna died last year, Parker had taken it on himself to return to the farm and stay with Grandpa on the weekends whenever he could.

Reaching the barn, Heather went out to the field and brought three of her ten horses into the barn and fed them: Queenie, an old, retired dun-colored mare and Heather's first rescue; One With Wind, a retired, all-black racehorse who had broken his leg and hadn't had it set correctly; and Sunstone, a golden Akhal-Teke, deemed unbreakable by the wealthy family who had purchased him for their young daughter.

Littlefoot still paced back and forth in his stall, and she wondered if he would settle down at all tonight. As she finished the chores in the barn, she noticed that One With Wind and Sunstone both appeared on edge and were eyeing Littlefoot carefully.

She considered letting them stay out in the field for the night, but Sunstone had a nasty habit of biting other horses who crowded her, and she didn't want to risk injury to them. And One With Wind, when left to his own devices, enjoyed jumping the fence at dusk and visiting the lady horses at a nearby farm.

"Sorry, guys, if you would behave better, I would trust you outside while Littlefoot gets used to being here, but you'll have to be good examples for him. Show him he's safe here and he can relax, okay?" She gave them each a nose scratch.

After she finished the inside chores, she filled the outside feeder and water troughs for the other six horses.

With the evening chores complete, she stood next to Littlefoot's stall and observed him for a long time. She'd been around horses her whole life and had seen a lot of negative behaviors trained out of them. She'd seen traumatized horses learn to trust again. So far, her rescue horses hadn't been too difficult. But Littlefoot was different; he might have issues she'd never seen or dealt with before. He would be a challenge.

"We have to help each other out, Littlefoot. What do you say? Will you work with me, buddy?"

The horse, paying no attention to her, kept pacing.

Chapter 2

Littlefoot hadn't touched his feed. He wasn't pacing, but he frequently shifted his weight from one side to the other and fear still swam in his eyes.

"Ready for me to look him over?" Mom asked as she entered the barn, pulling her light brown hair, that was beginning to gray at the temples, into a ponytail. Mom was a veterinarian specializing in farm animals, and she had given her expert care to every animal the Fletchers ever owned.

"Yes. He's calmer today, but he still looks nervous. I don't know if you'll be able to do a physical." Heather knew Mom had a busy schedule, and she always felt a little guilty asking her to examine one of her horses, even though she insisted it wasn't a problem. It was a major blessing to have free veterinarian services, especially with a start-up horse rescue ranch that had brought in little money so far.

The fundraiser helped, of course, but so far it had only covered feed expenses for the year. The horses grazed in the summer, and she was able to get some hay cut from their own fields or bought cheaply from neighbors. For the most part, she didn't have financial worries, but to grow the rescue and keep it going, she would have to bring in more income. She intended to make that happen before it was more of a need, and she hoped a good chunk of that income would come through rehabilitating and selling horses, as well as the riding lessons she offered. Her reputation in the community as a professional horse whisperer contributed to the success she was building.

The older horses, like Queenie, lived out the rest of their days in Heather's care and were used in riding lessons. The younger ones she trained, worked with, and sold to new homes. In the last four years, she'd sold five of her horses. The others had behaviors that took more time and care to train out of them.

One With Wind was getting close, thanks in part to Zeke's lessons and his desire to try barrel racing—if he could talk his mother into it. But it would still be a while before Heather felt One With Wind was ready to find a new home. She would have two more horses, Brazen Fire and Lady, ready by the fundraiser, and she hoped interested buyers would show up to see them in action.

Mom entered Littlefoot's stall, followed closely by Heather. The opening of the stall door caught Littlefoot's attention. He reared slightly and shook his head. The two paused, waiting to see if he would calm down or become more agitated.

"He definitely doesn't enjoy being in an enclosed space," said Mom. "Have you considered putting him outside in his own section of pasture?"

"I'm considering it, but I'm not quite ready to test him yet. I want him to know this is home now before I let him out, in case he's a jumper."

Mom nodded, moving closer to the horse and reaching out her hand, which held an apple slice, for Littlefoot's inspection. He flinched, tried to back away, and snorted. Mom lowered her arm. "I think you're right about the physical examination. From just looking at him, he looks healthy. I don't see any issues with his legs, his stance; his skin and coat look good. Nose is clear, mouth is clean, eyes are clear. As far as checking his hooves for damage, I'd say as long as he isn't showing any signs of pain, we can leave it for now and let him settle in. Has he eaten anything?"

"No, not yet."

"Well, monitor that. It's probably just stress. What about water?"

"I haven't measured yet, but just from looking, I'd say he's had little to no water so far."

Mom nodded again. "If he's not at least drinking by tonight, I'll be concerned."

"Okay. Thanks, Mom."

They left the stall. As she latched the door, she heard Mom sigh. "What?" asked Heather.

"I know you're already thinking about this, and I don't want to discourage you, but I'm worried about this one. The look in his eyes ... I just ... he might not be fixable."

"I know. My gut tells me that, too, but I can't put him down based on first impressions. I have to be certain there's nothing I can do first."

Mom smiled and held her arms out toward Heather, who stepped into her hug. "I know you do, and I love the way you trust yourself, and your skills, to know when you can and can't help a horse. But as a veterinarian who's seen a lot of different animals, I have to tell you, I'm uncertain anyone can fix a horse this badly damaged. But as your mother, I support your decision to try, and I know Littlefoot is in the best hands he could be."

"Thanks."

"All right, I have to go."

Heather lingered near the stall after Mom left, watching Littlefoot and thinking about Mom's warning. She'd heard of horses that couldn't be fixed but had never encountered one. Grandpa had told her most horses could be trained out of their misbehaviors and overcome their trauma, but they had to have a human willing to have patience and kindness and stick it out with them. If a horse could find a human like that, then that human wasn't likely to run into an unfixable horse.

Maybe Littlefoot would be the horse to test that theory.

After finishing her chores, Heather moved Queenie into the stall next to Littlefoot. She hoped that Queenie being the calm mare she was, would encourage Littlefoot to relax and make friends. She watched the two horses for a few minutes as Queenie curiously lifted her head over the wall between the two stalls and sniffed with interest at Littlefoot. Littlefoot made no movement toward Queenie, though, and Heather left them, heading to the back of the barn to work in her office.

She had vendors to follow up with for the upcoming fundraiser, and she wanted to see if she could get ahold of Ed Burton and get more information on Littlefoot. He had to know more than he'd told her. Getting the full story could help her decide how best to help the traumatized horse.

She flipped through the file on her desk containing Littlefoot's paperwork and found Ed's phone number. Picking up the phone, she dialed the number, flipping through the pages on her desk while the phone rang and scanning the information Ed had provided her. She got his voicemail and breathed a sigh of relief that it was actually his phone number and not a fake.

"Hi, Ed. This is Heather Fletcher with the Fletcher Horse Rescue. I had some follow-up questions for you regarding Littlefoot. Could you please call me back as soon as you can?" She left her cell phone number and hung up.

She closed the file and put it into the cabinet beside her desk before sitting down in her old swivel chair. The 1960s era chair had once lived in front of Grandma Edna's desk. After she passed away, Grandpa had offered it to her. The leather and springs were still in great condition, and it squeaked only a little when it moved.

She grabbed a notebook from the corner of her desk and flipped back a few pages, trailing her finger down the list of to-do items she'd written for the fundraiser. About half of them had been marked off so far, but with only a month left before the event, there was still a lot to do.

After making several calls and sending about a dozen emails, she got up, stretched, and walked out to see if Queenie and Littlefoot had made any progress in the introductions.

Littlefoot hadn't budged from his corner, and it appeared Queenie had given up for the time being. She was quietly munching her hay. Heather walked up to Queenie's stall and scratched her nose. "Thanks for trying girl."

She heard the phone in her office ring and jogged back to answer it.

"Fletcher Horse Rescue, how may I help you?"

"Hi, my name is Derek Rodenbaum. I saw an ad online for your horse ranch, and I was wondering if you offer riding lessons for kids."

"Yes. I typically do one-hour lessons on Fridays and Saturdays, and right now my time slots are pretty open. I currently have one student on Fridays and one on Saturdays." She flipped open her notebook and made a note to add riding lessons to her website and advertisements, something she'd been meaning to do but kept forgetting about. She'd started offering riding lessons when she opened the rescue as another way to bring in some money, but until now she'd relied on word-of-mouth customers. Currently she had only one paying student and Zeke, who did chores for her in exchange for his lessons. It was time to do something more.

"Oh, great. My wife and I have been looking into lessons for our son, Xavier. He's eight and has some special needs. I don't know if that will be a problem or not," said Derek.

She sat back in her chair. "I haven't ever taught special-needs kids, but ... what are his needs?" She wondered if that was a stupid question. She'd worked with special-needs horses, but never people, so she really didn't know what to ask.

"He has fetal alcohol spectrum disorder, or FASD. His birth mother drank alcohol while she was pregnant with him, and it caused some damage to his brain. He has trouble in school and struggles with emotional regulation. There have been studies done on kids who struggle with emotional regulation—not specifically FASD kids, but ones with similar issues—and it seems that working with horses helped those kids immensely. I realize you aren't a therapy ranch, but we can't afford the cost of a therapy ranch, and we're hoping that simple horse-riding lessons will help him in the same way, at least a little."

Emotional regulation. She wasn't one hundred percent certain what that meant, but she'd heard stories of autistic children having meltdowns from being overstimulated. Maybe it was similar to that. The only horse she had that might be able to handle something like that would be Queenie.

"Well, I'd like to do some research and maybe meet Xavier before I commit to giving him lessons. I just want to make sure I have the right horse for him to train with first."

"Oh, of course. Whatever you need. I could send you some articles on FASD if you'd like. It's kind of hard to explain and separate from other mental health issues. You're the fifth place I've called and the first to even consider our request, so I really appreciate this. Even if you can't teach our son, this really means a lot. Thank you."

"No problem. What time would work best to meet Xavier?" The man's desperate enthusiasm made her nervous, and she hoped she wouldn't be adding to their disappointment by turning them down later rather than saying no immediately like the other four people he'd called. But, as with Littlefoot, she couldn't say no based on first impressions. She'd talk to them and make a decision after learning more.

"Things work more smoothly with Xavier if we introduce him to new people in a place he's familiar with. New people and unfamiliar places all at once can be tricky. Would it be super inconvenient to have you come down to Ogden to meet him? There is a little neighborhood park. I think it's about halfway from your ranch to our house, judging by this online map."

For other riding students, this would be an odd request, but from the tone of his voice, it didn't sound as though he was trying to scam her or take advantage of her. It was a public place after all. She checked her schedule. She needed to pick up a few things in town for the fundraiser, so she could run her errands the same day she met Xavier. "Sure, that should be fine."

"Awesome. My wife usually takes him to that park every Tuesday afternoon. Would tomorrow work for you, or is that too soon?"

She checked the calendar on her computer. Nothing set in stone for tomorrow. "No, I think tomorrow afternoon should be fine. I actually have some errands I have to run in town this week anyway, so that will work out perfectly."

She heard Derek sigh on the other end of the line. "Thank you so much. I can't tell you how much I appreciate this. We've been looking for something for Xavier to do so my wife, Jan, can have a bit of a break while I'm at work. Sorry. I know this may not work out, and it's totally fine if it doesn't. It's just, after reading all the research, I'm really hoping we can find a place to teach him to ride so we can see if it will help him. I'm babbling now, sorry."

"Oh, it's okay. I'm looking forward to meeting Xavier. Let me give you my email address so you can send me those articles."

"Oh, right. Okay, I'm ready."

She gave him the email, verified the address for the park and the time to meet one more time, and hung up.

For the next hour, she did her own research on FASD and answered calls from people involved in the fundraiser. It was disappointing how little information she found on Xavier's diagnosis. From what she could tell, a person who had FASD could have a whole range of problems and health issues, and there was no guarantee that one person with FASD would have the same issues as another person who had FASD. The only way she would know for sure what Xavier struggled with would be to meet him and have a more in-depth conversation with his parents. She wanted to be prepared for her meeting with them—to know what questions to ask and the best way to ask them so she didn't accidentally offend them by saying the wrong thing.

One thing was for sure: if she agreed to teach this kid how to ride a horse, she would be out of her element in every way. She might not understand Xavier's situation yet, but she already had a pretty good idea of why the other places Derek had called had flat-out refused. She was starting to feel bad about getting his hopes up, because she wasn't sure she could handle it. Especially right now, with the fundraiser looming.

Forwarding her desk phone to her cell phone, she got up from her seat, stuck her cell into the back pocket of her jeans, and walked out to check on Littlefoot. He was pacing again.

She sighed, leaned on the door to his stall, and reached her fingers toward him. He snorted and moved to the corner farthest from her.

"You're safe here, Littlefoot. I promise. I'm going to do everything I can to help you realize that."

She watched him for a few more minutes before heading outside to work with her other horses.

Chapter 3

Driving to Ogden wasn't often on Heather's to-do list. Her family had developed relationships with families all over Mylin Valley, and they could obtain most of what they needed, in terms of farm supplies and food for the animals, locally without making the thirty-minute trek to town.

What she disliked about the trip was not the length of the drive but that it required her to travel down a narrow, winding canyon road. Normally she wasn't a nervous driver, and driving in the summer was much easier than in the winter, but the sheer rock walls on each side made her feel claustrophobic. It didn't help that she heard stories of horrific car accidents on this stretch of road more often than she actually traveled it. So every time she took the canyon road, she turned off the radio, clutched the steering wheel extra tight, and focused on every car she saw to make sure it wasn't crossing the yellow line in the center of the road—something that happened all too often on the sharp, blind curves.

At the bottom, she relaxed her shoulders and glanced at the address on the scrap of paper sitting on the dashboard. At the first light, she turned left and searched for the correct street number.

She was still nervous about this meeting. Even after reading the articles Derek had sent her, she still didn't understand what FASD was or what it looked like. They called it an *invisible disease*. Did that mean he would look and act normal for the most part? In her research she'd learned it wasn't the only "invisible" disability. People could also hide diagnoses such as learning disabilities, ADHD, and depression by pretending to be okay, finding ways to minimize their exposure to the things they struggled with, or by using medication to minimize their effects.

That left her feeling uncertain and full of questions. According to one article, FASD could look like ADHD, learning disabilities, bipolar disorder, and a host of other issues, which didn't mean much to her because she wasn't familiar with the outward signs of many of those illnesses either. She hoped that seeing Xavier in person and talking more with his parents would shed enough light on the situation to help her decide. Besides, she'd also researched horse therapy and found several articles showing evidence that kids with special needs did see a decrease in emotional outbursts with prolonged exposure to horses and other animals.

She turned right and saw a small playground up ahead on the left. The park was tiny, filling half a city block.

She pulled into a designated parking spot and turned off her truck, glancing at the handful of people scattered around the park. Four or five kids ran around the playground. A couple sat on a park bench near the swing set, and an older woman sat at a picnic table, knitting, on the other side of the playground.

Climbing out of the truck, she headed toward the couple. The man on the bench glanced her way, then stood and headed toward her, smiling. He looked out of place in the park with his business-casual black slacks and a tucked-in pale blue shirt. Heather realized he'd probably come straight from work and might even be here on his lunch break. He greeted her with a small wave and stretched out his hand. "Heather Fletcher?"

She nodded and took the offered hand.

"Derek. My wife, Jan, is over there."

Heather followed him back to the bench, where he introduced Jan to her. Jan was thin and pale, with blond hair that hung straight and limp on her shoulders. She had on a plain purple T-shirt and jeans and reminded Heather of someone recovering from a long illness. She gave Heather a brief smile that didn't reach her eyes and then focused her attention back on the playground.

"Have a seat," said Derek. "I can stand."

"Thank you," said Heather, taking the seat next to Jan.

"Xavier is over on the swings." Jan nodded her head toward the small two-seat swing set.

Heather followed Jan's gaze and saw a small boy sitting on a swing, motionless. He looked much younger than eight. The little boy watched two other children with curiosity. His jeans had large holes in both knees, and the wrinkled red-and-yellow-striped shirt looked much too big for his slight frame. His shoes were worn-out and frayed, and his dark brown hair was a tangled mess.

She glanced at Derek's outfit and wondered if the family was struggling financially. She recalled Derek's comment on the phone about being unable to afford the therapy ranch. However, Jan's and Derek's clothes looked clean and in good condition. She thought about Zeke, who, when he was younger, used to be really rough on his clothes, especially jeans. It drove Aunt Michelle crazy. Maybe Xavier was the same.

One of the other children approached Xavier and announced, "I claim you free of this horrible dungeon. You are free to go."

Xavier jumped off the swing and ran to the monkey bars, where he scrambled up and across, making whooping noises. Then he joined the other child and whispered conspiratorially to her, pointing at the boy who'd released him from the dungeon every so often. Whatever he'd said, the little girl apparently thought it was a great idea, because she nodded and giggled a lot. So far, he looked like a completely normal kid.

"So, I read the articles you sent me last night and, I have to admit, I'm still a little lost. I understand what FASD is, but everything I've read seems to indicate that it can present differently in every child who has it."

Derek nodded and sighed. "It can. As the name implies, there's a spectrum of symptoms and levels of disability, the worst case being FAS, or fetal alcohol syndrome. Xavier doesn't have it that bad, and although he has some facial features that come with FASD, they are pretty mild. The main things we've seen in Xavier so far are poor coordination, hyperactive behavior, difficulty staying attentive to one thing for very long, and a hard time learning math. His growth milestones are also delayed. The coordination we've been working on. He has therapy for that once a week, and he is improving. It's just a slow process. He takes medication to help with hyperactivity, but we don't want a zombie child, so it only helps a little. We haven't found a solution for the other issues yet. It's summer break right now, so we aren't seeing as many behavior issues as we normally do during the school year, but in a few weeks, as we get ready to transition back to school, we'll see an uptick in those negative behaviors. Change is hard, learning is hard, the school environment is hard with all its distractions, and all that combined comes out in negative behaviors."

Heather nodded. "What do those negative behaviors look like?"

Derek looked at Jan, who sat up straight and stretched her back. "It could be anything from arguing, to shutting down and not speaking, to worse things like hitting, kicking, name calling, or having a full-on tantrum or meltdown."

Heather considered that for a moment. Having a tantrum near or on a fifteen-hundred-pound animal would not be good. "Are there certain things that trigger each of those? For instance, would a fear of heights cause a tantrum, or sudden movements?"

Derek shrugged. "Honestly, we haven't really found a pattern to the behaviors. Sometimes he doesn't sleep well, and that will always make him grumpy and hard to work with, but it doesn't always mean he'll end up having a meltdown. Sometimes he just shuts down and falls asleep. If he gets angry, it's usually because he's overwhelmed by something, but even then, sometimes being angry will result in him saying angry words or calling us names, and that's the end of it. But sometimes it's like he just doesn't want to stop. Like, somehow the anger makes him feel good, so he just keeps stoking that anger until he explodes into a tantrum."

"Sometimes the tantrums come because a teacher, an aide, or a friend of ours doesn't know how to read him, and they don't back off and give him space," added Jan.

Heather looked at the little boy running around the playground. The way Derek and Jan described him made him sound like a live bomb, ready to explode any second and without warning. It would be risky to have him around horses, especially horses rescued from less-than-ideal circumstances. But the research on horse therapy was undeniable. And Queenie was calm. In the three and half years she'd had Queenie, nothing had ever startled her. She was a wise old mare, unsurprised by anything the world threw her way. If Heather trained

Xavier to ride, Queenie would definitely be the horse for the job. But could *she* do it? Could she learn to understand this little boy well enough to teach him without hitting the explode button? And would riding lessons really be as beneficial as horse therapy? She didn't even know what was involved in horse therapy. Did the horses need special training? She realized her research had been incomplete.

"So, if he gets upset or shows signs of being frustrated, it's best to give him a few minutes alone to calm down?"

Jan nodded.

She was certain she could manage that. After all, she had to be aware of any sudden changes in a horse's behavior, and whenever she gave riding lessons, she had to learn the temperament of each student in order to pair them with the right horse. Teaching Xavier shouldn't be too much different in that regard, although she suspected breaks would be frequent interrupters, and if he needed a break while he was on a horse, that could be tricky but not impossible.

"If you don't mind me asking, how did you find out he had FASD? From what I read, it sounds like it's difficult to diagnose." The question wouldn't help her decide, but it was something she'd pondered. Did Jan drink while she was pregnant? She was pretty sure she'd heard it wasn't good to drink while pregnant, but having never been pregnant, she really didn't know exactly what the guidelines were.

"It can be," said Derek, shifting his weight from one foot to the other. "We adopted Xavier from my niece."

Heather suddenly remembered Derek saying something about Xavier's *birth mother* on the phone. She felt heat rise to her cheeks and hoped her face wasn't turning red. Poor Jan. She wondered how often people judged Jan for the issues Xavier had because they didn't know about his adoption. She was ashamed of herself for making the assumption.

"My niece was fifteen when she found out she was pregnant. She didn't want the baby, but her parents—my brother and sister-in-law—wouldn't sign the consent for her to get an abortion, which is required in Idaho, where they live. As an act of rebellion, she did everything the doctor told her not to do, including drinking alcohol."

Heather's stomach twisted with disgust.

"When my brother told me about my niece's condition and what she was doing to herself, we looked into a private adoption," Derek continued. "We'd tried to have children of our own but had been unsuccessful. We had already been talking about adopting, so we approached my brother and sister-in-law about it. They warned us she wasn't taking care of herself or the baby, but they said we were welcome to talk to her and share our plan with her. We drove out for a weekend visit and explained to my niece that we wanted to adopt her baby. She was angry but seemed willing, because she had no intention of keeping him after she gave birth. We asked her to come live with us until Xavier was born. Explained it would give her time away from her parents, time to think about what she wanted to do after the baby was born, if she wanted to move back to Idaho, or whatever. We told her if she lived with us, she had to take care of herself and the baby. We told her to think about it, and before we left the following day, she agreed to our plan. When she went into labor, we told the doctor about her habits during the early days of her pregnancy, and my niece admitted it as well. For the next three years we went to a specialized developmental pediatrician who monitored his growth and milestones and she determined he does in fact have FASD. That's how we got the diagnosis."

"Wow, I'm sure that was a lot for you two, and Xavier. Is your niece still in Utah, or did she move back to Idaho?"

"She moved back. We worked to restore her relationship with her parents while she was with us, and she agreed to move back and finish school. I think she also wanted to move back because she didn't want to see us raising her son. She hasn't contacted us since. I know she's in college now and living in her own apartment, so she's doing okay for herself."

"That's good, at least. I hope I'm not prying too much. I'm just not familiar with any of these invisible disabilities and I want to understand." Heather glanced at Jan, who didn't acknowledge her words. Jan continued to stare at Xavier on the playground, her arms hugging her middle and her lips in a thin, tight line.

"No, not at all," Derek responded. "We prefer it when people want to understand. So many people judge us at first sight. They just think we're negligent parents and let our kid run wild with no discipline. If they only knew the truth, they'd realize we are actually pretty strict. We have to keep things consistent, otherwise life would be much more difficult than it already is."

"So, he likes routine and structure?" Riding lessons were always structured and full of routine, so no problem there, either.

"Yes and no," said Derek. "It's good for him. He does better when there is structure and consistency, but he also likes to test those boundaries a lot. He keeps us on our toes, that's for sure."

Heather smiled. "It sounds like it." She could handle a little boundary testing. It was important for the safety of horse, rider, and teacher that boundaries be enforced, and she wasn't afraid to be the enforcer of those boundaries.

"Let me call him over so you can meet him. He's been playing for a good hour now, so he could probably use a break," Derek said.

Jan reached into an oversized bag sitting at her feet and pulled out a bright orange water bottle.

"Xavier," Derek called, cupping a hand to his mouth.

Xavier glanced at his dad but didn't even hesitate in his step as he ran after the two kids he was playing with.

"Hey, bud, come get a drink of water and catch your breath for a moment."

Xavier glanced again in their direction, hesitated, looked at the two kids, then back at his parents, as if trying to decide if he wanted to stop playing long enough to obey his dad's summons.

"Come on, bud, just for a minute or two, and then you can go play again," said Derek.

Xavier's shoulders slumped and he made his way over, eyeing Heather as he approached. He continued to stare at her with wide brown eyes as he eagerly sucked water out of the bottle Jan offered him. He breathed heavily through his nose as he drank, his face red from his exertions and covered in a sheen of sweat and dirt. When he finished, he pointed a finger in Heather's face. "Who's that?" he asked, keeping his eyes on her instead of looking at either of his parents.

Jan grabbed Xavier's finger. "Xavier, remember it's not polite to put your fingers so close to someone's face. Especially when they're covered in dirt."

His face contorted and he whined, pulling his hand from his mom's. "Who is she?" he asked again, sounding irritated.

"This is Heather Fletcher," said Derek.

"Hello, Xavier. It's nice to meet you," said Heather, smiling at him.

He narrowed his eyes. "How do you know my name?"

"Oh, your dad told me your name."

Xavier glanced at his dad, then back to Heather. "What are you doing here?" The question was blunt, and although he didn't seem well versed in social etiquette, he wasn't being rude. He seemed curious about this stranger sitting with his parents.

"I'm talking to your parents about my horses."

"You have horses? How many?"

Heather nodded. "I have ten horses right now."

Xavier's eyes got even wider. "That's a lot."

Heather laughed. "It is a lot for one person to take care of, but I have some help."

"Xavier, remember how Dad and I talked to you about taking some horse riding lessons?" asked Jan.

Xavier shook his head and sucked on his water bottle again.

"Oh, come on, bud, remember all those videos we showed you of kids riding horses?" asked Derek.

Xavier nodded.

"Remember how you said you wanted to ride on a horse like those kids in the videos?"

Another nod.

"Well, we're talking with Heather here to see if she or someone she knows can teach you how to ride a horse."

Xavier shoved his water bottle into Jan's hands.

"Can I go back and play now?"

Derek sighed. "Sure, bud."

Xavier took off, yelling like Tarzan.

"So what do you think? Is he going to be too much for you to handle?" asked Jan in a tone that suggested she knew Heather would say no.

Heather considered. She could see Xavier had a lot of energy that might be difficult to corral and direct. Having an emotionally volatile kid near horses was risky. But she felt confident she had a horse she could use to teach him, and she was used to reading people and horses, so she thought she could manage his changeable moods. She also knew she could offer routine and structure.

The only worrying thing was the possibility of him having a tantrum on the horse. She was sure Queenie could handle it, but she didn't want to see the horse or the child get injured. On the other hand, he was small enough that she could pull him off the horse if needed, or catch him if he wriggled himself off mid tantrum.

The fundraiser was an issue. She wouldn't have a lot of free time right now to do any extra research, but from what she'd already learned, there wasn't much research left to do—at least not for his diagnosis. She wanted to look more into horse therapy and what that consisted of. But she lived and breathed horses. Whatever she might learn from researching horse therapy, she was confident she could find a way to implement it with Xavier.

"I'm willing to try it," Heather said.

Derek grinned, and Jan looked at her in surprise.

"I can't guarantee I'll succeed, but I have a horse I think would work well with him. I'll probably have more questions as we get going. I'd want one of you to be there for the first several lessons, just to be safe, but I'm willing to try."

"Thank you," said Derek, who looked as though he could barely contain his excitement.

Jan looked less enthusiastic but also thanked her.

Heather excused herself after they discussed cost and set a time for Xavier's first lesson on the upcoming Friday afternoon. As she climbed back into her truck and headed off to run her errands, she felt a mixture of excitement and uncertainty. Her decision to teach this boy could end up helping him—and by extension his parents—in ways she couldn't even imagine. On the other hand, it could end up an epic failure, one that resulted in Xavier, herself, or both of them getting badly injured. She shook her head. There was no point in allowing herself to think that way. She'd learn to read Xavier as well as she read her other students and her horses. If she wanted to succeed, it was her only option.

Chapter 4

A couple days later, Heather walked slowly to the barn, watching the rays of sun peek out over the mountains to her left. She loved this time of day, listening to nature wake up before human noises drowned out the soft breeze and birdsong. She unlocked the barn and entered the dark building, listening to the soft nickers from the horses who stayed there during the night as she felt for the light switch and flipped it on.

Her gaze landed on Littlefoot's stall, and she smiled. He stood in the middle of his stall, and Queenie lifted her head over the wall between them in greeting. He stayed just out of reach, but he was moving in the right direction and wasn't pacing. She walked over to check his food and water, and the positive feeling vanished. He still wasn't eating. However, he was drinking water. Mom had said not to worry if he ate little during the first week, as long as he drank water. But how could she not worry? Her intuition told her he didn't have much of a chance. If he didn't eat, things would only get worse. Neither she nor Mom could do a physical examination, so if he got sick, she wouldn't have a chance to even try to help him get over the trauma he'd endured.

Heading to the workbench opposite her office, she grabbed a pair of gloves, a shovel, and the wheelbarrow that sat propped against the wall in the back corner and got to work cleaning the stalls. She saved Queenie's and Littlefoot's stalls for last. Until now, she'd kept Littlefoot in his stall while she cleaned, working slowly so he would get used to her presence near him. He always reared, snorted, and pawed the ground, dancing around the stall to keep as far away from her as he could, but he hadn't completely panicked and the stall was big enough that she could stay out of harm's way. Today, she thought she might try Mom's suggestion of releasing him out into the barn while she cleaned to see what would happen.

First, she let Queenie out and took care of her stall. When she finished, she considered for a moment. Littlefoot seemed more accepting of Queenie now. Maybe more space would be an incentive to make friends. Of course, when she'd let him out of the trailer, he'd kicked and reared. She didn't want to risk Queenie getting hurt. Besides, she needed Queenie rested and healthy for Xavier's lesson tomorrow. She led Queenie back into her stall and closed the door.

"I know I usually let you outside right about now, but I want you here until I'm done with Littlefoot, okay?" Maybe simply having her calm presence in the barn would be enough.

Queenie snorted, and Heather scratched her nose and slipped her a carrot.

"That's my girl."

She slid over to Littlefoot's stall door and observed him for a moment. "Are you ready for this, big guy? Let's get you out of here, okay?"

Littlefoot didn't respond until Heather unlatched the door. His ears flicked and his attention focused on the door, as it always did. Heather swung the door open, staying behind it in case he kicked, and waited. For a moment he didn't move. Then all at once, he seemed to realize he could leave. He ran out the open door, kicking behind him. He galloped to one end of the barn, reared up, kicked, turned, and ran the length of the barn before repeating the process on the other side.

Heather realized he was looking for a way out of the barn. It was time to calm him down. She left her place behind the stall door and stood in the middle of the barn, raising her hands and shouting as she walked toward Littlefoot. He reared up at her. Heather gave him a firm "No" and stood her ground. When his feet were on the ground again, he nodded his head quickly several times before backing away from her.

"Hey, I see your frustration, Littlefoot. I do. But we've got to take baby steps here, and you've got to understand I'm the boss. You can't act that way. You're going to hurt yourself or the other horses, or break something. We can't have it, dude. Sorry."

Littlefoot snorted, pawed at the ground, and eyed her. But he wasn't kicking and running anymore. She observed him for another minute before going to clean his stall. He trotted past her and began pacing in the larger space. Occasionally she glanced in his direction while she worked. He wasn't panicky anymore but also didn't try to make friends with Queenie as she'd hoped.

When she was done, she made her way toward him to guide him back into his stall. When she got within six feet of him, he jerked his head up and trotted to the other side of the barn. She got in his way before he passed his stall, and he turned and trotted back to the other barn door.

Heather sighed. "You're going to be stubborn about this, aren't you?" She thought for a moment. She would be here all day, working on the fundraiser. If she let him out into the ring, she could monitor him. It might be worth it to test him.

She left Littlefoot where he was and made her way out back to move the fence panels so his only option when she opened the barn door would be to go into the ring. Once he was inside, she could move the two panels on either side of the barn door quickly to close the circle again.

After she accomplished that, she swung one side of the barn door open and clicked her tongue to get Littlefoot's attention. At the sight of the open door, he galloped toward it. As soon as he passed her, she lifted the fence panel closest to her and moved it back into the circle, then ran to move the other panel into place before he charged it. He reared up when he reached the other side of the ring and was now following the fence all the way around. When he reached Heather, he stopped, cut through the middle of the ring, and stood on the opposite side.

Heather leaned on the fence, catching her breath. After a moment of rest, she grabbed a bale of hay and tossed it into the feeder inside the ring. After that, she unwound the hose attached to the barn and filled the water trough. To her surprise, Littlefoot trotted over and munched eagerly on the hay.

"Well, okay, then," she said, crossing her arms. "I guess you have a fear of all small spaces, not just trailers. That's something I can work with."

Heading back to the barn, she freed Queenie from her stall and took her out to the pasture. As she walked alongside Queenie, the door on the other end of the barn opened. Heather glanced over her shoulder and saw Parker enter. Despite growing up on the ranch, Parker never really looked like he belonged in the barn. His dark brown hair was always meticulously combed, his typical collared shirts and creased slacks were always clean and free of wrinkles, and his hands didn't have the rough quality of Heather's and their parents'.

"Hey." She nodded at him and patted Queenie's rump as she exited the barn.

Parker joined her and pointed at Littlefoot as she shut off the water and wound up the hose again. "That's the new horse?"

"Yep."

"How's he doing?"

Heather shrugged. "Hard to say. This is the first time I've let him outside. He hasn't been eating inside, and now he's eating with gusto. I'm still trying to figure him out a little. If the guy who brought him here would return my calls, I could be farther along, but so far, I've heard nothing and I've been leaving messages every day this week."

"That sucks."

"Yeah. So what are you doing here? Aren't you supposed to be at school?" asked Heather.

"My Tuesday and Thursday classes are all in the afternoon, so on Monday, Wednesday, and Friday I've been staying the night at Grandpa's and having breakfast with him before heading to town."

"That's sweet. And Harry and Lisa are okay with it? I know you've been helping them at the restaurant."

"I only help in the evenings three days a week, and I head here after work, so mornings are fine," he said testily.

"Oh, sorry, I wasn't suggesting you're doing anything wrong. I was just thinking that you're really stretching yourself, helping them out, helping Grandpa, and all the work you have to do with six classes. You've really been there for Grandpa since Grandma died."

A pained expression crossed his face. "Everyone thinks I'm going to burn myself out, but I'm fine. I just want to spend as much time with Grandpa as I can before I start this job. After I move, I don't know when I'll be able to come visit."

Her heart twinged at his words. Ever since Grandma died last year, they'd all done their best to make sure Grandpa wasn't too lonely or sad. Out of all of them, Parker was most likely to overthink things and worry. She needed to get him out of his funk.

She placed her hands on her hips. "What about me?"

"What?"

"I know you're going to miss Grandpa, but what about me? Your one and only sister?"

Parker grinned. "Why would I miss you, Rainbow Unicorn?"

Heather's mouth gaped in mock offense. "You wouldn't miss me at all? Not even a little bit?"

He rolled his eyes, still grinning.

She pulled Parker into a headlock and tousled his hair. When they were four and seven, respectively, Heather had declared she was going to have a rainbow-colored unicorn when she grew up and would get very angry whenever anyone told her it wasn't possible or that unicorns didn't exist. But when Parker pointed at her and said "Rainbow Unicorn," she hadn't been able to escape the nickname for a good year. Occasionally, her brothers still pulled it out in social situations to embarrass her.

She released him and he combed his fingers through his short brown hair, the same dark shade they'd both inherited from their father.

"Seriously, though, Parker, I know it's going to be hard for you to move away from Grandpa. You've always been so close, and I'm glad you've been able to spend so much time with him. And next semester, when you only have one class, you'll have even more time with him."

"Yeah, when this semester is over, I want to come stay with him during the break. I haven't asked Harry and Lisa yet, but I hope they'll be okay with it."

She smiled. "I'm sure they'll understand."

"Also, since I'm supposed to move a couple of months after Grandpa's birthday, I want to have a special celebration for him this year."

"Yeah, you mentioned that at dinner the other night. I don't have a lot of extra time to help plan until after the fundraiser, but after that's over, whatever you need, you can count on me."

"Thanks. I better get going. I don't want to be late for class."

Heather nodded.

"Hey," she said.

Parker stopped and turned back to face her.

"You don't need to worry about Grandpa. If something happens, I know you'll drop everything and come home. Mom, Dad, and I are all close by. He'll be in good hands."

He rubbed the back of his neck. "Yeah, I know. But Dad's always out in the fields, Mom is all over the valley, and you're so busy all the time and only have lunch with him occasionally. He really needs more attention than that."

"Hey now, I admit I haven't been as attentive to Grandpa lately, but you know Mom checks in every time she's nearby and Dad rides over all the time. We all know how much time you spend with him, but you can't really think we wouldn't fill that gap after you leave?"

Parker shrugged. "I guess you're right. I better get going."

Heather nodded and watched him leave. She knew he had no reason to worry so much about Grandpa, but his concern about how little time the rest of them spent with Grandpa nagged at her. Parker made more time for him than any of them, even with his hectic schedule. With her working so close to Grandpa's house, she could check in with him more than she did. She decided she'd go visit with him this afternoon, after she finished up a few things.

She went out back to see if she could work with Littlefoot now that he was out in the open. Entering the paddock, she noted that he seemed content for the first time since he'd arrived. Maybe there was hope after all.

She clicked her tongue and Littlefoot turned his head and looked at her.

"Hey, boy."

She stopped. Littlefoot's ears had gone back, and he lowered his head. There was a challenge in his eyes, and she didn't like it.

"What, you think you're in charge now?"

Littlefoot snorted but didn't move. Heather stepped closer.

He pawed the ground and shook his head. She made a noise to

correct this aggressive behavior and took another step forward.

Then Littlefoot charged her. She yelled and waved her arms, but he didn't stop. At the last second, she twisted out of his path. He came to a stop on the other side of the enclosed space, content once more.

Heather shook her head and rested her hands on her knees, catching her breath. Dad had been mostly correct. Littlefoot had charged, only it wasn't out of panic—which made him much more dangerous.

She exited the paddock and headed to her office to leave Ed Burton another voice mail. This time, she didn't bother to hide the frustration in her voice. If he didn't call her back soon, she was going to drive to his house and hunt him down until she got the information she needed.

Chapter 5

"You're doing really great with those agility exercises," Heather told Zeke as he dismounted One With Wind.

"Thanks. I still feel slow, though."

Heather shook her head. "Your speed improves every week, I'm certain. But because you want to compete next year, I'll start tracking your time more carefully."

"Okay. Do you really think One With Wind will be ready for adoption by next spring?" asked Zeke, undoing the saddle strap and lifting the saddle off.

"Yeah, I do." Zeke wanted to use One With Wind to compete next year. He was the only horse Zeke had trained on. The idea of competing with an unfamiliar horse made him nervous. Plus, his mom wasn't likely to let him compete with any other horse. It had taken her long enough to come to terms with him riding at all.

"We might be able to work something out, at least for next summer. But keep in mind, he may not do well in competitions. His leg may be better, but as you know, it wasn't set right. And I'm only letting you train with him because he's still a racehorse at heart and needs the exercise."

"I know. Mom is just being impossible over this."

Heather patted his back. "More experience, especially with different horses, can only help you when you can take part in races. Make sure you tell Michelle that."

Zeke rolled his eyes. "Like she'll listen."

Heather gave him a sympathetic look and shook her head. She saw a silver minivan making its way up the driveway. Nervous butterflies flitted in her stomach, as they had been doing randomly all day whenever she thought about her first lesson with Xavier. "She will eventually. And you'll always be welcome to practice on my horses. They may not all be racehorses, but if you can train the younger ones, that's just another way to practice your skills."

"Like Sunstone?"

Heather nodded. "Exactly. After you give One With Wind his rubdown, will you let him back out into the pasture?"

"Sure."

Heather waved at the van as it pulled to a stop near the barn. A moment later, Jan and Xavier climbed out.

"Xavier, I know you're excited, but no running," Jan warned.

Xavier jumped up and down in place, pointing at One With Wind. "I want to go see the horse. I want to go ride the horsey!"

Heather stepped up to them and knelt in front of Xavier. "Hi, Xavier. Do you remember me?"

Xavier's eyes met hers for a split second before they returned to the horse behind her. He stopped jumping but vibrated with excitement. "I want to ride the horse."

"I can see you're very excited to ride, Xavier, but we won't be riding the horse that's behind me. Do you want to follow me into the barn to see the horse you get to ride?"

Xavier's brows knitted together, and he pointed at One With Wind. "I want to ride that horse."

"One With Wind is a really excitable horse, and he doesn't behave very well with brand-new riders," said Heather. "But I bet Zeke would let you meet One With Wind while I go get the horse you're going to use. Would you like that?"

Xavier nodded his head vigorously.

"Okay, but you have to promise me to stay right next to Zeke and do exactly what he tells you."

Xavier agreed.

She stood and turned to Zeke, who'd been watching them. "Do you mind introducing Xavier to One With Wind and explain to him what you're doing?"

"Sure," Zeke said and waved Xavier over.

"I'll go get the other horse and be right back," Heather told Jan, who followed Xavier over to One With Wind.

Jan gave her a tight smile and nodded. Her hair, pulled back in a ponytail, made the sharp angles of her face look more severe. The woman just did *not* look happy.

Heather jogged into the barn, grabbed a harness, and went into Queenie's stall to put it on. Once she finished, she let Queenie out of her stall and out front to the empty paddock she kept specifically for riding lessons.

Exiting the barn, she saw Xavier resting his head against One With Wind's side, his head barely higher than the underside of the horse's belly. He giggled every time the horse took in a breath and made his head move.

Heather tied Queenie's lead to one of the fence panels and called out to Xavier, who turned toward her. "This is the horse you get to ride today. Want to come over and meet her?"

Xavier shook his head. "I want to ride this horse. He's fun. That horse is stupid."

"Xavier, we don't call animals or people stupid. Please apologize to Miss Heather," said Jan.

Xavier crossed his arms and grunted out "mm-mm" while shaking his head.

Zeke resumed rubbing down One With Wind, occasionally glancing nervously at the changeable eight-year-old standing a few feet from him.

Heather wasn't exactly sure what to do. She'd had other people call her horses names before. But she never made a big deal about it. If the name caller was a student, she simply taught them why the horse wasn't those things. But because this was their first day, she decided to let Jan handle it and simply observe and learn. She glanced at Zeke, who met her gaze. He pointed at One With Wind, and then the barn. She looked back at the mother and son, who seemed to be in a standoff, Xavier staring defiantly at Jan and Jan staring right back, her arms folded, eyebrows raised. This could take a while. She nodded at Zeke, who looked relieved at the opportunity to remove himself from the situation.

"Xavier, if you don't listen, we're going to go home and you won't get to ride any horse. Now please apologize to Miss Heather."

The young boy stomped his foot, sending up a small cloud of dust that settled on his worn sneakers.

Zeke led One With Wind into the barn, moving much faster than he normally did. Usually Zeke took his time with the horse, knowing his mom would be there any second to take him home. He liked to drag out the rubdown and the putting away of saddle and blanket, just to spend more time here.

As the horse passed them, Xavier made a high-pitched whining noise, stomped his foot again, swatted his hand at Jan as though he wanted to hit her, and then took off after One With Wind.

Realizing he was heading right for One With Wind's back end, Heather ran after him. At the same moment, Jan gasped, lunged forward, and grabbed his arm.

Xavier let out a piercing scream that stopped Heather in her tracks. He fought against Jan, twisting around, slapping at her hand and wrist, and attempting to kick her. When that failed to get his mother to release him, he tried to bite her, but Jan maneuvered him so he wasn't able to. She never spoke to Xavier, just held him away from her.

Xavier, on the other hand, hurled hateful words toward his mother, some of which Heather understood, including a few swear words, and others she didn't that sounded more like slurred growls than anything in the English language.

Finally, Jan let go of Xavier but kept her hands in front of her in a defensive position. Xavier ran into the barn calling, "Horsey, horsey, horsey!"

Jan took a deep breath and closed her eyes.

A better understanding of why Jan always looked so tired and worn-out crept into Heather's consciousness. "I'll go keep an eye on him," she said softly.

Jan nodded.

Heather glanced down at her hands as she entered the barn. They trembled slightly. What would she do if Xavier started destroying things inside the barn? Or directed his violence toward her? What could she do? These were things she should probably inquire about.

He'd made his way to the opposite side of the barn and was leaning his head out and looking around. She didn't want to risk him climbing into the ring just to the right of the barn, where Littlefoot was, so she picked up her pace to catch up with him.

He stepped outside, eying Littlefoot, who stood at his feeder munching on hay. But Xavier didn't approach Littlefoot or the ring. Instead, he turned his attention to the wide-open fields on the left. One With Wind was much too far away to be any concern for Heather. She wondered where Zeke had disappeared to; she didn't see him out back. Looking back at the barn, she saw him peering around the barn door near her office. She smiled and turned her focus back to Xavier, who was whining again. "I want to ride the horse." He looked at her expectantly, as though she would do his bidding, no questions asked.

"We need to talk about the rules before we can ride a horse," said Heather, glancing at her watch. "So you need to come back with me and listen, or we'll have to wait until next week to see if you can ride the horse then."

He stared at her, his mouth ajar. "Can I ride that horse next week?" he asked, pointing behind him.

Heather shook her head. "If you want to ride one of my horses, it has to be Queenie."

He frowned, crossed his arms, and stomped his foot.

She remembered the advice about giving him a break if he was frustrated, so she left him where he was and leaned against the side of the barn.

Jan joined her a few minutes later. It took ten minutes before he relaxed the angry expression on his face.

Heather looked at Jan, eyebrows raised in a question.

Jan nodded. "It should be okay to engage him now."

"Xavier, are you ready to hear the rules?"

He glared at her and walked past her into the barn. Once inside, he turned to look at her. "Well, are you coming?" he demanded.

Heather raised her eyebrows at his attitude. She was seriously second-guessing her decision to help him at that moment but followed, reminding herself that today was a new, and probably overwhelming experience for him. Derek had said his negative behaviors could be caused by him being overwhelmed.

Back in front of the barn, she squatted down beside Xavier, who stood a few feet from Queenie, grimacing at her.

"Hey. You got pretty mad when your mom grabbed you, didn't you?"

Xavier nodded.

"Do you understand why she grabbed you?"

Xavier jutted his chin out and gave her a side glare.

"Do you?" Heather asked again, her irritation rising with every stubborn glance he gave her. Maybe it was growing up in the country, but no one she knew had ever been allowed to treat adults with this kind of disrespect.

He shook his head, swinging it as far as it would go one way and then the other. It had to hurt his neck.

He's not like other kids she reminded herself. He learned differently, which meant the set of consequences she was accustomed to probably wouldn't work with Xavier.

"How heavy do you think this horse is?" She could tell her question caught him off guard, because he dropped his arms to his sides and looked from her to the horse and back again before he shrugged.

"Really heavy. At least twenty-five of you. If a short kid like you were to go stand behind Queenie here and she kicked, guess what part of your body her foot would connect with?"

He looked down at his body and pointed to his stomach.

"Nope." Heather pointed at his neck. "Her foot would connect with either your chest or your head and you would have to go to the hospital because you would have broken bones."

His mouth dropped open.

"So, why do you think your mom grabbed you?" asked Heather.

He looked over his shoulder at Jan, who stood a couple of yards away, listening to their conversation, her arms crossed. She didn't know if this was the correct way to handle this situation, but she would not allow any student of hers to get away with mean words or violent behavior toward her or their parents. She wanted to make that clear from the start.

He didn't answer for several minutes, and she repeated the question.

He scowled at her. "She didn't want me to get kicked."

"That's right, because you were running after One With Wind, and if she hadn't grabbed you, you would have been in the danger zone. So was your mom trying to protect you?"

He nodded.

"Was it nice of you to say all those mean things to her?"

He shook his head.

"Do you think it was nice of you to hit her, kick her, and to try biting her?"

Another shake of the head, this one more slight.

"Do you think there's something you should say to your mom for acting that way?"

He looked back at Jan again, but didn't say anything.

Heather cleared her throat and Xavier glanced up at her. She nodded her head in Jan's direction. "What do you need to say?"

He sighed, then slowly turned and, without getting closer to her, said, "Sorry, Mommy."

Jan gave him a tight-lipped smile that didn't reach her eyes. "Thank you for apologizing."

Xavier turned back to Heather. "Can I ride the horse now?"

"We need to talk about some other rules first," she said, standing up and crossing her arms.

Xavier clenched his fists and kicked at the dirt, sending up a cloud of dust. Then he took off toward the barn again. He sat down next to the open door and buried his head in his hands.

"I'm sorry," Jan said. "It's easy for him to get stuck on one idea, and it's hard for him to let go of it. And when he gets frustrated, it takes a while for him to settle. Once he's upset, it's easy to set him off again."

Heather waved her off. "I wasn't certain what to do when he went after you like that, or how to handle it. He seemed pretty calm in the barn, though, so I figured I would at least try to get him to apologize to you."

"You're doing really well with him," said Jan. "The way you spoke to him. Your voice sounded calm but firm, and you asked good questions, which got his mind off the horse."

Heather looked at Jan, surprised by the compliment. She'd acted on instinct, said what her parents had said to her and her brothers growing up, and tried to keep her temper in check. And the whole time she'd felt self-conscious, as though she was doing it all wrong, being too hard on a kid who might not understand what he'd done wrong.

"It's hard to be patient when he says the things he does, I know," Jan added. "And it probably doesn't seem like it, but he listened to your questions and responded. That's pretty huge. It could be the honeymoon stage, but still, it's a positive thing."

The way Jan's shoulders hunched, the way she hugged herself, and the fact that Heather hadn't once seen a genuine smile from her made it hard for Heather to believe the woman. The words felt hollow, almost as though she knew they were the right things to say, but she herself didn't believe them to be true. Did Jan always look so closed-off and disapproving, or was she just not really on board with Derek's horse riding idea?

"What do you mean by 'honeymoon stage'?"

"Whenever he meets someone new or finds himself in a new situation, he does a better job of minding his manners. It's when he gets comfortable with the new person or situation that the behaviors escalate. With Xavier, the honeymoon phase typically lasts about a month, but it's unusual for him to show any violence in the honeymoon phase, so I'm a little perplexed by that."

Heather nodded, thinking. It couldn't be easy living with a child who got angry so easily. In fact, she couldn't even imagine how two parents could handle what she'd witnessed today all day, every day.

She remembered the day at the park. Xavier had seemed normal, mostly. So maybe this wasn't a constant, everyday occurrence. But even if Xavier had episodes like this once every couple of days, or once a week, it would still be a lot to handle.

"If we get to a point where we can trust him in my care without you or Derek here, what should I do if he gets violent with me, the way he did with you just now?"

Jan stared at Xavier, her expression unchanging, and for a moment, Heather thought she might ignore her.

"His therapist taught us something called a therapy hold, which prevents him from being able to harm himself or anyone else. We could probably teach it to you, but out here, it might be best to just let

him be, as long as he's not in any danger. And if he is in danger ..."
She shrugged. "Do what you would do with any other student to get
him out of harm's way, I guess. I'll talk it over with Derek and see
what he thinks."

Heather nodded and glanced at her watch. Today's lesson was
nearly over. Clearly she had a lot more to learn about how to teach
Xavier than she thought. But she couldn't expect everything to go
smoothly at the start. Things would get better.

Xavier still sat on the ground, with his head buried in his arms.

"Hey, Xavier. We're running out of time, so if you don't want to
go over the rules right now, we'll just have to go over them next week
before you can ride Queenie."

He didn't even lift his head in acknowledgment.

"I guess I'll just tell your mom the rules and let her feed Queenie
some treats," shouted Heather.

Xavier's head popped up, but he said nothing and made no move
to get up. So Heather began telling Jan the rules, making sure she
spoke loud enough that he would hear what she said. It was a trick
that had always worked on Parker when he was little. Maybe it would
work on Xavier too.

"Okay, Jan, first, we can't stand behind the horses or crawl under
them."

Jan gave an exaggerated nod to show she understood the rule.

"The next rule is we can't run and goof off around the horses.
They might get scared and kick or run away, or they might get excited
and kick or chase us."

Another nod from Jan.

Heather lowered her voice to a normal volume and said, "We only
have about twenty minutes left, so obviously he won't get to ride
today. Do you think if he comes over here, he'll be able to tell me
those two rules I mentioned?"

Jan bobbed her head from side to side, uncertain. "Probably."

"If he comes over here, we'll go over those two rules and he can
show me how well he can stand next to the horse. I'll let him feed
Queenie a few apple slices, and next week we can go over more rules
and try to get him up on the horse."

"That sounds good," said Jan.

Raising her voice again so Xavier could hear, she invited Jan to follow her. "I have some delicious apple slices in my pocket for Queenie. She loves apples."

Jan followed her over to Queenie and Heather handed her an apple slice, making sure Xavier saw the exchange.

"Hold your hand out flat, and Queenie will do the rest."

Jan did as instructed, and Queenie scooped up the apple slice with her lips.

Xavier got up and raced over, but Heather put up a hand to stop him. "What's the rule about running around horses?"

He slowed to a fast walk. "Don't run around the horses."

"Right. And what is the other rule I said to your mom?"

Xavier reached them and stared at the apple slices in Heather's hand. "Um ... don't run around the horses?"

"You already said that one. What is the other rule?" asked Heather.

"Um ... don't crawl under them?" he asked, pinching his bottom lip with his fingers.

"Good. Where else shouldn't we stand?" asked Heather.

"Behind them?"

Heather smiled. "Exactly." She held out an apple slice to Xavier. He beamed and held his hands open.

"Now, when you feed the horse, you want to keep your hand flat so Queenie doesn't accidentally nibble on your fingers instead of the apple, okay?"

Xavier nodded, and Heather let the apple slice fall into his hands. He placed it on his open palm and held it up, holding his wrist with his other hand. "Like this?"

"Yep, just like that. Now put it in front of her nose and she'll pick it up."

He walked around Jan to stand in front of Queenie, still stretching out the hand with the apple slice and holding his wrist with the other.

Queenie went for the piece of apple, and as her lips scooped the fruit between her teeth, Xavier's body wriggled and he contorted his face.

Heather laughed, but pressed her lips together to stop herself. She didn't want to appear rude. "Does that feel weird?" she asked.

Xavier wiped his hands on his jeans. "Yeah. I don't like that."

"Well, you don't have to give her any more if you don't want to. Do you want to show me where it's safe to stand near a horse?"

Xavier shrugged his shoulders.

"Do you want me to show you?"

He nodded.

Heather showed where it was safest to stand near a horse and then had him walk around the horse, showing her he understood what she'd told him.

"Good job. Our lesson is over now, but I'll see you next week," said Heather.

"Will I get to ride Queenie next week?"

"I don't know. We'll have to see how well you can listen next week. We still have a few more rules to learn. If you can learn those rules, then you can go for a ride on Queenie next week, okay?"

He nodded, turned away from her, and headed toward their van.

"Thank you," said Jan.

"Sure. See you next week."

As she watched them climb into the van and drive off, she rolled her shoulders and stretched her arms. She'd assumed this first lesson would be awkward, but it had been harder than she'd expected. What would she do if he got angry while he was on the horse? She sighed, released Queenie from the fence, and walked her back into the barn, trying to shake off the unease twisting around in her gut. It was eerily similar to the feeling she had whenever she checked on Littlefoot. Complete inadequacy.

Chapter 6

Mucking out stalls, feeding animals, and doing health checks were a daily routine, but on Sundays, when the ranch hands had the morning off, Heather and Dad worked together to get his cattle and her horses taken care of so they wouldn't be late for church.

Heather had been helping Dad like this since long before she had her own animals to care for. Of course, when she was a little girl, he had forced Scott and Harry Jr. to get up and help before school, but as she got older, she got up willingly to help, and, just as Harry Jr. had taken over the cooking, she'd taken over the farm chores with Dad. Once she was old enough to complete most of the tasks without help, Dad stopped waking the boys, and father and daughter would go out into the dark morning to work, talk, and enjoy a thermos of hot chocolate, which later became a thermos of coffee.

When she started the horse rescue, their mornings together dwindled to three days a week, until she had more horses than she could handle and they came up with this new Sunday morning routine. Each week they switched off whose animals were attended to first, as well as who made the thermos of coffee. This morning, Heather made the coffee.

By the time they finished with Dad's cattle and moved on to Heather's horses, the bright morning sun had given them a splendid show as it rose above the mountains. Now they were moving horses out to pasture so they could clean the stalls.

"I see Littlefoot is outside. Is he doing okay out there?" asked Dad.

"He's eating, so that's good. But he's more aggressive than he was in the barn," she said, releasing Queenie into the pasture.

"I take it you haven't gotten hold of the neighbor who took him in and brought him to you?" After he released One With Wind, they walked back into the barn together, grabbing shovels, gloves, and wheelbarrows.

"Not yet. I'm going to have to track him down in person, because phone messages aren't getting me anywhere."

Dad nodded and rolled a wheelbarrow into one stall and started working. Heather did the same in another stall, and for a time they worked in silence.

"You're awfully quiet this morning," said Dad as they brought their wheelbarrows back from the compost pile. "Usually you talk my ears off with all you're doing and all your plans. Is everything okay?"

"Sorry. I have a new riding student. Friday was his first lesson, and I feel like it didn't go very well. He has special needs. After talking with his parents about his needs, I thought I understood what to expect, but it was harder than I thought it would be. My confidence is a bit shaken, and I've just been processing it all. We didn't even get through the rules of being around horses. That part usually takes five minutes."

Dad frowned. "When did this happen? I don't remember you mentioning anything about this new student before now."

"Yeah, sorry. I've been so busy with getting the fundraiser ready, I've barely had time to breathe. Derek, the boy's dad, called me this past Monday and explained their situation to me. I met with them in town on Tuesday since I had to run errands for the fundraiser. I met Xavier and asked his parents questions. I did a bunch of research Monday night and Tuesday morning so I'd have questions to ask, and I felt pretty confident I could help Xavier learn to ride. But he was all over the place on Friday. He wanted to ride One With Wind, and no matter what I tried, I couldn't get him to focus on anything else until the last twenty minutes."

"His parents didn't stick around to help?"

"Oh, his mom, Jan, was there, and she helped. But even she couldn't get him to focus on meeting the horse I wanted him ride, which was Queenie. He got pretty upset over it, called his mom names, tried hitting her." She shook her head. "Jan told me he sometimes gets stuck on an idea and he takes a while to move on. She also complimented me and said I handled the situation well." Heather blew out a breath. "It doesn't make sense, though."

"What doesn't?" Dad leaned on his shovel.

"She told me I did a great job, but I didn't do anything I wouldn't have done with any other kid. What I mean is, I didn't know I was doing anything. All I did was try to distract him from One With Wind so I could actually teach him something, and it wasn't a success, at least not in the way I'm used to looking at things. I want to help this kid if I can, but if I did anything on Friday that was actually helpful, then it all feels a little upside-down and backward."

"Well, I'm sure they'd understand if you changed your mind."

"I haven't changed my mind. It just wasn't what I expected."

Dad nodded. "You have a lot on your plate already, and the first lesson was harder than you expected. Are you sure you have the time and energy to devote to this kid right now?"

"Yeah, I mean, the fundraiser is taking a lot of my time, but that will be over in three weeks."

Dad sighed. "He sounds like a handful. Maybe too much of a handful. If you're so busy you hardly have time to breathe, can you really devote time and attention to this new student?"

Dad might be a third-generation farmer, with his leathery skin and thin, wiry frame, but he'd always been a worrier when it came to his kids. That's probably where Parker got it from, Heather thought. She couldn't put her finger on it, but this seemed a little different from his usual worry over a decision she'd made.

"It was only one lesson, and now I have a better idea of what to expect. He's only eight, and his disability makes him act younger. And now that I know what to expect, I can be better prepared. Quitting now would be the same as giving up on Littlefoot as soon as we got him out of the trailer."

Dad raised his eyebrows. "Like your mother has?"

Heather's cheeks flushed. "That's not what I mean. Mom wouldn't have put him down then, either. She would have given him a week at least."

"Do you think her opinion will have changed by this afternoon, which will mark a week?"

Heather shook her head, feeling deflated. "So you're convinced he's a lost cause, too?"

"I think if you weren't in the business of rescuing horses, then yes, it would make sense to put the horse down, but if it had been my horse, I wouldn't have brought him to a rescue ranch. I would have taken care of the issue myself. But because Littlefoot was brought to you and you are in the business of rescuing horses, it makes sense to see what you can do for him. I trust you with that decision. Right now, there's no harm to you or him, and this isn't your first rodeo with making the choice to put an animal down."

She nodded.

"The same isn't true with this boy," Dad continued. "Kid like that? This could be asking for trouble, serious trouble. Anyway, I don't want to see you putting yourself in the same position with him, where you push yourself, possibly too much, to get a result that might not happen."

Heather wiped her hand across her face, pushing the wisps of hair that had come loose from her braid during chores, and tucked them behind her ear. His words stung. Did he think she was being irresponsible with Littlefoot and wasting her time on lost causes?

"Thanks, Dad. I don't think that will happen, but I will keep it in mind."

"I hope so. Now let's get these chores finished up before your mom comes out here and scolds us for being late for breakfast."

When they arrived at church, they gave their usual greetings, caught up with friends, and enjoyed coffee and pastries before finding a row of chairs long enough for the Fletcher family. Since it was a rural small-town church, most people wore jeans and boots, which was just fine with Heather. She hated wearing dresses. Most of the farmers and ranchers who attended the church wore their good cowboy hats, Dad and Grandpa included. The older women always dressed up, many of them donning fancy hats.

Harry and Lisa attended a different church down in Ogden and only came to the little church in Mylin Valley for special occasions.

Scott usually joined them, though for the past couple of months, he'd been AWOL. But Parker and Grandpa Sam were there, and the five of them nearly filled a row near the front, saving a seat for Scott in case he showed up.

The worship service was upbeat and lively for the first two songs, and people swayed, clapped, and raised their arms as they sang. The final two songs of the service were slower, more worshipful.

Heather tried to put aside her stress over the upcoming fundraiser, the disappointment over her lesson with Xavier, and the pang she felt from Dad's words that morning. She tried to focus on the words of each song, thanking God for his faithfulness, his kindness, and his goodness, and considered how blessed she was to live in such a loving family, where they all cared so deeply for one another. She knew Dad had said what he had out of love and concern for her. Maybe she *was* taking on too much.

When the worship songs ended, the announcements were given and the offering taken up. Pastor Richard Barker took his place on the stage behind the wooden lectern, which was carved to look like a tree trunk with vines growing up and around it. He leaned over it, resting his arms on the slanted top, and looked out at his congregation with a frown behind his gray and white beard.

"How many of you are aware that relationships with people are important?" he asked in his deep voice.

A few hands went up, including Heather's. Several people nodded.

"How many of you know *why* our relationships with people are important?"

No one responded.

"That's not a rhetorical question. If you know, shout it out. No need to be shy—we're all family here."

"Connection," came an answer from the back.

"Good one," said Pastor Barker.

"So we aren't lonely," said someone else.

"Yep." Pastor Barker nodded. "Anyone else?"

Heather thought about how close she and her family were. Although it stung to have Dad point out a potential flaw in her, she knew it was because he loved her and didn't want her to get hurt or burned-out. She needed his advice and encouragement. "We learn and grow together," she heard herself say.

"Excellent," said Pastor Barker. "Today, and in the coming weeks, I want us all to better understand why God created us to need relationships with other human beings. And I'm going to show you, using the Bible, of course, but I'm also going to share some interesting information that science has discovered about why we need relationships and why, as much as we like to think dogs are our best friends, a dog as our only companion will leave us feeling lonely and unsatisfied." He licked his thumb and turned a page in his notes.

"Science has discovered our brains are wired for joy. Think of all those Bible verses that tell us to be joyful. Proverbs 17:22: 'A joyful heart is good medicine, but a crushed spirit dries up the bones.' Philippians 4:4: 'Rejoice in the Lord always. Again I say rejoice.' First Thessalonians 5:16: 'Rejoice always.' Galatians 5:22: 'The fruits of the spirit are love, joy, peace, patience, kindness, goodness, faithfulness.' Note that several of these verses tell us to rejoice or have joy all the time. Do you have joy all the time? And what is joy?" He stroked his beard.

"It's not happiness. We don't have to be happy all the time. Joy is internal; happiness is external. I like the way one man said it: 'Joy is the smile we cannot help but share.' Don't you just love that?" He paused, looking around the room. "Joy means someone is glad to be with us. Who are you glad to be with? And why are you glad to be with them? What is it about people we like that makes us like being around them?" He chuckled and his eyes slowly scanned the room before returning to his notes.

"Listen to this. Neuroscientists have discovered that, when we're babies, our brains are shaped by our joyful interactions with those around us. Isn't that something? It is during our first year of life that we develop a foundation of joy, and that foundation helps us attach to people, influences our identity, how we think about ourselves, how we view ourselves and our relationships, throughout the rest of our lives. Without a strong foundation of joy as infants, other emotions will fill that place.

"A baby who experiences more fear than joy will become a person who struggles with anxiety later in life. This is what science has discovered about how our brains work, because all of our emotions come from the brain. I don't know about you, but this is fascinating information."

Heather nodded her head and looked around the room. Several other heads were nodding as well, but she also saw a few annoyed expressions.

"Now, you might think having joy all the time sounds impossible in a situation where a baby didn't get the joy they needed to build a good foundation. You might be asking, 'How can God expect us to have joy all the time if we don't have any control over how much joy we receive as infants?' Good question. There are things you can do now, no matter your age, to grow your capacity for joy. In biblical terms, it's pretty easy—you renew your mind to God's way of thinking by being in a relationship with him and reading his word. Easy to say, not so easy to do, right?"

There were chuckles around the room.

"Science is giving us some help in this area, too. I'm going to spend several weeks, maybe even months, digging into this, but for right now I want to focus on relationships. Our relationships with people are important. Our joy foundation is built from our relationship with our parents and caregivers.

"We have a tiny little spot in our brains called the thalamus. It's where we learn to attach to people, and it's the first area of our brain to develop when we're babies. The thing is, we don't form attachments or friendships, or any kind of real, meaningful relationship, with platitudes. We don't form attachments by being irritated with people, either. A baby knows they are loved because Mom and Dad still love that baby, no matter how many diaper blowouts happen or how many times they get thrown up on, right?"

Laughter rose throughout the room.

"As adults we develop real relationships with people when we choose to keep loving them even after they lash out at us, after a disagreement, or we learn something about the other person we might not like very much. We love them through the hard stuff. You spouses out there know what I mean. After the honeymoon, you start to find out some things about your spouse."

More laughter.

"If we see someone once or twice a week and say, 'Hi, how are ya?' and 'I'm fine,' and go about your business, those relationships aren't worth much. No, I'm talking about the relationships where you hang all your dirty laundry out on the line and people still love you and want to be around you. They want to see you get all that dirty laundry cleaned up. It's about doing life together. Being in the trenches with one another.

"Our relationships with one another are so important. God designed us to need one another. To function at our very best, we need to receive love from other people, and give it. We need to give and receive joy and peace from others as well. So how do we do that? Well, we're going to talk about that next week."

Heather gathered her things and pushed her way through a small crowd of older church members heading toward the front platform. Most were frowning. She stopped, waiting for the rest of her family, and watched the group surround Pastor Barker. Something he said today must have made them unhappy. She couldn't imagine what; she'd found the whole thing fascinating. Her family joined her, and they made their way outside.

"Rosie's Café for lunch okay with everyone today?" asked Mom as they stepped out into the hot early-afternoon sunshine.

Everyone agreed with the plan, and they walked the half block to the little café. Crowds of people stood outside waiting for a table. Rosie's was one of only two restaurants in the valley open on Sunday. Not only did many of the members of their church eat out after service, others came from the Latter-day Saints church a block away and the Catholic church two blocks away, not to mention some of the people who came to the nearby lake every summer weekend and those who liked to hike, bike, and rock climb in the mountains surrounding the little valley.

Dad went inside to put their name on the list, and the rest found a bench for Grandpa to sit on in the small square behind the restaurant. The entire block contained small buildings sitting close to the sidewalk, most painted in pastel colors or left as natural wood. Behind them was a beautiful square shaded with large oak trees. The grass was lush, and there were plenty of places to sit and enjoy the small-town chatter. A small stage for the occasional entertainment stood in the center, and often the town hosted local musicians and bands in the summer. It was also available for rent, and many weddings were held there.

Grandpa took a seat on the bench, Parker sat next to him, and Heather perched on a large rock near the bench while Mom stood nearby.

"How is the Fletcher family doing this fine afternoon?"

Heather turned toward the voice of Sheriff Daniel Dixon, one of two sheriffs who patrolled the valley. His daughter, Cleo, had been Heather's best friend since high school, but she'd moved to Salt Lake City three years ago after being accepted into the University of Utah School of Medicine. The sheriff and his wife lived in Ogden but attended Mylin Valley Life Church when he wasn't on duty. Instead of his uniform, he wore black slacks and a bright purple button-up dress shirt.

"We're doing pretty well, Sheriff. How are you and your family?" asked Heather.

"Oh, well, we're doing adroit," said the sheriff, grinning mischievously.

Heather glanced at her mother, never sure how to respond in these situations. Mom smiled and pointed a finger at the sheriff. "Did Beth get you another word-a-day calendar?"

"Yes, ma'am, she did," said the sheriff, laughing.

"All right, well, I'm stumped. What does 'adroit' mean?" asked Mom.

"Well, the calendar says it's someone who is skillful in using their hands or their mind, but I looked it up in a thesaurus and it's also a synonym for 'good.' I do like throwing out all these crazy words and watching people react to them," said Sheriff Dixon.

Heather hated the sheriff's word-a-day calendar. The first time she met Cleo was at a barrel-racing competition. They'd competed against each other and tied for third place in the beginner category. After the race, they congratulated each other, got to talking, and became fast friends. When the sheriff came to collect Cleo, she introduced her father to Heather. He'd congratulated them both on scoring third and said, "You're the tertian twins!" Heather looked up the word when she got home and read that it was a form of malaria that caused a recurring fever. For the next week, she'd tried variations of the spelling, trying to make sense of what he'd said.

At the next race, she cornered Cleo in the barn and demanded an explanation. Cleo laughed so hard she cried. She explained the word-a-day calendar and how "tertian" is also a term in music theory, something to do with the interval of thirds. Her dad had been trying to tell them they were the "third place" twins. Ever since, any time Sheriff Dixon used one of his word-a-day calendar words, it made her cringe.

"How is Cleo? We haven't had a chance to talk much lately," Heather said, hoping to change the subject.

"Cleo is studying for finals. After this semester is over, she'll be done with her undergraduate degree and will start working on her MCATs."

"That's amazing. Be sure to tell her we're all proud of her," said Mom.

"I will. She also wanted me to tell you, Heather, she will be available to help you out at your fundraiser."

"Oh, awesome," Heather said.

"And how about you, young man? How are your studies going?" Sheriff Dixon nodded to Parker.

"They're good. I'll be graduating in the spring."

"Excellent, excellent. These kids with their college studies—it sure takes an adroit person to handle all that learnin'."

"Yes, it does," said Mom.

Beth and Dad joined the group, and the two families chatted until their tables were ready.

"Oh, Heather, I meant to ask you this while we were doing chores this morning and I forgot," said Dad after they sat down and looked over their menus. "There's some fence that needs repairing, and I wondered if you could help me this afternoon."

"Oh, sure."

Dad nodded his thanks.

"A lot of my calls lately have been about fencing injuries," said

Mom.

"Really? That's weird," Heather said.

"It seems all the animals have the same idea. Escape!" Mom said with a laugh. "Luckily, none of our cattle have been injured, and your horses don't seem to be participating in the escape plot, either."

Heather laughed. "Thankfully not. One With Wind is my only jumper so far, and he prefers to make his escape under cover of darkness."

A server came to take their order, and after they'd all ordered, Grandpa said, "Fall must be coming."

"Why do you say that, Grandpa? It's only August," said Parker.

"Because all the animals are actin' strange. They know when the seasons are a-changin', and their moods change."

"That's true. They know if the weather is going to change before we do," said Dad.

"So what did you think of Pastor Barker's message this morning?" asked Mom.

"I thought it was really interesting," said Heather. "The whole science-proving-the-Bible thing is fascinating, and it confirms we need each other not because it feels good, or right, or whatever, but because God made us to need each other. And now science backs it up too."

"I agree," said Parker. "It was interesting, but it made me sad."

"Why?" asked Dad.

Parker shrugged. "Because I'm about to leave everyone I know. I kind of wonder if taking this job is worth it."

Grandpa patted Parker's shoulder. "Your family will always be here, just a phone call away. You're working hard in your schooling, and I think this company must have people with good heads on their shoulders, since they picked a talented young man such as yourself. Not even graduated yet and they want you to work for them. That's pretty special. Just don't get so caught up in working all the time you never take vacations or come home for visits."

Parker folded his arms and looked down at the paper place mat in front of him and nodded.

Heather knew Parker's real concern was the possibility of not being here when Grandpa's days came to an end. A twinge of guilt twisted in her stomach. She realized she hadn't checked in on Grandpa since Thursday, when Parker had pointed out how busy she was. The fundraiser took more of her time the closer it got. Once that was over, she would resume her regular visits to Grandpa. She reached across the table and squeezed Parker's shoulder.

He glanced up at her and gave her a small smile.

She thought again about what Dad had said to her that morning. She'd learned to read horses well enough over the years that she knew and understood her own limits and abilities. Dad said he trusted her to know if and when a horse needed to be put down, and she knew when to stop spending her time and effort on Littlefoot. The same would not apply to Xavier. She'd agreed to teach him how to ride a horse but was quickly finding out it would be more difficult than she'd imagined.

Parker faced a situation filled with uncertainty, too. He didn't have to take the job. He could stay near home, look for something close by until Grandpa passed away, and then find a job out of state. It wouldn't be as adventurous, and he might have to start at the bottom and work his way up instead of getting a shot at the top from the start. Either choice had consequences, but neither choice was bad. He simply had to choose the best option for him. Weigh the pros and cons of each. And with each choice, he would have to give something up to get something else he wanted.

She'd chosen to teach Xavier based on information that suggested she had the ability to teach him. But the first lesson showed her something different—that she might not be as capable as she thought. A simple choice based on available information. She could keep going and find out if she was as capable as she had first thought, or she could quit now and continue life as it had always been, training horses.

But what about what Pastor Barker had said? Choosing to love people no matter what? Her family members were the type of people who were in the trenches together, who did choose to love one another, no matter what ugliness popped up. There had to be a balance, though. She couldn't jump into everyone's problems and love them through them. So she had to choose whom to simply treat with kindness, whom to love in action, and whom to get into the trenches with. Which category would Xavier fall into?

59

Chapter 7

Back at the ranch, Heather parked her truck in front of Dad's barn and got out just as Dad walked out, carrying the tools they would need to repair the fences.

"Let's take your truck," he said, placing the tools in the bed. "I was going to fill the gas in mine on the way home, but your mom got an emergency call, so I had to come straight home."

Heather nodded and followed him back inside to get the rest of what they needed.

Once they were loaded up, Heather gave her keys to Dad and hopped in the passenger side.

"You can drive if you want," he said.

"That's okay. You know where the broken fences are."

He nodded and started the truck. Putting it in gear, he drove around the barn and out into the field. There was no road or path to follow, so they made their way gingerly through the knee-high grass that was nearly ready to be cut and baled. The truck squeaked and rattled on the uneven ground, and neither spoke.

Heather let her thoughts drift back to Pastor Barker's message. For the most part, her family operated the way he said relationships should. They talked to, supported, and corrected one another, even when it was uncomfortable. Of course, Scott was acting a little strange lately and didn't seem to have a valid excuse for it. But did she treat other people the same way she treated her family?

Cleo, definitely. They were best friends and had been for a long time. They'd navigated high school together and all the drama that went with it. But she didn't feel really close to anyone else at church or in the community. She knew people, of course. Knew lots of things about them, too, because it was hard not to in a small town like Mylin Valley. Just because she knew things about people here didn't mean those people wanted her to know those things.

Dad pulled to a stop and turned the truck off. They climbed out, grabbed the tools, and got to work.

He cut away the old, broken strands of barbed wire, unwrapping it from two posts until he reached a length that was in good condition. Heather handed him the end of the new wire and a small, round piece of metal called a ferrule.

Dad threaded the new and old wires through the ferrule, then crimped them together.

While he finished that up, Heather measured the amount of new wire they would need, cut it, and attached the come-along tool that would stretch the fencing.

Dad joined her after grabbing another ferrule, threaded the other side of the old and new wires into it, and waited for Heather to ratchet the come-along tool so that the wire was nice and taut before crimping the ferrule. She removed the come-along, and they started the process all over again with the next broken strand. There were five strands of barbed wire that made up the fence, and three needed replacing.

"What did you think of Pastor Barker's message today?" asked Heather. "You didn't say at lunch."

He shrugged. "I thought it was interesting. It's nice to get a different perspective on things you've heard over and over."

"Yeah. I'm really curious to hear what he'll say next week. The attachment thing makes so much sense. I've been thinking about the different relationships I have, and I keep analyzing them."

"Analyzing? Why?"

She ratcheted the come-along tool on the second strand before answering. "I don't know. I guess I've been considering who I'm attached to and why." They started the third strand. "I guess I never paid attention to the fact that there are levels of relationship, and wondering how we know when to get in the trenches and *do life* with people, as Pastor Barker said."

"I suspect it's a mutual thing. One party in the relationship can't decide. It's a give-and-take. Both people involved have to be willing to trust each other and be open and vulnerable. You can't force love on anyone. I mean, I guess you can love someone by respecting their boundaries, if they aren't ready to open up or take part in the relationship, but there won't be much of a relationship if both parties aren't invested in it."

"That makes sense."

They finished the section of fence, loaded up, and moved to the next section that needed repairing.

"I've been thinking about what you said this morning," Heather said over the rumble of the truck.

Dad glanced at her. "What's that?"

"About pushing myself too hard."

He nodded.

"My gut feeling about Littlefoot is there is no hope for him, and maybe I should trust that instinct and the advice of Mom and you, but Littlefoot didn't choose to be in that accident. He was a good horse at one point. I can't help but believe he can be that again. And until I'm certain he can't, I can't give up on him, even though, at the moment, it looks like he isn't willing to be a partner in his rehabilitation."

Dad pulled to a stop at the next section of broken fence and turned the truck off, twisting in the seat to face her. "I know that, sweetheart. And I know you have parameters and limits that will help you determine that. I hope what I said this morning didn't make you doubt your abilities with horses, because I'm not worried about the horse."

She smiled. "I know. And it's true I don't know Xavier the way I know horses, but Xavier's disability isn't something he asked for, either. It was out of his control. I'm not going to fix what's wrong with him, I know that. But I might be able to help him learn a skill that can help him along the way. Maybe. I don't know yet. I'm still trying to figure that out."

He nodded thoughtfully. "I'm not saying you shouldn't try. I only want you to pay attention to your limits. You've got a lot on your plate, and you're a dreamer. You always have big ideas and plans floating around in that pretty head of yours. I want you to get all the things you want in life." He reached over and squeezed her hand. "I want you to see all those dreams become reality, but I don't want you to get burned-out in the process because you're so eager to do it all at once.

"And, Heather, you're putting yourself in a situation that's risky for you, and your horses, and your whole plan here, for a boy you don't even know. I don't want you thinking I don't support what you want to do, because I do. You have a good heart. I just don't want to see it get broken."

"Dad. It's one little boy. His parents and I communicate, and I've explained the risks to them. I'm not trying to dismiss your concerns. I always take your advice to heart."

Dad sighed, nodded, and reached for the door handle.

"Dad?"

He looked at her, eyebrows raised.

"I'm really glad I'm attached to you on a brain level," she said.

Dad smiled ruefully. "I'm glad we're attached at the brain, too."

They finished repairing the fence and headed back to the house. Heather helped Dad unload the tools, then headed to her barn to check on the horses. She cut up two apples, placed them in a pouch she attached to her belt, then went out to her fields.

Sunstone, Queenie, and Brazen Fire were all close by, and she gave them each a slice of apple. The others were scattered around the ten acres. A few headed her way, curious about her handout. After giving treats to those who wanted them, she trekked back to Littlefoot's paddock. She watched him for a moment. Outside, in the pen, with no one near him, he looked like a perfectly normal horse.

She entered the paddock and approached him. He laid his ears back and lowered his head. The closer she got, the more agitated he became. When she was a couple of yards from him, he reared. Heather stood her ground, making noises to correct him. When his feet were on the ground again, she praised him. She took a few steps toward him, and he tried to trot past her. She blocked him and corrected.

He turned and trotted away from her, but then turned quickly and ran straight for her. Heather shouted, raising her arms quickly. At the last second, Littlefoot veered and passed her. She jumped to the side, away from him in case he kicked. She yelled in frustration and turned to Littlefoot again. They stared at each other, both panting. "I'm trying to help you!" She wiped the back of her hand across her forehead. "Am I wasting my time? Should I just end your life, like everyone seems to think I should?"

Littlefoot raised his head in the air and neighed.

"Yeah, I didn't think you'd like that option. But something has to give, and you're not helping me." She thought for a moment, watching Littlefoot as he pawed the ground and shook his head. "Unless we can figure out a way to make some progress, things don't look good for you, Littlefoot. It's time to pay Ed Burton a visit."

After looking up Ed Burton's address, she hopped in her truck and headed down the canyon as the sun began it's decent in the west. Ed lived on the outskirts of Ogden, where urban development hadn't yet encroached on the remaining farmland. As she drove, she thought about how to approach the man, since he'd ignored her calls and emails. She didn't want to be brusque or angry, but he had been avoiding her, so she needed to be firm. Firm but polite.

Twenty minutes later, she pulled up to the house. She spotted a man standing inside, in front of a window—hunched over the kitchen sink, from what she could see. At least he wouldn't be able to pretend he wasn't home.

Heather climbed out of her truck and made her way to the front door. As she mounted the steps, Ed looked up from what he was doing and their eyes met. She gave him a smile, but he didn't return it. Instead, his eyes widened, and he froze. On the porch, she could no longer see Ed or the window. She knocked on the door.

A moment later, the thick wooden door creaked open about six inches and Ed's spectacled face peered through the crack.

"Mr. Burton, I have some questions for you about Littlefoot."

Ed's eyes shifted from her face to the handle of the screen door and back again.

Heather sensed he might not let her in, so she added, "Please, I'm not angry or anything. I just need some information so I can help him better."

The man's eyes narrowed, and for a moment neither of them

moved. Finally, he seemed to resign himself to her being there, opened the door wider, and unlocked the screen door. Heather released the breath she didn't realize she'd been holding and followed Ed inside.

"Thank you." She stepped into the small cottage-style house.

Ed was a short, skinny man, with a slight hunch. He rubbed his thin hands together as he led her to a small, worn green Formica table with chairs upholstered in a gold-colored fabric, before motioning for her to take a seat.

He sat in the chair opposite, removed his glasses, and polished them on his gray button-up shirt. Heather watched him, wondering if he would say anything or if she should just jump in and start asking questions.

A clock chimed somewhere in the house as he placed the glasses on his nose again and cleared his throat. "What do you want to know?"

His voice was frail and shaky, and again she wondered how this man had managed to get Littlefoot into a trailer. He didn't seem like the type of person who could handle a horse easily, but then, people probably thought that about her Grandpa Sam, and he'd been around horses all his life. Of course, Grandpa wouldn't be able to handle Littlefoot now. Was the same true for Ed?

"I really need more information about the accident Littlefoot was in."

His eyes shifted away from hers. "I told you what I know."

"Mr. Burton, I looked up the news articles on the crash, and they gave me more information than you did. Please, I'm not getting very far with Littlefoot, and I don't want to have to put him down. He's afraid of small spaces, which is understandable with what I know about the accident, but the usual methods of desensitizing him aren't working. In fact, I can't even get close to him, which makes me think there is more to the story than just a bad accident. If you know anything, even the name of the vet who treated him, it will help."

A pained look crossed Ed's face. "I wanted to help him. I raise ponies, so I thought I could handle Littlefoot. Especially since I knew him before the accident. He was always at the fence line, friendly, calm, interested in the ponies." He paused, took a handkerchief out of his pocket, and wiped his nose. "Well, I suppose if you're talking about putting him down, the rest won't matter much. The news articles mentioned how the accident happened, yes?"

Heather nodded. "Yes, it was night, and the roads were wet. A semi swerved into the oncoming lane hitting the truck. Both truck and trailer tipped over, and when help arrived, they declared the owner dead at the scene."

Ed shook his head. "The news articles got it all wrong. The horse and trailer rolled off an embankment. The first responders also thought Littlefoot was dead. They couldn't get close enough to him to be certain because of how the trailer was situated, but he wasn't moving or making any noise, so they assumed he was also dead. After getting my neighbor's body out of the vehicle, they brought in a crane to lift the truck and trailer back onto the road before doing anything with the horse."

Heather covered her mouth with her hand.

Ed nodded and ran a hand across his face. "They cut the truck away from the trailer and lifted the truck up to the road. As they were attaching the crane to the trailer, the horse kicked and whinnied. They stopped what they were doing and called a vet to come assess the situation. But because of the wet conditions of the road and traffic piled up because of the accident, it took almost two hours for a vet to arrive. By the time he got there, Littlefoot had been pinned nearly five hours, and at least three of those hours he'd been conscious.

"The police had to use the Jaws of Life to open the back of the trailer so the vet could get inside, and after he was in, he immediately administered a sedative and a painkiller. All the windows had shattered, and even though it was safety glass, Littlefoot had some embedded in various parts of his body. The divider in the trailer came off its hinges and was bent and mangled.

"Luckily Littlefoot wasn't impaled by it, but it covered his head and much of his body like a claw, and when he started kicking, the edges gave him some minor cuts on his back. They lifted the divider off him after the sedative kicked in. Littlefoot got to his feet, but he wouldn't put weight on his back right foot, and the vet determined it was broken. He put a splint on it, but the horse was so scared, he wouldn't go up the embankment. They made a type of sling to wrap around his midsection, attached it to the winch on the crane, and hauled him up. The vet blindfolded him for that, of course, and he was still blindfolded when he got him into his trailer, which worked out all right because by that time he was pretty dopey from the drugs. At least until the truck moved. The vet had to give him an extra dose of sedative at that point."

Heather's heart sank. This was much worse than she expected. Littlefoot had suffered a kind of trauma he might never recover from. "Did the vet tell you all of this?"

Ed nodded. "A week after the accident, the vet showed up at my neighbors', looking for any living relatives. But his wife died five years ago, and his kids have all moved away. The vet paid me a visit and asked if I'd be willing to take the horse in when he was all patched up. I had a soft spot for Littlefoot, and he'd always gotten along with my ponies, so I agreed. But when he got here, he wasn't the same horse. I had to keep him sedated or he would kick and bite. Even sedated, he was pretty feisty. There isn't a lot of space here, so I didn't have a choice but to keep him in the barn. I kept him until his foot was completely healed, but I couldn't keep him with my ponies. It was too dangerous. That's when I called you."

"But why didn't you tell me the entire story?"

He sighed. "I called one other place before I called you. I told them everything, and they told me to put a bullet in his head. That was the last thing I wanted to do. I don't have the skills to fix him, but I hoped a rescue ranch would. I was afraid if I told you everything, you wouldn't take him either. He was such a good horse. I wanted to get him somewhere in hopes he could be fixed."

Heather sighed. "I have gotten the advice to put him down." She paused, pressing her lips together, considering her options. Littlefoot had to learn to trust people again. Every person he'd come in contact with since the accident had forced him into situations that made him afraid.

Ed hung his head and rubbed his hands together. "So there's no hope for the poor fella, then. I guess I should have taken care of it myself after all."

"I'm not quite ready to give up on him just yet."

Ed looked up at her, surprised.

"I may not be able to fix him, but now that I know just about everything that happened, I can try a different approach."

Ed nodded, his eyes glistening with unshed tears. "Thank you. I'm sorry I didn't get back to you. I probably made things worse instead of better. I just didn't want to be the reason he was put down."

Heather reached over and patted his arm. "I'm glad you brought Littlefoot to me. I have one more question for you, though."

"What's that?"

"How did you get Littlefoot into your trailer?"

Ed smiled sadly. "I blindfolded him like the vet did, gave him a sedative, walked him around outside for about twenty minutes, then led him right into the trailer. He resisted after he got up the ramp, but he was too doped up to fight much. He seems to do fine with a blindfold as long as there aren't any loud noises."

"But he didn't have a blindfold on when we let him out of the trailer."

"I took it off after he was inside. I figured the medication would be enough."

Heather nodded, remembering how feisty, to use Ed's term, Littlefoot had been when she'd let him out of the trailer and the noise of Ed's diesel engine in the barn. It seemed Littlefoot had experienced many people who had thought more about their own desires, fears, and needs than of his traumatized ones. No wonder he wanted nothing to do with her. He'd lost all trust in humans to care for him when he needed it most.

"Thank you, Mr. Burton. That answers all my questions. I think I have a better idea of how to help Littlefoot now." She stood, her desire to leave his small house and get back to her horses growing by the second.

Ed stood too and followed her to the door. "If you think of more questions, call me."

Heather turned and looked at him, eyebrows raised.

He held his hands up in front of him. "I promise I'll answer."

She gave a quick nod, smiled, and opened both sets of doors. Stepping onto the porch, she took a deep gulp of fresh air and headed down the steps, waving at Ed as she reached the driveway.

He waved back before stepping back into his house and closing the door.

She started the engine and put her truck in reverse. She had a better idea of what to do to help Littlefoot. There was no guarantee it would work, but at least it was something to try.

Chapter 8

For three days, Heather tried getting close to Littlefoot using a different method. Instead of forcing him to accept her presence near him, she found the edge of his limits and simply waited, watching to see if he would make any move toward her. There was no progress yet. She needed to add more to her plan, but only now had she found an opportunity to talk things over with Mom. The fundraiser had been keeping her busy, while Mom was swamped with vet calls.

"Obviously, the traditional methods aren't working," Heather explained. "Since he's had a major traumatic experience, I was wondering if I could keep him on a sedative while I work with him."

Mom bit her top lip, a sign she was thinking, and watched Littlefoot. "I guess it can't hurt to try. How sedated do you want him to be?"

"Not so sedated that he can't walk straight."

Mom nodded. "All right. Let me see what's in stock. I'm still not sure anything you try is going to work, so I'll give you a one-month supply. I'll need to see some progress in that time before I agree to anything else."

Heather's stomach knotted. One month wasn't a lot of time, but she understood where Mom was coming from. "Okay."

"I assume you want to add it to his food, since you can't exactly give him a shot or a pill."

"Yeah. Thanks, Mom."

"You might talk to Grandpa and William about Littlefoot, too. Don't forget, they both have a lot of experience working with horses. They might have some ideas you haven't thought of." Uncle William was another of Mom's siblings who lived on a hundred-acre spread on the opposite side of Mylin Valley.

She nodded, heat filling her cheeks. She should have thought of that herself.

"I hear you have a new riding student," Mom said.

"Yeah, Xavier."

"Your dad mentioned he has special needs and that the first lesson didn't go so well." Mom's raised eyebrows made Heather wonder how Dad had presented the information to her. Had he been upset? Annoyed? Or just worried?

"Yeah, it's a little more challenging than I expected, but I'm learning."

Mom nodded. "Are you sure it's a good idea to take on a student like that when you have a horse that needs so much attention?"

"Teaching Xavier doesn't take up much more of my time than any other student. I'm still giving Littlefoot the attention he needs. All the research I'm doing to best teach Xavier is done in the evening, after I'm done with everything else. Besides, I thought you said I should put Littlefoot down."

Mom folded her arms. "I did say that. But you've chosen not to take my advice and are trying to train him. He's going to require a lot more training than any of the other horses you've brought in."

"I know, Mom. I'm not neglecting him. The only reason I haven't done more until now is because you've been so busy."

"Ah, I see. So it's my fault Littlefoot hasn't improved in the last week and a half." Her eyebrows arched again.

"No, I didn't mean it that way. I have been working with him. So far, nothing has made a difference. But I finally talked with Ed Burton a few days ago and got more information. Now that I know more, I can do more. I just haven't been able to implement the new plan yet because I haven't had a chance to talk to you about the sedative. Sorry."

"Well, your father thinks you might be in over your head, and I'm beginning to understand why."

"Yeah, he told me. But it only looks that way because of the fundraiser. Once that's over with, I'll have tons of time for both Littlefoot and Xavier."

Mom gave her a wry smile. "All right. I have clients to see, so I better get going. I'll get the sedative to you tonight if I have it on hand; if not, I'll order it and get it to you as quickly as possible."

"K, thanks." Usually, her parents were more understanding with her process. Why did teaching Xavier make them doubt her?

Heather headed back to her office to check messages and continue working on details for the fundraiser. How could it be that the event was only two and a half weeks away? It felt like there were still a million things left to do.

Two hours later, a knock on her door interrupted her progress. Looking up from her computer, she saw Scott standing at the door, looking disheveled, pale, and tired.

"Can I borrow a few of the horse racing barrels you have?" he asked before she could greet him.

"Um, sure. Are you okay?" she asked, getting to her feet.

Scott rolled his eyes and turned away from the door. "I'm fine."

She followed him to the back of the barn, where she kept her old race stuff in case any of her students ever showed an interest in learning barrel racing, pole bending, or jumping. "You don't look fine."

He let out an exasperated sigh. "I'm fine. I just need a few barrels to practice for an upcoming race."

Heather leaned against the wall and folded her arms, watching her brother as he inspected the barrels. She wondered if the low light in the barn was playing tricks on her eyes because it looked like his hands were shaking.

Her office phone rang, and she hesitated to go pick it up.

Scott glanced at her. "I can get these by myself."

Heather frowned at him, but he obviously didn't want to talk to her, so she jogged back to her office and picked up the receiver. "Fletcher Horse Rescue, this is Heather."

"Heather, this is Arlo Hanlon with the yoga studio in town."

"Hi, Arlo. What's up?"

"Hey, I promised to donate some tickets to your fundraiser coming up for a free session of yoga with goats, but we just found out our two does are both pregnant and we're taking them off the rotation until their babies are born, which means our classes are all full. We're working on a new class, yoga with ferrets, but it's not set in stone yet. Turns out ferrets aren't that easy to work with, and I don't know if they'll be trained by then. Would it be all right if we offered a certificate to our regular yoga class? The one with no animals?"

Heather bit the insides of her cheeks to keep from laughing. Arlo and his wife, Meadow, had opened the yoga studio three years ago. When they announced they were going to start a yoga with goats class a year after they opened, everyone thought they were crazy, but it ended up being their most popular class. That led them to trying out other animals, too. Last year they'd tried yoga with llamas, which might have worked out if they had figured out how to keep the llamas from spitting on everyone.

She'd never been one for yoga. The ranch gave her plenty of exercise opportunities every day. But she'd gotten to know Arlo and Meadow through her fundraiser, which they had supported every year.

"A certificate for a regular yoga class should be fine."

"Oh, great. We were worried it would be too boring or something."

"Nope, people will love any class at your studio. Besides, they can still visit and watch the goats, right?"

"Oh, yeah, good point. All right, we'll get that certificate ready and have it delivered to you by Monday."

"Sounds good. Thanks, Arlo."

"No problem. Have a Zen day, amiga."

Heather smiled and shook her head as she placed the receiver back into its cradle, then went to check on Scott. He was loading a third barrel into the back of his SUV and securing them with a ratchet strap.

"Need help?"

He shook his head and avoided looking at her. It was unusual for Scott to be anything but upbeat and jovial.

"Are you sure you're feeling all right? You look exhausted." Her gut twisted in worry. He'd never acted this way or looked so ill, even when he had a bad day or was sick.

"I'm fine." He finished tightening the strap, then turned toward her. "I'll be back later for more barrels." And he moved to the driver's side door.

She followed him there and leaned against his car. She didn't want to annoy him further by asking him again if he was really all right. He obviously wasn't. All of this seemed so out of character. Of her three brothers, she'd always been closest to Scott. Their mutual love of the outdoors had fostered their closeness over the years. He'd confided in her more than anyone else, and when he'd done something he knew would get him in trouble, he sought her advice. When he liked a girl in school, she was the first to know. It was strange to find him being so evasive.

He climbed into his SUV and looked at her. "By the way, I probably won't be able to help with your fundraiser."

"What? Why?" She stepped back, shocked. He was supposed to be giving horse rides to kids on Queenie. Her mind raced through replacements for him, but came up empty.

"I have a race that day," he said, breaking his brief eye contact with her.

Her mouth fell open. "A race?"

Scott shrugged and started the engine. "I have to go." And he closed the door.

Heather stepped back from his car and watched him drive off, feeling as if she'd been punched in the gut. What hurt wasn't so much that he was backing out of helping her with the fundraiser, but the fact that in twenty-three years, Scott had never treated her as less important than his extreme sports. He'd been to every one of her riding competitions and had encouraged her to keep going when things got hard. He saw the adventure in reaching new goals. What was going on?

She remembered her conversation with Dad about Pastor Barker's message and how relationships are a two-way street. If someone didn't want to be fully part of a relationship, it wouldn't be a very deep or meaningful one, no matter what the other person did. Why was Scott pulling away?

She dug her cell phone out of her pocket and dialed Harry Jr.'s number. He answered after the second ring, a clang of pots and pans almost drowning out his "Hello?".

"Hey, have you talked to Scott recently?"

If there was anyone capable of bringing Scott back to reality, it was their big brother Harry. He'd helped resolve arguments between Scott and the rest of them many times, including arguments with their parents. Harry Jr. was the voice of reason and compromise on both sides.

"No, not since family dinner. Why?"

"Something's wrong." A lump formed in her throat as she explained what had happened.

"Yeah, that definitely sounds weird."

"Do you think you could try to talk to him? I don't care if he doesn't help with the fundraiser. I'm just worried."

"I'll try."

"Thanks."

After hanging up, she went to her office and sat down at her desk. She would need to find a replacement for Scott to handle the children's rides at the fundraiser. It all seemed preposterous. She'd always been able to count on Scott. She opened her laptop but couldn't bring herself to look through her contacts to find a substitute.

Chapter 9

Jan rinsed off a handful of grapes, pulling them off the bunch as she rinsed them, then set them on a napkin on the counter. After she'd removed all the grapes, she carefully wiped each one so they weren't dripping with water and didn't have any little pieces of vine left on them before placing a handful in the shallow well of Xavier's divided plastic plate—the blue one with dinosaurs on it. Then she added some vanilla yogurt in a little bowl that she placed in the other small well of the plate. In the large space, she placed a slice of cheap white bread spread with a thin layer of peanut butter and an equally thin layer of jam on top, before folding it in half.

"Xavier, your lunch is ready," she called, setting the plate on the table.

Xavier skipped from his bedroom to the kitchen, sat down, and ate, smacking his mouth loudly on a grape.

"Chew with your mouth closed, please," Jan said.

Xavier sighed but closed his mouth, moving his jaw in exaggerated circles as he chewed.

Jan watched him for a moment before walking down the hall to check on his progress with putting his laundry away. She'd tried to get him to help her fold earlier, but after folding a pair of pants into a sloppy heap, he had been distracted, as usual, and because she was feeling impatient with him today, she had finished the job herself instead of trying to keep him on task. The one thing she had insisted on was that he put his clothes away in his dresser.

At the end of the hall, she glanced back at Xavier. He still sat facing the window, bouncing in his seat and humming to himself while he ate. Sticking her head inside his room, she saw the pile of clothes still sitting on his bed and all his dinosaur figurines scattered on the floor. She sighed and returned to the kitchen, sitting down in the seat across from him.

He gave her a toothy grin, and bread crumb–speckled yogurt seeped through the holes where two of his teeth were missing.

She smiled back, hoping her face didn't show her disgust at the display of his chewed-up food. "Is it good?"

He nodded.

"Good. After you're done eating, I want you to finish putting your clothes away and pick up your toys. Then we'll go to your riding lesson. Okay?"

Xavier cocked his head to one side and looked at her like he didn't understand, but then he shrugged. "Okay."

She wasn't sure if the confused look meant he'd forgotten that today was Friday and he had a riding lesson, or if it was something else entirely, but she didn't ask. Asking too many questions could upset him, and because he'd had three meltdowns already this week, and today had been going well so far, she didn't want to rock the boat.

Once his plate was clean, he got up from the table and headed back to his room.

Jan closed her eyes, realizing her mistake. *Stupid, stupid, stupid.* "Hey, Xavier, wait a minute."

He turned back toward her but didn't return to the kitchen.

"I still need you to put your plate in the sink. Then you can put your clothes away." Routine and order were important for Xavier, but without constant and specific communication, routine didn't happen. Without routine, or a schedule, or a plan, he could play with his toys or watch TV for hours without stopping to eat or go to the bathroom. But changing something in the routine or not explaining things correctly could prompt a meltdown.

"You told me to put my toys away after I ate," he yelled, pointing at his bedroom.

"I know I did. I should have done a better job explaining. Will you forgive me?" she asked, clasping her hands together when she felt them tremble.

"No!" he stomped his foot. "You didn't do it right, but I did it right and then you tell me to come back. Well, make up your mind!"

Jan opened her mouth to speak.

"Well?!" he yelled, spreading his arms wide, then slapping them against the sides of his body before she could get a word out.

She took a deep breath and closed her eyes—something a therapist had told her to do when she was feeling anxious or angry. It never seemed to help when Xavier got this way, though.

"I'm waiting," he said.

She took another deep breath and released it before opening her eyes. "Xavier, I would like you to put your plate in the sink, then put your clothes and toys away."

"No, I'm not doing it, you stupid bitch." He sat down on the floor with a thump and crossed his arms, watching her defiantly.

Jan's hands visibly shook now, despite being clenched, as they always did whenever she had to handle one of Xavier's episodes on her own. She carefully got up from her seat, left his line of sight, and started washing the dishes in the sink. When that was done, she wiped down the already clean counters, rinsed the dishrag, and hung it over the faucet. She leaned against the sink and listened to her shaky breathing. Waiting. Hoping. There was no use demanding him to do anything. It would only escalate things until she had to restrain him, and she hated restraining him.

After a few minutes, she asked quietly, "Xavier, can you please bring me your dirty dishes?"

She heard rustling, and a moment later, Xavier appeared at the table. He picked up his plate, bowl, and spoon and brought them to her, dropping them into the sink so they clattered loudly.

"Thank you. Now, can you please put your clothes away?"

Without answering, he turned and left the room.

Jan washed the dishes, then went to their small living room to recover for a few minutes before checking on him. They could still make it to his lesson on time.

Getting up, she headed to his room to check on his progress. All his clean clothes had been tossed all over his room, and Xavier was in a completely new outfit. "Xavier, what happened? Why didn't you put your clothes away?" she asked, trying to keep her tone even. Too much emotion on her side would trigger him.

"Oh, I forgot." He looked around at the mess he'd created, then back at her. "Will you help me?"

After they gathered his clothes and piled them on his bed, she started folding. Xavier took each item of clothing, one at a time, and carried it to his dresser. As he carried the last item, she checked her watch. They might still be able to make it on time if traffic was good.

"Great job. Now can you put your toys away?"

In the same leisurely fashion, he carried one toy at a time to his closet and dropped them in the bin.

"Xavier, do you think you could clean up a little faster? We're going to be late for your riding lesson."

She scolded herself for the request as the words left her mouth. Being on time or not didn't mean anything to Xavier, except that one made his parents upset and one didn't. One effect of FASD was the inability to understand the concept of time passing, so telling him they'd be late meant nothing to him, and neither did time-related consequences, like sitting in time-out for five minutes. They'd had to learn a whole new system of consequences and rewards. Eight years in, and it was still a struggle to get it right.

He scowled at her and started kicking his toys into the closet. Once they were all inside, he slammed the door shut and gave her that defiant look she hated so much.

"Xavier, please put your toys away where they belong." Her voice caught and she swallowed hard.

He kicked the closet door, but then opened it and tossed each toy into the bin, glaring at her after each throw.

"Thank you," she said as calmly as possible when he'd finished. "Now can you please put your shoes on so we can go to your riding lesson?"

Xavier grabbed a pair of sandals from his closet and jammed his feet into them.

Jan sighed. "Hey, remember, you need to wear shoes that don't show your toes for your riding lesson."

"I'm wearing my sandals!" he screamed at her.

"Heather won't let you ride the horse if you wear sandals."

"Shut up. You don't know anything. You're just a stupid mom."

She got up and walked out the door. Something soft hit her back, and she turned to see one of his stuffed animals on the floor at her feet. "One point." She clenched her jaw and fists before turning and going into her bedroom.

Xavier let out an ear-piercing scream.

Each day, Xavier started with ten points. Every point was worth five minutes of electronics in the evening. He might not understand the concept of time, but he treasured the hour of television he got each evening after dinner, marked by a large timer next to the TV set. He understood what it meant when the timer was set to a lower value, and they had a list of specific reasons he could lose points. Violent behavior toward people and animals was one of them. She closed the door to her bedroom, sat on the edge of her bed, took several deep breaths, and listened to the sounds of items being tossed, kicked, or hit in her son's room.

Chapter 10

Heather paced in front of the ring, occasionally stopping to scratch Queenie's nose, and checked the time. Jan had sent her a text saying they would be late but hadn't answered her responding question asking how late they would be. She wanted to get Xavier on the horse today, but they had to finish going over the rules first.

"Hey, Heather?" called Zeke from the barn.

"Yeah?"

"My mom just texted me. Her appointment is running even later than she thought, and she won't be here for another thirty minutes at least. Can I hang with the horses in the field and give them some carrots?"

"Sure."

Zeke let out a whoop.

A dust cloud appeared at the entrance to their driveway. Heather squinted to make out the car. It was Jan's. Finally. She checked her watch again: fifteen minutes late.

After their car stopped, Xavier hopped out and ran toward her. "Do I get to ride that horse today?" he asked, pointing at Queenie.

"That depends," said Heather, rubbing her chin. "Do you remember the rules we talked about last week?"

He shook his head. "Nope."

"You don't? I bet if we think really hard, we can remember." She screwed up her face and tapped on the side of her head to appear to be thinking extra hard.

Xavier laughed.

"Now, let's see. One rule had to do with our feet. What was it?"

She observed Xavier from the corner of her eye to see if he was participating. His mouth hung open a little and he seemed absorbed in watching her pretend to think.

Suddenly his eyes got wide, and he gasped. "Don't run!"

"That's right. That was one rule. Great job!" She held up her hand, an invitation for a high-five, and he waved his whole arm in a circle before slapping her hand and beaming at her. "What's the other rule we talked about?"

Xavier stared up at her, his mouth slightly open again. He didn't appear to be thinking at all, but she waited anyway.

Finally, he shrugged.

"Something about where we stand?" she offered.

His gaze went skyward for a moment, then returned to her face. "Don't get kicked?"

"And where is the danger zone for getting kicked?"

"I don't know."

"Sure you do. Look at Queenie and see if you can remember."

He looked at Queenie for a moment. "Behind her?"

"Yes! Good! Are you ready for a couple more rules?"

"Sure."

"Okay. First, I want you to look at Queenie's ears and tell me what they're doing."

Xavier walked over to the fence and squinted up at the horse's ears. "They're going like this." He lifted his hand and swung it back and forth.

"Right. What do you think that means?"

"I don't know."

"When her ears are straight up like that, it means she listening to what's going on around her. And she's interested in what's going on around her. What do you think it would mean if she laid her ears back?"

"That she didn't want to hear what's going on?"

Heather chuckled. "No, if her ears are back, it means she's mad or upset."

"Oh."

"If we look at her ears every now and then, we can see what kind of mood she's in. If a horse is angry, it's a good idea to give them some space until they aren't angry anymore."

"Like me!"

Heather smiled impressed he'd made that connection, "That's right. Now, do you see that strap around Queenie's head and neck?"

Xavier nodded.

"That's called a bridle and reins. When you're riding the horse, you'll use the reins to tell Queenie what you want her to do and where you want her to go."

"Cool."

"It is cool. But there's something very important to remember about that strap. Never wrap it around your hands or your arms. Do you know why that's a bad idea?"

Xavier shook his head.

"If you were to slip off the horse and your hand was wrapped in the reins, you'd be dragged around."

"That might be fun."

Heather shook her head. "I promise, it wouldn't be."

"Have you done it before?"

"No, I haven't, but I have fallen off a horse before. Which brings me to the last rule we need to talk about today before you can ride on Queenie."

"What?"

"Whenever you ride on a horse, you need to wear a helmet."

Xavier scrunched his face. "I don't want to do that."

"Well, if you don't want to wear a helmet, you can't ride on the horse."

Xavier stomped his foot and grunted in frustration.

Heather glanced at Jan, who had stayed near their car, her arms folded. She remembered what Jan told her last week, about him getting stuck on an idea and it taking him a while to come around. So, instead of saying anything more, she walked toward the barn, where a metal locker stood near the door. She unlocked the keypad and swung the door open, then leaned against the side of the barn and waited. Xavier stared angrily at her, his arms straight at his sides, his fists clenched.

She glanced at her watch. Thirty-five minutes left of their lesson. Plenty of time to get him on the horse and walk him around the ring for a while—at least, it would be if he cooperated. Who knew how long it would take him to decide? And if he decided he wouldn't wear a helmet, that would be the end of their lesson.

She realized there were many things Xavier could refuse to do that would end his lessons, boundaries she couldn't allow him to cross in order to keep him safe. The opportunity to ride a horse was his for the taking, but he had to be a willing participant in this relationship. She could only do her part. Dad's words, and Pastor Barker's message, came back to her. Dad didn't want her to push herself too hard trying to help Xavier. Limits and boundaries were more than just rules. But in this case, her limits were clear, and there was no danger of her pushing Xavier or herself too hard. If he didn't want to wear a helmet, there was nothing more she could do. Simple.

Glancing at Jan, she wondered why she seemed so distant today. Last week, she'd appeared interested and engaged. Today she seemed ... well, like a horse with its ears back. Upset. Not even a hello or an explanation for being late, she realized. Had Xavier had a meltdown? Had he been mean to her, as he had last week? If so, how could he appear as if nothing had happened?

Dumb question, she told herself. She'd experienced his changeable behavior for herself. She checked the time again and looked at Xavier.

He no longer wore an irritated expression on his face. Instead, he seemed lost in thought. Far away. Maybe it was time to try again. She pushed herself off the side of the barn and walked toward him. His attention snapped back to her. "Are you going to wear a helmet so you can ride Queenie today?"

His gaze fell to the ground, and he didn't answer. Heather glanced at Jan, unsure what to do. She didn't want to push him. Any other student, she would, but Xavier had limits of his own and she didn't want to accidentally push him past those limits and set the bomb off. A moment later, Xavier started walking to the locker, so she followed him. He stopped in front of the hanging helmets and continued to stare at the ground.

"Can I try some helmets on you?"

He nodded once, not looking up.

She grabbed one and set it on his head. Too small. She grabbed the next size up and tested it. Better. She wrapped the straps under his chin but didn't buckle them and checked to make sure they sat where they were supposed to on the sides of his head. Perfect. "Can you lift your chin up a little so I can buckle this? I don't want it to pinch your neck."

He threw his head back and seemed surprised that the helmet didn't fly off his head.

"Maybe not that far."

He straightened his head and tried to hide his amusement but failed and shook with laughter. She grinned, buckled the strap, and stepped back to take a better look at the fit.

The laughter disappeared, a scowl replacing it. "It's too tight," he whined.

She reached forward and stuck a finger between the strap and his chin. "It's supposed to be tight."

"I don't like it."

"Sorry, bud. If you want to ride, you have to wear it."

He tried to push the strap off his chin, whining while he did so.

Heather glanced at Jan to see if she would come and assist, but she just watched from her spot near the car.

"Hey, you're going to hurt yourself doing that. Do you want me to take it off?"

"Yes. I don't like it."

"Okay, but if I take it off, you can't ride Queenie."

He moaned, and his body slumped. "I want to ride the horse," he whined, letting his head flop around as if the helmet were weighing him down.

"Well, then, you have to keep the helmet on," she said, crossing her arms.

He tried lifting the helmet off his head without undoing the straps and whined a little louder. Heather leaned toward him and unsnapped the strap. Xavier removed the helmet and threw it as hard as he could. Heather felt her own agitation rising and glanced at Jan again. Was it too much for her to step in here and say something to her kid? Give her some advice on how to handle this? She walked back into the barn and paced in front of the stalls, checking her watch while she walked. Twenty more minutes. She only had to last twenty more minutes. She could handle that.

Blowing out a breath, she went back outside to see where things stood with Xavier. He'd retrieved the helmet and was attempting to fasten it on his head again. He was grunting and yelling in frustration at being unable to connect the straps, which were twisted.

"Need help?"

He twisted away from her. "No."

"The straps are twisted," she said in a sharper tone than she intended.

He pulled the helmet off and stretched his arm out to his side, his back still turned toward her. She took the helmet, fixed the straps, and set it on his head. He connected the straps under his chin and then turned toward her.

She folded her arms and waited.

"Can I ride now?" he asked impatiently.

"You're going to keep the helmet on?"

He nodded.

"Do you think we can try not to throw the helmets from now on?"

He rolled his eyes but nodded again.

"Great. Let's go ride."

They entered the ring where Queenie had patiently been waiting for the past forty-five minutes. Heather picked up a set of movable wooden stairs and set them down next to Queenie.

"You can use these stairs for right now, but when you get a little bigger, you'll have to learn to mount a horse without stairs. Climb up here."

Xavier cautiously climbed the three stairs. When he reached the top, he clung tightly to her shoulders and his breath came in quick, short pants.

"You're okay. I know it looks high, but it's not, really. I bet you could jump down from there and be just fine."

"Mmm-mm, I don't want to jump."

"No, you don't have to. I'm just saying—never mind." She tapped his left leg. "You're going to put this foot into this stirrup and then swing your other leg over Queenie's back."

Still clinging to her shoulders, he lifted his left leg and tried to put it into the stirrup.

"It'll help if you hold on to the saddle instead of me."

He let out a fearful whine but moved one hand to Queenie's back, the other still clinging to Heather, then tried the stirrup again. He got his foot inside the hole this time, then looked at Heather, his eyes wide.

"Great job. Now you need to let go of me and grab this right here: it's called a saddle horn. Grab it with both hands and swing your leg over to the other side."

"I'll fall."

"No, you won't. I'm right here and I won't let you fall. See, I'm going to hold on to this leg so you can't fall off. Okay?"

"Uh-huh," he said pitifully before grabbing the saddle horn with first one hand and then the other. "I can't do it."

"Yes, you can. Stand on this foot," she said, patting the leg in the stirrup. "Then swing your other leg over. I'll help you."

He lifted his right foot off the top step, putting all his weight on the foot in the stirrup, and tried to lift his other leg over the horse's back, but his left knee was bent and prevented him from being able to swing the other one over.

"Straighten this leg," she instructed.

"I can't," he snapped.

"Sure you can. Remember, I'm right here and I won't let you fall." She placed a hand on his back and pressed on it. He slowly straightened his left leg, and she pushed him up and on to the horse.

"See, you're up!" she exclaimed, jogging around to the other side of the horse to help him get his other foot into the stirrup.

He beamed down at her. His eyes were still wide, and he clung so tightly to the saddle horn, his knuckles were white.

"Hey, you okay up there?" she asked, not wanting to walk Queenie until he looked a little more relaxed.

He didn't respond. Heather patted Queenie's neck and waited, watching him. Queenie shifted her weight. All the color drained from Xavier's face and his eyes got wider, which didn't seem possible, and his arms trembled from clinging so tightly to the horn.

"You're all right, Xavier. We'll just hang out here until you're more comfortable."

He was panting now, but he nodded.

"Take a deep breath. You're okay."

Queenie shifted her weight again and Xavier let out a piercing scream, and when he didn't have breath to continue, he hyperventilated.

"Xavier, you can climb off. Just swing your leg back over."

Queenie stomped her foot, and Xavier let out another scream.

Heather took his right foot out of the stirrup and ran to the other side. Queenie had her ears back now and was snorting, which made Xavier scream even louder, if that were possible.

Removing his left foot from the stirrup, she scrambled up the steps, plucked Xavier off the horse, carried him down, and set him on the ground.

He ran to the fence, climbed through, and ran to his mom's car.

Heather's whole body shook from the adrenaline coursing through her bloodstream, and when she saw Jan still standing near the car, her arms still folded as she watched her son climb into the backseat, irritation radiated through her to a degree she hadn't known herself capable of.

She noticed another car parked next to Jan's van. It belonged to Aunt Michelle. Great. She looked around, wondering how much her aunt had witnessed or if she'd been out back looking for Zeke. She didn't see Michelle anywhere.

She heard the sound of a horse galloping behind her, and she turned to see Dad riding up to the ring where she stood.

"Is everything okay?" he asked. "I heard screaming."

Heather rubbed her forehead with the back of her hand. "Yeah, everything is fine."

"What happened?" he asked, still sitting on his horse, his gaze flitting from her to Jan and back. Heather took a deep breath, trying to calm herself down, knowing she didn't appear calm.

Dad slipped off his horse and climbed into the ring. "Heather, what happened?" He grabbed her shoulders and bent down, forcing her to meet his eyes.

A lump formed in her throat, and she coughed to clear it. "Xavier panicked when he got up on the horse. That's all."

Dad visibly relaxed and released her shoulders.

"I'm sorry about that," Jan called.

Heather looked up and found Jan standing beside the ring, just a few yards away. "He can't process when he freaks out. He gets tunnel vision. But he's okay, or he will be. You handled that perfectly, Heather. Really." She smiled, lifted her hand, then slowly turned and made her way back to her car.

Heather stared after her, completely dumbfounded.

"Are you sure you're all right?" Dad asked.

She nodded her head, walked over to Queenie, and started undoing the saddle. "I've never had anyone scream like that before. My ears are still ringing, but I'm fine."

"Well, that was dramatic," Michelle said.

Heather looked toward the barn and saw her aunt leaning against her car, looking out of place in the country with her black pantsuit, four-inch heels, and jet black hair in a French twist.

"Yeah, a little," Dad responded to Michelle's remark. "How are you, Michelle?"

"Fine. I had an impromptu parent-teacher meeting this afternoon, so that's why I'm late picking Ezekiel up today."

Heather lifted the saddle off Queenie and carried it to the fence. Dad lifted the panel open for her, and she headed inside the barn.

"Zeke's out back with the horses," she said. "I'll get him."

Michelle nodded. "Thanks."

Heather put the saddle away, rested her hands on a workbench nearby, and blew out a breath. The anger she'd felt at Jan's flippant, unhelpful behavior ebbed, and the trembling produced by the mixture of adrenaline and anger was subsiding. She pushed off the workbench and headed out back to find Zeke.

He appeared to be having an in-depth conversation with One With Wind. She smiled. She'd done her fair share of confiding in horses herself.

"Zeke, your mom's here."

He turned and jogged her way. Not waiting for him, she headed back through the barn.

Dad and Michelle stood near the car talking, but they broke it off when she approached.

"He's coming," Heather said.

Michelle nodded.

"Are you sure you're okay?" Dad asked.

"Yeah, I'm okay."

"All right, then I better get back. See you later."

"Nice chatting, Harry," said Michelle.

He lifted a hand and climbed onto his horse.

"So I take it the screamer is your new student?" asked Michelle. "The one with special needs?"

Heather nodded.

"Zeke mentioned him to me last week. Sounds like a handful."

"Yeah, he is." Heather attempted a smile.

"You know, being a music teacher in the public school system, I have some experience with kids like him."

Heather looked at her aunt. "Really? I guess I didn't realize that." A tendril of hope rose in her.

"Mm-hmm. He didn't say much, but your dad doesn't seem too thrilled with your new endeavor. I can't blame him. Special-needs kids are so difficult to work with."

"Yeah, I'm figuring that out. It's taken two lessons to explain the rules to him, when normally it only takes five minutes."

Michelle chuckled. "If I'm totally honest, they're not my favorite kids to teach," she said in a low voice.

The tendril of hope withered. What helpful information could her aunt provide if she didn't like working with special-needs kids?

"Hi, Mom. Sorry, I was out back with the horses." Zeke's face was red and he was panting from running.

Michelle looked him over. "Your cousin and I need to chat for a few minutes. Why don't you go visit with Sam and clean yourself up?"

Zeke nodded and ran off.

"Why don't you like working with special-needs kids?" Heather asked.

Michelle sighed. "Well, it's not entirely the fault of the children. Since I work with junior high students, the special-needs kids have periods just like everyone else. Typically they start their day in a self-contained classroom, which is just a fancy term for a class with other special-needs kids. And most of their school day takes place in that room as well. All the basic school stuff—reading, writing, and arithmetic—is taught by the special-education teacher. But they usually have two periods where they have out classes so they can interact with the normal kids." She made air quotes around the word *normal*.

"Music is an elective class for all the kids in my school, so students, special needs or not, have to meet certain requirements in order to be able to take my class. If they meet those requirements, which are softened for the special education kids"—she rolled her eyes—"then they can take my class if they want to. There aren't always special-needs kids in my classes, but when there are, the entire dynamic of the classroom changes."

"How so?"

"Well, it depends on the needs of the child. For instance, I had a little girl who had Down syndrome one year. She was well behaved and didn't cause any problems, but I had to give her so much one-on-one time that I had several other students suffer in their progress because of it. If they had an aide in the class to help them, that would be incredible, but most of the special-education aides know nothing about music, so they can't do much. I've been asking for a music aide for those students, but because I don't consistently have special-needs students in my class, they won't set aside the funds for it. It's very frustrating."

"So what about students who don't behave well? What do you do for them?"

Michelle rolled her eyes again and huffed. "Those kids rarely last long in my class. The requirements for them to get into the class are softened because of their level system, and they go up and down the levels like a professional piano player doing scales."

Heather cocked her head to one side, not understanding.

"Sorry, I forget not everyone knows about music. A scale is a sequence of notes, and it's one of the most basic things you learn in music."

"Oh, I see. They go up and down the level system a lot then."

"Exactly. So, often they'll spend a week in my class, there will be some kind of issue where they aren't behaving or causing chaos, and they lose a level, so they no longer qualify to be in my class. The frustrating part about it is, as soon as that child makes it back to the top level, they can start coming back to the class. So a child might come to class for a week, not be able to come for three weeks, then they come back for another two weeks, and leave again.

"Meanwhile, my other students are learning all the things they need to learn until this one student comes back to class. Then I spend more time with that one child than I do with the rest of my students, trying to teach them the very basic music skills. But really, I don't think I've ever had a special-needs child learn anything more than two or three notes." She shook her head. "It is extremely frustrating."

Heather's brows knitted. "It sounds like it. But do you think if they were placed in an environment where they could learn at their own pace, they would succeed?"

"Maybe. It's hard, because they all have their own special needs, and every single one of them learns differently. One might be great at math but only on a computer; another might be great at math as long it's all done on paper; another might never understand the basic concepts of math but excel in reading. There are so many variables, and I don't know what the answer is, but ..." She glanced around and leaned closer to Heather. "I don't think the public schools are doing very well in this area. Don't tell anyone I said that."

"If you had the time and resources, would you want to figure out a better way for the students who do come to your class?"

Michelle hesitated. "I know this sounds bad, but if I had the choice, I would choose not to have special-education students in my class." She held up a hand. "Don't get me wrong. They deserve an education. But most parents sign their child up for this elective because they read some article about how learning a musical instrument can help a special-needs child cope better. It may be true, but in my opinion, a dedicated music teacher outside of the school environment would be a better fit for them. Besides, I wanted to become a teacher to teach music. I love music. I love seeing kids catch a passion for music. But I didn't become a teacher to teach special-needs kids. It takes a special person, with an abundance of patience, to teach a special-needs child. And I am not that person."

Heather nodded. "I guess that makes sense."

Michelle rested a hand on her arm. "Your dad is concerned, and rightly so. You need to decide if you're going to teach this boy to ride a horse, or teach this special-needs child. There is a difference."

Heather bit the inside of her lip. It wasn't the advice she'd hoped for, but everything her aunt said made sense. There was only one problem: she didn't know how to teach a special-needs child.

Chapter 11

The sanctuary was mostly empty as people drank coffee and caught up with one another in the foyer. Heather took a seat and set her Bible and purse on a couple of chairs near her to save them for her family before burying her head in her arms.

She hadn't slept well the last two nights. She hadn't heard from the Rodenbaums and knew Xavier might never want to try getting on a horse again. Regardless, the things her Aunt Michelle had said about kids with special needs created a cacophony in her head. Somehow she felt the failure was hers, and she wanted to make it right. On top of that, Scott's strange behavior still weighed on her.

This morning, when she and Dad had done their chores, they had worked in an awkward silence. In fact, things between them had felt awkward since Friday. She knew he was concerned, but even he should be able to recognize the likelihood that Xavier would never want to come back.

She sat up and fished her phone from her purse. She had to shake off this negative mood. Derek had told her there were therapy ranches out there, but they couldn't afford to take Xavier to those places, which meant she could probably call and talk to people at one of those places and find out what they do for the kids, what their programs are like, and their opinion on what she was trying to do. Maybe she could even tour one of them. That might help her figure out if she was even close to doing what was right in trying to teach Xavier.

The difference between teaching a child how to ride a horse and teaching a special-needs child: she understood what her aunt meant. Xavier needed someone who could focus on him and his needs, more than on the task at hand, which was teaching him how to ride a horse. He was missing basic skills he needed to survive in the world, skills he needed more than he needed to learn how to ride a horse. Horses could teach a lot of lessons, she knew, but were they the lessons Xavier needed? For most kids, riding a horse was a fun skill to learn, a pastime, a way to get some exercise. For Xavier, it was an opportunity to equip him to survive in society.

As she began an internet search for therapy ranches on her phone, she hesitated. Maybe, she thought, she should wait and find out if there would be any more lessons first. She was still busy getting things ready for the fundraiser. Looking into this immediately could end up being a waste of time that she couldn't afford right now.

The band started the first song for worship. Looking up, she saw many seats filled already, and a crowd had just entered the sanctuary, pulled away from their conversations by the music.

She turned the sound off on her phone and tucked it back into her purse. She would have to finish puzzling that out later. Her parents appeared, and she stood to let them pass. Then she gave her full attention to the worship service, which always helped her refocus her thoughts.

After worship, announcements, and offering, Pastor Barker rose to speak. He looked as tired as she felt this morning. He opened with prayer and was silent while he flipped through the pages of his Bible. "Today we're going to look at Acts 4. Last week, I started talking to you about discoveries in the field of neuroscience that are confirming and giving us new insight into what the Bible tells us about relationships. I briefly explained that our brains are designed to develop on a foundation of joyful interaction with our caregivers. We attach to our parents, siblings, and extended family through our early interactions as infants. As we age, our brains continue to develop. When we reach puberty, or those early teen years, we start developing our identity. Who we are as a person. We find our people, our tribe, a group where we belong.

"In Acts 4:32, it says, 'All the believers were one in heart and mind. No one claimed that any of their possessions was their own, but they shared everything they had.' I want to focus on the first part of that verse: 'All the believers were of one heart and mind.' Does that mean they agreed about everything? The color of the carpets, whose turn it was to do the dishes? I doubt it. So what are they talking about here? Verses 23-31 show the believers praying together after Peter and John reported back to them after being in jail. They'd been told not to teach in the name of Jesus. What did they pray for? Verse 29 says they prayed for boldness to continue speaking God's word, and for more signs and wonders. They were of one mind and heart when it came to sharing the good news of Jesus.

"Now consider. Are we, as a church family, of one mind and heart about the things of God? Are we a tribe of people who all feel welcomed here? When you enter this building, do you feel that everyone you come into contact with is glad to be with you? I would venture to say, the answer to most of those questions is no."

Guilt filled Heather. Lately, she'd been getting a lot of advice regarding Littlefoot and Xavier. It wasn't exactly what Pastor Barker was talking about, but her parents sure seemed of one mind and heart when it came to their doubts about the wisdom of taking on a traumatized horse and a damaged child. Was she being stubborn about both? Refusing to see the truth about her own limitations? Her relationship with Scott was on shaky ground for reasons she didn't understand. Parker's accusation that she was too busy to give Grandpa enough attention came back to her, and the guilt deepened. She glanced down the row at her grandfather. His slightly hunched form rocked slowly back and forth in his seat, his gray eyes fixed attentively on Pastor Barker.

"As the pastor of this church, that makes me sad, and I want to find a way to bring about this sense of belonging for each and every one of us in this church. Now, that doesn't mean I can be best friends with each one of you. I'm only one man. But I do hope that each of you, when you come to me, feel seen, heard, and understood. Even if I ultimately don't agree with you, or you with me, I hope you'll feel I took the time to really listen and understand your views.

"All of this I'm talking about, and will be talking about, has to start with me. And I'm making the effort to put into practice what I'm teaching you. I hope you'll each, in turn, catch the excitement for this process and will want to begin implementing this yourself in your relationships with others in our community. If I'm the only one trying, none of this will work. It has to be done in relationship with one another.

"So, what am I talking about? You may think I'm putting a new spin on an old message, but I intend to change the way we do church. Starting today, there's going to be more interaction from you. I am here to teach you, so you can walk out these doors and be a light to the world. If we're sitting in church each Sunday, listening to a nice message, then leaving and going about our regularly scheduled program, nothing much is going to change. I know not everyone will like this change, because I intend to get you out of your comfort zones, but if you stick with me a while, I think you'll catch the vision.

"So today, I want everyone to stand up and face someone next to you. Don't leave anyone out. Everyone face someone."

Heather glanced around. People were slowly getting to their feet, looking uncomfortable. She was on the aisle this morning. She turned to Mom, sitting next to her.

"This is different," Mom said under her breath. "I wonder what we're going to do."

Heather shrugged, hoping it wouldn't be anything ridiculous like doing trust falls or a silly dance.

"Okay, now, I'm going to start my watch for thirty seconds. All I want you to do is make eye contact with the person you're paired with and smile. Simple enough, right? Don't break eye contact for thirty seconds. Here we go."

Heather met Mom's eyes and smiled, wondering what the purpose of this was. To her surprise, she felt herself wanting to look away after ... she wasn't sure how long, but as the seconds stretched out, she found it impossible to believe they hadn't been standing there for more than thirty seconds already. Her eyes twitched with the desire to look away, but she forced herself to keep contact.

"Okay, all done," Pastor Barker said.

Mom laughed. "I can't believe how hard that was," she murmured.

Heather blew out a breath. "Glad I'm not the only one who thought so."

"How was that?" asked Pastor Barker. "Did anyone find themselves wanting to break eye contact before the thirty seconds were over?”

Almost every hand went up.

“Even though you are all smiling, you wanted to break eye contact. Anyone willing to share how it felt?”

“Intense,” shouted someone.

“I almost felt giddy,” said another.

“Those are great answers. Take a seat and I’ll explain what happened.”

The room buzzed as everyone sat down. Pastor Barker stood in the pulpit, grinning.

“Notice how the atmosphere of the room has changed. It’s not quiet, and everyone looks and sounds a little more relaxed.”

Heather looked around the room. People grinned at one another, fidgeted, and talked in low voices. Her own mood had improved, and she felt like she had a little more energy than she had when she first got to church.

“As infants, we grow our joy foundation through joyful interaction, and most of that is done through eye contact. But even babies will break eye contact sometimes. What’s happening is we take in joy when we meet the gaze of someone who is glad to be with us. We know they’re glad to be with us because of the genuine smile on their face. How much capacity we have for joy depends on how long we can keep taking in joy through that eye contact. When we reach a point of being overwhelmed by joy, we break eye contact and rest. The rest is just as important as the joy exchange. Over time, if we have a lot of these joy exchanges, we’ll be able to endure longer periods of eye contact because our capacity for joy will grow.

“In the age of technology, we’ve lost a lot of opportunities to make joyful connections with people. When we don’t have joyful connections with people, we feel alone, isolated, anxious, and a host of other things. If we go too long without joyful connection, and then experience joy to an overwhelming extent, it can look like hyperactivity, or invading someone’s bubble.

“I want our church to be a place of joyful community that reaches beyond these four walls. I want us to share each other’s joy, allow ourselves to experience and share in one another’s sorrows, and become a tribe with one heart and mind in sharing God’s love with one another and the world."

There was so much Heather needed to digest. Pastor Barker's sermon made her look at her situation with Xavier and his family in another light, one that took into account what her Aunt Michelle had said, but in a more positive way. What if she took the focus off Xavier learning to ride a horse, as her aunt suggested, and instead looked into this brain science stuff a little more and what it might teach her about helping him?

Pastor Barker hadn't specifically said anything about special-needs kids, but Xavier scared easily, angered easily, blew up easily, got hyper easily. Last week Pastor Barker said science had discovered ways to grow our capacity. What if that is what Xavier needed? To grow his brain's capacity for joy so that the other emotions wouldn't take over so easily? Since FASD affected the brain while the infant was in the womb, maybe this information could help Xavier learn the skills he needed. The information Jan and Derek had shared with her all dealt with his behaviors, but they hadn't specifically mentioned if any of that research came from this knowledge about brain science or if it stemmed from other kinds of research. But Jan seemed to struggle as much as Xavier did to find joy or even to make those connections Pastor Barker said were so essential.

Heather realized how her relationships with beautiful, sensitive, and sometimes troubled horses had brought her joy since she was a little girl, even when she felt misunderstood by the people in her life. She could look into it more this afternoon, make a list of lessons a horse could teach a child like Xavier, and see if there were ways to combine the two.

This morning, she'd been discouraged. But she'd learned early on that things worth doing didn't come easily. Horses had taught her that. Xavier needed to learn that. You had to learn their language, and know their signals and what those signals meant. People told her she had a gift for reading horses, but in reality, she'd spent every spare second of her child and teen years studying them, working with them. Helping Xavier couldn't be much different. She just needed to learn his language and figure out his signals. Of course, she also needed more opportunities to work with him, which she might not get.

"Ready for lunch?" asked Mom.

"Actually, I wanted to ask Pastor Barker something. Go on ahead. I'll catch up."

"Okay. We're going to the barbecue place today. We'll save you a seat."

Heather nodded, gathered her things, and headed toward the front where four older ladies appeared to be giving Pastor Barker an earful. She stood a respectful distance away and waited. One woman was Mrs. Eberly, the town gossip. When she wasn't happy about something, everyone knew it. Harry Jr. and Scott had experienced more than one run-in with her as kids. Since Mrs. Eberly lived in the small Mylin Valley town, she monitored everything, including what the kids were up to. And she never failed to inform parents whenever she saw their kids doing something she didn't think was right. Heather had thankfully escaped Mrs. Eberly's notice as a child because she was always riding horses and hardly ever came to town without one of her parents. Mrs. Eberly could probably use a good dose of joy.

Jan's unsmiling face flitted through her mind. Raising a child who had frequent emotional outbursts had to be terribly difficult. If she could find ways to increase her joy and peace, maybe it would help her as well as Xavier.

"Ladies, ladies," Pastor Barker said, holding his hands out in front of him, trying to get them to quiet down. "I understand what you're saying. Really, I do. Your arguments are valid, and I promise this week I will call and schedule a time to visit with each of you personally and hear what you have to say. But let's not cause a scene here in the aisle. Go enjoy your families, and I'll be in touch this week. Promise."

One lady shook her finger at him before turning to go. Another huffed indignantly, and Mrs. Eberly linked arms with two of them and pulled them down the aisle with her. "Come on, girls. We can discuss this further over tea at my place."

Pastor Barker blew out a breath and shook his head as he watched them go.

Heather smiled and stepped toward him. He held his hands up as if protecting himself from her, and she laughed.

"Do you come in peace? Or do you also have a complaint?"

"I come in peace."

He dropped his hands and smiled. "What can I do for you today?"

"I wanted to let you know that I'm really enjoying this series you're doing."

"Oh, I'm glad. I haven't been hearing that much lately."

Heather was shocked. "Really? I can't imagine why. It's really interesting. I love all the information you've shared about the science that backs up what the Bible has always said."

"It's pretty fascinating, but many people believe science and God don't mix, and they don't want to hear about scientific theories in church." He nodded his head in the direction of the ladies who'd just left.

"But ... didn't God *create* science?"

Pastor Barker pointed a finger at her, grinning. "Bingo."

"Well, I'm enjoying it and was wondering if you'd come across anything in your research or learning on the subject about special-needs kids."

Pastor Barker furrowed his brow and stroked his beard. "I can't think of anything I've read about that topic. Why do you ask?"

She explained Xavier's situation and how she wanted to be helpful.

Pastor Barker's face lit up. "I can't tell you how much this encourages me, Heather. To know someone is taking this information to heart and wants to put it into practice. This is exactly what I was talking about today, reaching beyond our walls to share to joy." He paused for a moment, looking into her eyes thoughtfully. "It won't be easy. Introducing a new way of looking at and thinking about things … well, people don't readily accept that kind of change. It will take time and a lot of patience. But I get the feeling you already know that. You're doing the right thing by trying to learn as much as you can, from science and the Bible. Now, I can't think of any books to recommend, although you're welcome to borrow anything from my library you like. But I can get you the websites to the organizations where I've been getting all of this information. Maybe you can find something there, or find someone you can talk to about it. And if you want to talk about what's in the books I give you, call me anytime."

"That would be perfect. Thank you," she said, grateful for his encouragement as much as his help.

"Can I email it to you this evening?"

"Sure."

Pastor Barker nodded. "All right, then."

They said their goodbyes, and she left the building. She crossed the street to the barbecue place and joined her family, feeling more hopeful than she had that morning.

Her parents, Grandpa, and Parker were ordering their food at the counter as she joined them.

"Oh, I was just about to order you your usual," said Mom.

"My usual sounds great," she said, glancing at Parker and wondering what he thought of Pastor Barker's sermon and whether it had made him even more conflicted about moving to another state. Once they had their food, they found a table outside and sat down to eat.

"Grandpa, you know my new horse? The traumatized one?" Heather asked. "Do you have any advice on how I should help him?"

She'd already come up with a plan and had a pretty good idea what Grandpa's answer would be, but he might have a nugget of wisdom she hadn't thought of yet. Maybe if she showed Parker that she was invested in keeping Grandpa involved and making sure he didn't get lonely, he would be more comfortable taking the job.

"Oh, traumatized horses. They're either the most impossible horses to work with, or they become the best, most loyal horses a person could own. If they make it through the journey of trauma, they'll probably still have a few little oddities, but they'll know who they can trust. It just takes time, patience, and a lot of attention. Those trauma horses, whew-boy, they can be difficult. But if you succeed, it's always worth it."

Just like Xavier, Heather thought.

Chapter 12

"There are a couple options for sedatives, but I think this one will be the best because it comes in a pellet treat," Mom said, handing her a small box. "That means he'll be more likely to eat it, because he won't take treats from anyone and we can't get close enough to give him another type of oral medication or a shot."

"Thanks. Should I just put it in his food every morning?"

"Yes, but watch him, especially after the first time. It takes thirty minutes to kick in. I don't foresee any issues, but look for signs of trouble breathing, high blood pressure, the usual stuff."

"Okay."

"And let's start him with just one treat, two times a day. That's the lowest dose possible. I know you want him alert to work with him, so let's see how he responds on this dosage, and if we don't see a change, we can up it to two treats twice a day. You'll want to give one treat, morning and night, unless you only want him sedated during the day when you want to work with him. Then I would only give him one in the morning. However, it might be helpful to have him sedated around the clock at first; it might help him see that his world has become safe again."

"Great! I'll give him his first dose now, because I haven't given him any grain yet. That way I can keep an eye on him while I finish up the chores, before all the phone calls start pouring in about last-minute details for the fundraiser next weekend."

Mom smiled. "I've noticed all the equipment coming in, tables and tents. Are you excited?"

"Yeah, and a little overwhelmed. I almost can't believe how much it's grown in such a short time."

Mom squeezed her arm. "You're doing great things, child of mine. I better go. I have a full list of animal patients to visit today."

"Okay. Thanks again for this."

"Sure thing, sweetie. By the way, have you had lunch with Grandpa recently?"

Heather shook her head guiltily. "I keep meaning to. I've just been so busy."

Mom nodded. "If you have a chance, he'd really like to see you. He's been asking questions about your new student."

"Oh, okay. I'll go over today."

"How are things going with that, anyway? Your dad told me about Friday, how he panicked on the horse."

Heather rubbed the back of her neck. "I haven't heard from Jan or Derek since then, but knowing what I do about Xavier, I'm not confident he'll want to come back."

Mom smiled. "Guess your dad and I did all that worrying for nothing."

"Yeah, I guess so."

"Well, I better be on my way. See you later."

After Mom left, Heather made a list of what she needed to accomplish that morning. She needed to finish her chores and take care of the messages on her machine before visiting Grandpa.

In her office, she took one medicated treat out of the box, then slipped the box into a drawer and locked it. She didn't like having medications, even if they were for animals, sitting around. The last thing she needed was for someone to misread the box and feed the horses handfuls of medicated treats.

She tucked the treat into her shirt pocket, then grabbed her shovel and filled a small bucket with oats for Littlefoot. He already had hay on hand, but she'd have to check it and replace it if it showed any signs of getting moldy.

Out back, she dumped the oats into a small feeder set aside for that purpose, fished the treat from her pocket, and crumbled it in with the grain. Littlefoot might be slow at finishing his hay, but he never neglected his grains. She walked over to the hay feeder and dug through it. There hadn't been much moisture lately, so she didn't expect to find any mold, but she checked anyway, just in case.

Littlefoot continued to eye her warily while she worked, but as soon as she headed toward the barn again, he trotted over to the grain bin and munched.

Heather smiled and went about the rest of her chores. Once done, she checked on Littlefoot again and made her first phone call of the day.

"Hello?" asked a groggy voice.

"Scott, it's Heather. You said you couldn't help with the fundraiser. I just wanted to confirm that was really the case and not a fluke because you were annoyed with me or something." Harry Jr. had sent her a text the evening before. He had not been successful in getting a hold of Scott.

He groaned on the other end of the line, and Heather checked her watch. Just after eight in the morning. Not early enough to feel guilty about waking her brother up.

"I'll help," he said finally, and Heather raised her eyebrows in surprise.

"Are you sure? What about your bike race?"

He grunted. "I don't have a chance in hell of winning, anyway. I may as well help you instead."

"Gee, thanks."

Scott sighed. "Anything else?"

Heather hesitated. She needed to be able to count on her brother, and this spur-of-the-moment change of decision wasn't giving her confidence. "You're sure you'll be here?"

"God, yes. I said I'll be there, so I'll be there."

"Okay. Will you be here the evening before for setup?"

"Why? I just need Queenie, a saddle, and a bridle, right?"

"Yeah, I just wasn't sure if you were planning on stopping by or not."

"No."

"Okay. I'll see you in a couple of weeks then."

"Yep."

Heather stared at her phone after her brother hung up. Her gut told her she couldn't trust him, but who else could she ask? She didn't have any other volunteers, and it would be difficult for anyone to fill two positions. Maybe she should drop something. She headed to her office to check the schedule of events and her messages to see what she could move around.

Two hours later, she emerged from her office bleary-eyed and exhausted. She'd decided there was nothing she could drop. But her family would all be at the fundraiser, and she might ask one of them to fill in at the last minute if Scott failed to show up. She'd also returned a dozen messages and finalized details on at least half of the vendors and volunteers who were coming.

Now she needed to get away from her phone and the computer and visit with Grandpa Sam. Leaving the barn, she walked the short distance to his house, mounted the steps, and knocked loudly to announce her presence before letting herself in. His door was never locked, hadn't been as long as she'd known him.

"Hello?" she called, entering the small living room. The old fabric couch sat in the middle of the room, empty. But the television was on, the volume turned up to accommodate Grandpa's hearing loss.

Otherwise, the house seemed quiet. She wondered if Grandpa might be taking a nap, but the sound of a spoon against glass came from the kitchen to her right. She found him sitting at the table with a mug of tea. "Grandpa?"

He tried to twist his body around to look at her, but his stiff joints didn't allow for much twisting, and she walked to the table and took a seat.

"Well, hi there," said Grandpa. "I haven't seen you around here for a minute."

"I know. I'm sorry."

He patted her hand. "Don't be sorry. Young people have things to do."

"Yes, and one of those things is to visit with my grandfather more often."

He chuckled, looking pleased. "Do you want some tea?" He started to get up, but she reassured him she was fine for the moment.

"Mom said you had questions about my new riding student. I'm sorry for all the noise."

"Oh, that's no bother. I've been watching you out there with him. He's a feisty one, isn't he?"

She smiled. "Yes. He has some special needs."

"Some what?"

"Special needs," she said a little louder.

"Special needs? What's that?"

She thought for a moment. "He has a disability called fetal alcohol spectrum disorder."

"Oh? I've never heard of that."

"It's brain damage from his birth mother drinking alcohol while she was pregnant."

"That's too bad. You know, in my day, doctors told women a glass of wine was good for babies in the womb. Funny how things like that change."

She nodded.

"So that's why he's so feisty, then?"

"Yep."

Grandpa carefully lifted his mug with shaky hands and took a sip. "I'd like to meet him, the next time he's here."

Heather straightened in her chair. "Really?"

"Sure. We can take him for a ride on my golf cart."

Heather laughed. "I'm sure he would love that, Grandpa."

"When does he come again?"

"Well, actually, I'm not sure if he's going to come back."

"Oh? Why's that?"

She explained what happened at Xavier's last lesson. "I'm not sure he's going to want to try again." She needed to call them but had felt too overwhelmed over the weekend to do so.

Grandpa's eyebrows knitted together. "I saw you help him up on that horse and heard the screams. But a young boy like that can't know what he wants. He should face his fears and get back up there. That's what I always had to do."

Heather smiled. "I know, Grandpa, but Xavier is pretty stubborn. If he gets it in his head that he doesn't want to do something, it's difficult to get him to change his mind."

"Reminds me of my granddaughter," he said, carefully lifting his mug again.

Heather grinned, and the gray eyes that met hers over the rim of the mug sparkled mischievously.

Finding Purpose

She sat with Grandpa until he finished his tea and he declared he needed a nap. She made sure he got to his bed safely, then headed to the barn to work her horses, starting with Littlefoot. She'd only spent about twenty minutes with Grandpa, but it reminded her how much she enjoyed slowing down in the midst of her busy schedule to visit with him. Parker was right: she had been too busy lately to give Grandpa the attention he deserved. She promised herself she would do better.

She filled a pouch with carrot sticks and apple slices and tied it to her belt before climbing over the gate and into the corral with Littlefoot. He stood on the other side of the ring, watching her warily.

She moved toward him slowly but purposefully, opened the pouch, and took out one carrot stick and one apple slice, then pulled the drawstring closed again, never taking her eyes off Littlefoot while she completed the task.

When she got within six feet of him, she stopped and held out her hand, offering the treats. Littlefoot didn't move.

After a few minutes, she stepped closer, her hand still stretched out. Still nothing. He simply stood there, watching. But he also wasn't flinching, and there were no signs he was thinking about bolting or rearing.

Another two minutes passed, and she took another step forward, letting her eyes communicate her intentions to the horse. This time Littlefoot stepped backward but still didn't show signs of bolting or rearing. She let him have his extra space for another minute before stepping forward again. This time her arm with the treats was just inches away from the horse's nose. His nose twitched a little as he sniffed the offering, but he made no move to take it. Their eyes stayed locked on each other.

Heather took another small step forward. Littlefoot's eyes glazed over. She frowned. An unexpected result. Instead of bolting, he disassociated. Escaping to some other, hopefully happy, place in his mind and was no longer present with her. She placed the treats back in her pouch and stepped back. It was progress, kind of. He hadn't tried to get away from her or charge her. And the disassociation she could work with. It was simply a matter of getting him used to having people closer to him over time so that it didn't completely overwhelm him. Without the aggressiveness, there was a small chance she could do something with this horse.

After climbing out of the ring, she leaned against the fence, watching him as he came back to the real world. She thought about the brain science stuff Pastor Barker was teaching at church. Even though he was speaking specifically about human brains, she could see a correlation in information with Littlefoot. Humans who didn't get enough joy interactions had trouble with other emotions taking over or getting easily overwhelmed. Littlefoot felt overwhelmed by having humans too close because it had been a long time since the interactions he had with them had been pleasant. Only time would tell if her efforts in showing him kindness and gentleness would have an impact, or if he would ever choose to trust her.

She smiled. "Good job, Littlefoot."

Back in her office, she found she had a message from Jan. No details, just "Call me back when you get this."

Heather wondered if all her worrying and planning about what to do would be wasted. Had they decided not to continue with the lessons? She wanted to read the books Pastor Barker had loaned her and look into the resources he'd sent her last night, but she hadn't had time to do any of that yet. She wanted to offer a solution, to let them know she was at least trying everything she could to help them. But if they'd lost hope, or Xavier refused to come back, what could she do?

Picking up the phone, she dialed the Rodenbaums' number and waited.

After four rings, Jan picked up, sounding relieved to hear Heather's voice.

"Hey, I just wanted to let you know Derek and I talked about what happened last Friday," Jan said. "We've talked with Xavier about it and even consulted his therapist on the subject. Xavier isn't so sure about riding anymore, but he still wants to visit with the horses. Derek thinks we should keep taking him to lessons in hopes he'll gain more confidence over time."

Heather's shoulders relaxed a little, but she heard hesitation in Jan's voice. "Okay."

"I'm not entirely sure Xavier will ever overcome his fear, though, and I feel like that isn't fair to you. I thought, maybe, instead of a lesson this Friday, we could meet at the park where we first met with you and talk more about it?" Jan asked.

"Oh." She knew where Jan was coming from. But Heather had gained a lot of new insight this past weekend and hoped she would be able to show Jan she could adjust to Xavier's needs. "Sure, that works fine." The fundraiser—she should invite them.

"Great. Noon still work?"

"Yeah, it does. Actually, I don't know if you would be interested, but I'm holding a fundraiser in two weeks here at the ranch. It's my third year doing this. There will be food, games, horse rides, all kinds of things. We're a nonprofit, so this is a way for me to bring in enough money to keep the rescue up and running. And who knows? If Xavier sees other kids riding horses, it might help him regain confidence."

"Oh, that sounds neat. We'll try to make it for sure."

"Great. It's from nine to two a week from Saturday. And I'll see you this Friday at the park at noon."

"Sounds good. Thanks."

After hanging up the phone, Heather tapped it against her hand, thinking. Now all she had to do was learn enough about this brain science stuff before Friday so she'd have something to talk about.

Chapter 13

Jan watched as Xavier climbed the steps to the larger of the two slides on the playground, she winced as he launched himself down it, not waiting for the little girl who'd gone before him to scramble off the bottom of the slide. Fortunately, the little girl moved herself out of harm's way before he reached the bottom.

Crossing one leg over the other, she rested her chin in her hand. A nap would be heavenly right about now. But of course, unless Derek was there to keep an eye on Xavier, no nap would be possible. Even when Derek *was* there, a nap usually wasn't possible. Her neck was stiff and sore, and she wished they could go home. But this time of getting energy out was important for Xavier. Besides, she still had her meeting with Heather.

She glanced toward the parking lot as the thought crossed her mind and saw Heather coming her way. The poor girl. She really didn't know what she was doing with Xavier. It was sweet of her to try, but over the past eight years, Jan had seen professionally trained people give up on her son. Heather just wasn't cut out for the job. No one was, apparently. Why had Derek insisted on these riding lessons? It would end up like everything else they'd tried. Disappointment for her and Derek, and another lost connection.

"Hi," said Heather, taking a seat on the bench next to her.

Jan smiled and scanned the playground.

"You look exhausted," said Heather. "Is everything okay?"

She shrugged her shoulders. "It's been a hard week. We took Xavier to see his new classroom at school, and we've slowly been trying to get him into the school routine, packing his lunch and making him get his backpack loaded and ready to go each day. Little things like that. But change is hard, and he knows school is going to start soon, which is a big change. We try to prepare in every way we can, like with the backpack, but it's never quite enough to prevent the season of meltdowns."

"Oh, I'm sorry. I can't imagine how difficult that must be for you and Derek."

She frowned. People said that all the time, and although it was true, they really didn't know, and their words of comfort did nothing to ease the stress of not knowing what would cause the next meltdown, or where, or how bad it would be. An afternoon of taking Xavier off her hands would do more than their words of sympathy ever could. But that never lasted long either. Something always happened. She and Derek were always called to return home, and sitters always quit, never repeating a visit more than three times. It made it difficult to relax when she and Derek did get the chance to get away for a date night. They were always waiting for the call or text that would end the night.

She cleared her throat and took a sip of water from one of the two water bottles she kept in her purse. "I told you Xavier and Derek are still willing to move forward with the riding lessons, even though Xavier isn't sure about riding, and I'm a little hesitant. I know it takes a longer time to determine if it will be good for him or not, but with school starting, I'm worried about putting too much on him. Derek wants this to work because of all the articles he's read on the benefits other kids have experienced, but he also feels a lot of guilt."

She was silent for a moment, looking off into the distance. Then she added: "I think he just wants to find things to keep Xavier busy so I get a break, because I'm the one who's with him all day and adopting him wasn't really my choice." *Crap*. She hadn't meant to say that.

Heather drew back in surprise.

Jan sat up straight and held her hand out defensively. "I was on board with adopting Xavier, but he is Derek's blood relative. His niece's baby. And when he heard she didn't want Xavier, he suggested to his brother and sister-in-law that we adopt him before he consulted me about it. We'd already been talking about adopting because we couldn't get pregnant, so it wasn't like he was going against my wishes or anything. He knew we'd been discussing adoption, and here was a child who needed a home. But I think he has guilt over not including me in the decision, especially because we didn't realize things would be this difficult when we signed the papers. And because it was a private adoption and not a state one, state resources are pretty much impossible to get, and everything else is too expensive and isn't covered by insurance."

"I see. Gosh, I know I keep saying this, but the more I learn, the more I understand how hard it is for you guys. Not just from the point of raising Xavier, but from every side. The lack of professional supports, the lack of understanding about special needs in general. I really want to help in whatever way I can. And I think it would be great if we could get to a place where you can leave him in my care, to have a break."

A lump formed in Jan's throat, but she smiled and swallowed until it lessened. People said that too, but it only took one outburst for them to change their minds. "That's sweet. It really is. But you have your business to run and I don't want you overwhelmed with our issues. Especially since it's unlikely Xavier will ever get back on a horse."

She scanned the playground again for Xavier. He was watching two other children about his age build a sandcastle with brightly colored buckets of various sizes that had decorated bottoms to look like castle spires. He was a little closer than social norms allowed, but the kids didn't seem to mind. She glanced around at the other parents and saw one woman watching the two kids intently. She was alert but didn't seem worried about Xavier being so close to her kids.

"I've actually been doing some research on my own that I've found interesting," said Heather. "I'm not sure if it's anything that would be useful for Xavier or not, but I thought I would ask you about it. I know you've both done a lot of research, and it's possible you've heard of this already."

Jan looked at her. Heather's hands were clasped casually in her lap, but the red half-moons on her nails suggested she was anything but relaxed. If there was one thing she'd learned from being Xavier's mom, it was how to read people. She could always tell when someone had passed from sincerely wanting to help to simply being polite and giving lip service to the idea. It always meant they were going to quit soon. But so far, Heather seemed sincere. She had good reason to be nervous about bringing up some kind of research, though. Many people had assumed she and Derek hadn't looked into every possible resource for Xavier, and it always rankled when they went through the litany of their sources.

"I've been trying to learn more about FASD to better understand how I can help, but haven't found much. The information I came across is really fascinating, but I can't find anything about it specifically helping special-needs kids of any sort, so I don't know if it's anything to pursue or not, but there are interesting brain science studies that suggest ways we can heal the brain with special exercises."

Jan felt the usual annoyance welling up in her, the kind she experienced whenever someone presumed to make recommendations. Although she hadn't heard of such "exercises," that hardly mattered. Xavier had brain damage in the womb. *Damaged.* As in, not fixable. Not developed correctly. Not normal.

Xavier's angry scream cut through her thoughts, and she twisted her head toward the playground.

He still stood near the kids with the sandcastle buckets. He pointed at the large purple one sitting near one of the little girls, unused. The little girl shook her head and pulled the bucket closer to her. Xavier stomped his foot.

"Xavier, honey, if they don't want you to play with their toys, you need to listen, okay?"

Xavier glared at her and folded his arms but didn't move away from the girls. Jan stared at him, her eyebrows raised. She counted to twenty in her head, then said, "Do you need a drink of water?" Often changing the subject completely jarred him out of his bad mood enough to defuse the situation. She could tell he was thinking about her question, but he finally shook his head no.

"Okay." She glanced at the woman sitting on the other side of the playground, who was observing Jan and Xavier's exchange. "Can you show me and Heather how you can get across the monkey bars?" she asked, anxiety squeezing her chest as she tried desperately to move her son away from the two little girls.

Xavier's gaze shifted to the seat next to her, and his expression changed to one of surprise. He hadn't realized Heather was here, but now, of course, he had someone to impress, so he agreed to her idea and ran off. Jan forced her shoulders to relax a little.

"Sorry about that."

"It's all right," said Heather.

"What do you mean by 'healing the brain'?"

"Well, I've only started to learn about it, but the book I'm reading right now explains, in layman's terms, how the brain works in processing emotions and stimuli, and things like that. According to the introduction, the later parts of the book explain how we can do things to strengthen connections in the brain that are weak, for whatever reason. So if calming down from anger is a struggle, you can do things to make that easier, by strengthening the connection to whatever the brain needs to connect to in order to help someone calm down faster and easier, or not get so worked up. At least, that's what I'm understanding so far. I really haven't gotten very far into it yet," she said apologetically.

Jan's annoyance returned. If Heather wasn't even that far into the book, why bring it up at all?

"I haven't heard of it, but Xavier doesn't need to be *fixed*. He just learns slower, gets overwhelmed easily, and needs people who can understand that and support him, not try to *fix* him."

Heather's hands flew to her mouth. "Oh, no, that's not what I meant at all."

Xavier's scream came again, and Jan blew out a breath as she looked to the playground. Xavier was hanging from the middle monkey bar. Another boy had started on the monkey bars opposite where Xavier had started, and now they were at an impasse. Xavier kicked his legs at the boy but didn't connect. Jan got up and rushed over. "Xavier, there's enough room for you to get around him. Just put your hand here." She showed the space where he could place his hand.

He shook his head and screamed again, kicking his feet while doing so. His hands were red from the effort of trying to keep his grip.

Jan looked at the other boy, whose eyes were wide and hands just as red, and wondered where his parents were and why they weren't coming to save their kid. Xavier was stuck on making it across and wouldn't move with this boy there. But she couldn't ask the boy to keep crossing with Xavier kicking like this. And from the look of things, asking or waiting for Xavier to drop might cause a meltdown. It wasn't fair to ask the other kid to drop to the ground and start over, but it was the easiest solution. "Hey, I don't want you to get hurt with him kicking like this. Do you mind letting go and giving him some space?"

The boy stared at her and back at Xavier, then dropped to the ground and ran off.

"There, he moved. Do you want to finish crossing now?"

Xavier grunted and kicked at her.

"Hey, that is not okay. Do I need to take a point away?" She hated taking points away in public places, but he couldn't be violent. One day he would be big enough to do serious damage to people or property. This was one lesson they wanted him to learn while he was still small.

He grunted again and wiggled his entire body, still clinging to the bar.

"You need to be nice with your body, then. Now, decide if you want to cross or drop, then come and get some water, okay?"

Xavier let himself drop, then sat in the sand and crossed his arms in full pouting mode.

"Can you make him move? I want to cross," said a little girl who was now standing on the top ladder rung of the monkey bars.

Jan blew out a breath of irritation. "He's going to need a few minutes."

Xavier picked up a handful of sand and threw it toward the girl.

"Mommy!" the little girl screamed and ran off.

Jan rolled her eyes. The sand hadn't even come close to hitting her. "Xavier, we don't throw sand," she said sternly.

He picked up another handful and threw it at her legs, then glared up at her.

"Okay, one point."

He let out an ear-piercing scream, got up, and started hitting, pinching, and kicking her.

Jan stepped behind him, wrapped her arms around his torso and upper arms, then dropped into a sitting position, which forced Xavier to do the same. Then she wrapped both her legs over his. A classic therapy hold they'd learned in the adoption classes, meant to prevent injury to the child and the adult until the crisis was over.

Xavier fought against her with every ounce of strength he had and tried to twist his arms to scratch and pinch any part of her body he could reach. He also pounded his head against her chest.

"What can I do?" asked Heather, who'd run over the instant Jan restrained Xavier.

"Call Derek. Tell him what's going on," she said over Xavier's screams.

"Okay."

Heather dug her phone from her pocket. She almost dropped it twice because her hands were shaking so badly. Finally, she found Derek's number and called. She paced, watching Xavier struggle against Jan's hold as she listened to the ringing. "Come on, come on." The phone went to voice mail.

"Hi Derek, this is Heather. I'm with Jan and Xavier at the park, and Xavier is having a meltdown. Jan is ... um ..." What was the word? "Holding him down. She asked me to call you and let you know. Thanks. Bye."

She hung up the phone. What now?

She glanced around the park at the other parents and children. Many parents were packing up and leaving, but two or three stood around watching and talking on their phones while they tried to get their children off the playground.

Her heart raced and her entire body felt shaky. She tried to take deep breaths to calm herself, but she couldn't catch her breath. Not knowing what else to do, she tried Derek again, and again got his voice mail.

There had to be *something* else she could do.

But nothing came to mind, so she paced near the park bench, hoping Jan would ask her to do more so she didn't have to stand here feeling completely useless, and waited as Xavier continued to thrash in his mother's arms.

After a few minutes, she managed to regulate her breathing and noticed that, by degrees, Xavier was calming down. He wasn't fighting as hard. She couldn't wrap her mind around it. Why this explosion? She'd seen little children get upset and kick and scream, but this was different. Bigger. Scarier, somehow. Out of control. Her phone rang.

Glancing at the screen, she let out a sigh of relief.

"Derek, hi."

"Hey, are you still at the park?"

"Yeah, it looks like he's calming down, but Jan is still holding him."

"Are you okay?"

"Me?" Heather was surprised he would even consider her at this moment.

"Yeah, I know something like this can be a shock at first. It gets the adrenaline pumping."

Heather chuckled, an inexplicable lump formed in her throat. "Yeah, it does. But I think I'm all right." Her voice shook, and she looked around the playground again. All the parents except one had left. One woman stood halfway between the playground and the parking lot, shifting her weight from one foot to the other, her cell phone clutched to her chest. Her children, the two who had the sandcastle buckets, played tag in the grass nearby. She looked toward the street. Heather followed her gaze. Two police cars had just pulled up, and the officers were climbing out. Surely the woman hadn't called the police on Jan and Xavier!

"Tell Jan I'm on my way."

"Okay, it looks like the police are here, too."

She heard Derek sigh. "Yeah, that happens pretty frequently. They know us pretty well by now, though."

"You're kidding."

"Nope. I've got to go. I'll be there soon."

"Okay." Heather couldn't believe any of this was actually happening. The meltdown was one thing, but to have to deal with having the police called on you as well? And for this to happen frequently? She shook her head. What was wrong with people?

"Derek's on his way," she shouted to Jan.

Jan nodded. Xavier wasn't fighting anymore, and Jan rocked him back and forth as he whimpered softly.

The police officers took their time in approaching them. They glanced at Heather, clearly uncertain about her role in this. She decided to let them come to her and kept her eyes on Jan and Xavier.

"Are you thirsty?" asked Jan after another minute passed.

Xavier nodded.

"Why don't we get up and get some water? I have some in my bag."

Xavier nodded again and slowly climbed to his feet. His pants were wet at the front, but he didn't seem to notice or care.

Heather saw Jan eye the officers as they walked toward Heather. Once Jan and Xavier reached the bench, Jan told the boy to sit down and drink his water. He complied, his eyelids drooping, as he sat sipping. He seemed zoned out; he didn't look her way or at the police officers standing a short distance behind him.

It reminded Heather of Littlefoot and how he disassociated whenever she came too close. For the horse, disassociation was a reaction to too much stimulation, which basically prompted the horse's mind to shut down until it wasn't overwhelmed anymore. After what she'd just witnessed, she could easily believe Xavier was experiencing something similar.

Jan walked over to the officers and spoke with them. After a few minutes, the officers left and Jan rejoined Heather and Xavier.

Heather hoped for an explanation but didn't want to ask. The ordeal had left Jan looking more tired than ever, and although she wanted to understand what had happened, she realized getting answers might have to wait.

Derek pulled up at the park and joined them a moment later, and Heather suddenly felt like a third and unnecessary wheel. What was she doing just standing around like this? She took a few steps away to give them some space.

Derek leaned over Jan and whispered to her, then straightened and smiled at Heather. "I'm going to take Xavier home and let Jan recuperate for a while."

Heather nodded. "Is there anything I can do?" she asked quietly.

"No. Jan usually just needs some time to be quiet and alone after an episode like this, and Xavier will most likely take a nap."

Heather nodded again. "I guess I'll head home then. Please let me know if I can do something."

"Thanks, I will," said Derek.

Heather headed toward her car, feeling as though she'd just woken from a nightmare. She thought she understood now why Jan never smiled. What she'd just witnessed was Jan and Derek's life. Day in, day out. She thought about her own parents and wondered if she or her siblings had ever caused their parents this much pain and stress. From her perspective, there was always laughter and joy in their home. There didn't appear to be much joy in Jan and Derek's experience of parenting.

Chapter 14

Heather parked her truck in front of the horse barn and stared out the front window for a moment, wondering how she'd made it home. She remembered nothing of the drive. Climbing out, she headed for her office, then closed the door behind her and sat at her desk, where she burst into tears. Sobs wracked her body as the events from that afternoon played over again in her mind.

She wasn't even sure why she was crying. Was it the shock and helplessness she felt? The sudden awareness of what Jan and Derek endured on an almost daily basis? Her inability to help, either in that moment or with the horse lessons?

The calm determination on Jan's face as she held her thrashing son flashed through her mind. How did they live like that, never knowing what would send Xavier off the deep end? The physical and mental stress of it had to be immense.

Her sobs subsided, and she glanced around her office for something to wipe her face with. She found a stack of clean, worn cloths she used to dust and tidy up her office, grabbed one, and covered her face with it as a fresh batch of tears surfaced. How could she have been so stupid as to suggest she knew something about brain science that might help them? Jan had been irritated at the suggestion, she was sure. But she wasn't really trying to *fix* Xavier, was she? The whole point was to help him learn to ride. She thought over the past few weeks. All the advice she'd gotten, all the research she'd done. Maybe she *had* veered off course. She fixed behavior issues in horses for a living, so transferring that idea to her work with Xavier wasn't that far-fetched, was it?

But human beings were a lot more complicated. Pastor Barker had told her she was doing the right thing by learning as much as she could from science and the Bible, but how could it be the right thing if she used what she learned the same way she used her knowledge about horses—as a way to fix people. Who was she to think she could "fix" a boy she'd barely known for a few weeks? Jan was right to feel offended.

A light knock sounded at her door, and she wiped her eyes and blew her nose with the rag.

The door opened, and Dad stepped in.

"I stopped by to see if I could borrow—" He stopped and frowned. "What's wrong?"

She waved a hand in his direction and attempted a smile. "Oh ..." She shook her head. "All the stress from being so busy is catching up with me. No big deal. What did you need to borrow?" She set the rag she'd been using on the corner of her desk and grabbed a fresh one.

"Stress? This looks like a little more than stress. Did something happen with that kid?"

Her lips trembled as she tried to hold back tears, but they burst out of her and she doubled over in her chair, covering her face with the rag.

His hand rested on her back, heavy and comforting. He massaged her neck lightly with his thumb and forefinger, not speaking, until she was calm enough to speak herself.

"What's going on, darlin'?" he asked, gently pushing her shoulders back to make eye contact with her.

"I met Jan and Xavier at the park today instead of having a lesson with him." She explained how Derek wanted Xavier to continue with the lessons, but Jan had doubts. Wiping her face and taking a deep breath, she continued. "I wanted to ask Jan if she'd heard about this brain science stuff Pastor Barker has been teaching about in church, to see if it was even worth pursuing for Xavier. She hadn't, but she thought I was trying to 'fix' her son. I don't know. I don't think that was really my intention, but I've been fixing horses for so long the idea might have transferred over to Xavier."

"I'm sure that's not true," said Dad.

"Before we cleared the air, Xavier got upset with another boy on the playground and had a meltdown. Jan had to restrain him to keep him from hurting anyone. It was awful."

Dad rubbed her arm. "It sounds awful. But no one got hurt?"

She shook her head. "No, but someone called the police." Her lips trembled again. "I couldn't believe someone did that." Tears filled her eyes again, and she dabbed them away with the rag.

"They've probably never seen a child restrained like that before. I might have been concerned myself."

Heather shrugged. "I guess so. I just can't imagine being a parent who's wrapped up in trying to get their out-of-control child to calm down and then have to be questioned by police. What if the police had decided she was abusing Xavier? To have to worry about being arrested for child abuse, or have your child taken away from you, on top of everything else? It's not right."

"No, but I suspect those people who called the police didn't know what they were seeing. A kid like that, completely out of control. There's bound to be trouble." He shook his head.

Her father's defense of the bystanders irritated her. He was trying to get her to see the other side of things, but she already knew about that side—she was on it, and now her eyes were open. People needed to be aware of what Jan, Derek, and Xavier were going through. There needed to be more understanding about children with special needs. She nodded but said nothing more.

Dad straightened and stuck his hands in his pockets. "So what are you going to do?"

She looked up at him. "About what?"

"About teaching Xavier to ride."

"I don't know." She hung her head.

He sighed. "Sweetheart, this sounds like a good time to back out."

"What?" she asked, looking up and searching his eyes. She only saw concern.

"Look how upset you are, and you were only a witness to what happened today. What will you do if you're alone with Xavier and he has a meltdown like he had today? What if it happens when he's on a horse?"

Last week could have been just as bad as today. She knew that. Instead, he'd frozen with fear on the horse and simply screamed. Still,

Dad had a point. It would be dangerous for both of them if he acted out around a horse, the way he had at the park today. "I'm not sure what I would do."

"It's dangerous. There are organizations and programs out there that help these kinds of kids. The people there are trained to handle these kinds of situations. You aren't."

Heather buried her face in her hands. He was right. But why couldn't she learn? Why did she have to be another person in a long line of people who'd already given up on the Rodenbaum family?

"Sweetheart, I don't want to tell you what to do, but consider what will happen if you have a neighbor drop by, or someone comes to buy one of your horses, or drops off donations, and Xavier is in the middle of a meltdown, you having to pin him down to keep him from harm. What will people think? They'll see that and won't want their kids taking lessons from you, or they might wonder if you're rough with the horses. And seeing you like this ... well, I hate it. Your mother and I are worried about you, about the danger you're taking on with this boy. It could destroy everything you've worked to build here."

She looked up at him through fresh tears. "The Rodenbaums need help. If you spoke with them for just five minutes, you'd see it in their eyes."

"I believe you, Heather, I do. But you aren't qualified to help them, and there's too much risk for you in even trying. Perhaps your role in all this is to help them find the resources that can help."

Heather remembered the irritation on Jan's face when she brought up what she was learning about brain science. He might be right, but how could she send them to another place that might just turn them away, or worse, a place that was perfect but unaffordable for them? She nodded, ready to be done with this conversation. "Maybe."

She needed a day or two to think through everything. So many voices had entered her head she felt pulled in all directions. She thought about Pastor Barker's warm encouragement, Derek's desperate hopefulness, Dad's fear, verging on anger, Aunt Michelle's stress over teaching special-needs kids, and Jan's anger from today and her doubts about Heather's ability to help them.

Dad sighed, and his jaw worked back and forth. "Just think about it?"

"I will. I have been. Promise."

Dad went back to his chores, and Heather, feeling exhausted but less emotional, prepared some treats for Littlefoot and headed out to work with him. Some physical exercise would do her good and help get her mind off the situation with Xavier.

She'd made progress with Littlefoot over the past week. The sedative seemed to be working. She could now stand next to him, and he only disassociated when she touched him. It was more progress than she'd anticipated, but it probably wasn't enough to convince Mom and save him from the threat of being put down. There was still a lot of work to do. Once she could touch him without him disassociating, she would work on leaving her hand on his nose for an extended period, then moving down the rest of his body, where he wouldn't necessarily be able to see her.

She clicked her tongue to get Littlefoot's attention as she climbed over the fence. He had his back toward her, but at the noise, he turned and watched her approach. She moved at her normal pace now and didn't pause. Littlefoot still looked a little wary and stepped back, as if he had considered protesting her approach but decided against it.

Yesterday he'd finally taken a nibble of a treat she'd offered. Today, she left the apples and carrots in the pouch on her belt to see if he would still accept her approach. He did.

He flinched slightly when she reached up to touch his nose and disassociated after five seconds of touch. She removed her hand and stepped back, letting him come back slowly. Once he was alert again, she repeated the process.

"Good boy," she cooed in the few seconds she had his attention before he shut down again. She removed her hand but stayed standing next to him this time.

Sometimes the process of helping horses through their issues was guided by looking for microscopic improvements. A tiny speck of new trust from one day to the next. Sometimes, you really had to look for it. And sometimes those slight improvements came after weeks or months of no change. If you weren't looking for the small things, you might never realize you were making a difference.

She thought about Xavier. Was it the same with him? Jan said he learned slower than other kids. Did they look for minor improvements in him? If so, how long did it take, typically?

She sighed, closed her eyes, and rested her head against Littlefoot's neck. Yet another question she didn't have an answer to. Littlefoot flinched, and she realized what she'd done.

Opening her eyes, but not moving, she waited. Littlefoot adjusted his weight from one side to the other and snorted softly. She felt his head cradle hers and she lifted her forehead from his neck, met his gaze, and smiled. He was alert, watching her. "You can sense I've had a rough day, can't you?" She wasn't touching him anymore, although the urge to do so was strong. He nuzzled her shoulder.

"If anyone knows what a rough day is like, you do. Don't you, bud?" The wariness in his eyes vanished for the moment as his desire to comfort shone through. Only time would tell if this was a breakthrough moment or a momentary fluke that would disappear after she was in a better mood, but she enjoyed every second of seeing Littlefoot's true nature shine.

"I can't tell you how much I needed this today, Littlefoot," she whispered to him, fresh tears filling her eyes.

He grunted and nuzzled at the pouch on her belt. She laughed and loosened the top, pulling out an apple slice. He happily took it from her hand before turning away from her, ready for a break from their interactions.

"What do you think, Littlefoot? Should I help Xavier's parents find some other resources for him?" she asked, offering him a carrot, which he sniffed at but didn't take.

"Oh, you don't like carrots? What's wrong with them?" she asked, trying to get him to take the carrot, but once more he refused. "All right, apples it is." She took the last three apple slices out of her pouch, holding one out to him. He hesitated, and the wariness returned to his eyes.

"People told me I shouldn't expect too much from you, either, you know. That I shouldn't put too much effort into your rehabilitation because you're a lost cause. Until this very moment, I thought they were right. But look at you now." She paused, watching as he stepped toward her and took the offered apple slice from her hand. "I don't know what to do, Littlefoot. I wish there was some kind of sign to show me the right path to take with Xavier. Like the sign you've just shown me." She glanced toward the sky, offering a silent prayer. *Show me what to do, Lord.*

She needed to talk to someone, vent, get a new perspective. But who? She already knew her parents' opinion. Parker and Harry were busy, Scott was ... well, not reliable. Not Jan or Derek. Someone she could express all her opinions, fears, and frustrations to who wasn't already involved. She pulled her cell phone out and called Cleo. She needed her best friend.

Chapter 15

The next afternoon, Heather drove to a café forty-five minutes away to meet Cleo for lunch—the halfway point between their homes.

She paced in front of the small eatery, watching for her friend's car, and didn't relax until she saw it. As Cleo climbed out, Heather walked toward her, grinning. Cleo's thick black hair was styled in a short, poofy Afro. She wore bright yellow capris, a white T-shirt, and white flats. They hugged.

"It's been too long, girl," said Cleo.

"Yes, it has. You've changed your hair. I love it." They pulled apart and made their way inside.

"Yeah, I'm trying to embrace my natural hair, but I did that forever ago. I thought I told you? I know, it's my fault. I had to go and move to the big city."

"Right, but we agreed it was for a worthy cause—so you can become a doctor, move back home, and take care of all my horse-related injuries."

They laughed.

"That's right, and I'm getting there. Had my last pre-med final yesterday, and then I'm moving on to the MCATs."

"That's so awesome! I hope when you go through your residency, you get to work in a hospital closer to home."

"Me too, girl, me too."

They followed a waiter to a table and looked over their menus. Neither had been here before; they liked picking a new place every time they met up.

"This place is cute," said Cleo.

The interior was decorated to look like a French bistro. The floors were made of brick-red cobblestone, the walls a light cream color with vines painted along the top. Plants were on every surface that could hold a plant without being obnoxious or in the way.

"Yeah, I love all the plants." She reached out and touched one. "They're real. That's neat."

"Mm-hmm. So what's going on? You didn't sound so hot on the phone yesterday."

The waiter returned and took their order. Heather waited until he left before answering Cleo's question.

"I need some perspective, and maybe some advice."

"Perspective? Are you having a midlife crisis or something?"

Heather smiled. "No. I have a new riding student, and I don't know if I should keep trying to teach him or give up." She told Cleo about Xavier and everything that had happened since Derek called her three weeks ago. Their food came while she told the story, and they were half done with their meal before she finished.

When she ended, Cleo sat back and blew out a breath. "Girl, you sound all kinds of confused."

Heather buried her face in her hands. "I do, don't I? I'm completely overthinking this and making connections where there are none, right? Like between Pastor Barker's message and how to help Xavier?"

"I don't know about that."

Heather raised her head.

"Will you be needing to-go boxes today?" asked the waiter, returning.

They both declined the offer.

"How about some dessert?"

"Yes, sir," said Cleo. "I want a slice of that cheesecake I saw in the display when we walked in."

The waiter smiled and nodded.

"I didn't see the cheesecake, but that sounds good. I'll have a slice too."

"Very good," said the waiter, and he left.

"In school I did a whole semester learning about brain function. It's fascinating and incredibly complicated. There's so much we still don't know, especially about problems like FASD. But I don't think the connection you've made is all that far-fetched."

"Really?"

She shook her head. "There are all kinds of studies out there showing how the brain is capable of healing after traumatic injuries, and in areas where the brain has been damaged, there are cases where the brain actually made connections around the damaged area and functioned like normal. It's an amazing piece of equipment we have behind our eyes."

The waiter returned with their cheesecake and cleared their plates.

"My main question for you is, what do *you* want to do? You wanna teach this boy or not?"

"I want ..." She shook her head as Jan's never-smiling face came to mind. "I want to bring them some joy. All of them." Her voice shook as she said it.

Cleo nodded, took a bite of her cheesecake thoughtfully, then pointed her fork at Heather. "How are *you* going to do that?"

Heather sat back in her seat and shrugged. "I don't know. Jan's right—Xavier may never get back on a horse. In which case, my skills are pretty useless."

Cleo cocked her head to one side. "I don't know about that. You're Miss Horse Whisperer. You could teach him a bazillion things other than just riding. Maybe you haven't figured out how to teach him yet, but that doesn't mean the information and the skills to do it aren't there. You think you've identified the skills he could learn just by being *around* the horses, right?"

"Kind of. I'm still working on that. I mean, the obvious ones are trust, perseverance, responsibility, and patience. But those things all come with what I can do with a horse—training them, taking care of them, things like that. I'm not sure I can go about it the same way with Xavier."

"And this big blowup happened yesterday, so you haven't talked to them since." Cleo tapped the fork tines against her lip.

"The problem is, until the fundraiser is over, I don't have a lot of extra time to look into all this stuff. And I don't feel confident in moving forward until I can learn more, but I can't learn more until I talk to Jan and Derek and get that straightened out. I thought about seeing if I could take a tour of some therapy ranches. Derek mentioned them when he first called me but said they couldn't afford to send Xavier there, which is why they called me. If I can get a tour, ask some questions, I might have a better idea of what to do."

Cleo set her fork down and wiped her mouth with the napkin. "Sounds to me like you know exactly what you need to do. Call them. Everyone's cooled off by now. Maybe call them tonight, when they're both home and have fewer distractions. Then go for that tour thing. That sounds like a great idea."

Heather nodded. "But what about my dad? I can't just ignore his concern. He really isn't comfortable with me teaching Xavier. In fact, as much as he tries to hide it, I think he's angry with me for persisting with something he thinks is risky and foolish."

"No, you can't just ignore it, but you have to get this situation resolved first, or it's gonna keep eating at you. I don't think you're a people *fixer*; you're more of a people *pleaser*. You want to help these folks, but you want to make your dad happy, too. Maybe if you get things straightened out with this family and take the tour, you'll be able to explain to your dad why it's important for you to keep helping them. And why you think you can make a difference for this little boy. I'm sure he'd understand."

Heather shrugged. "I don't know."

"Think about it this way: if you call them tonight and apologize and they don't want Xavier coming back for more lessons, then problem solved. All the issues go away. But if they hear you out and want to keep up with the lessons, then you have a chance to say what you really meant to say to them and decide what you want to do. And after you know exactly what you want to do, you can explain it to your dad."

Heather sighed and took a bite of her cheesecake. Cleo made it all sound so easy. A clear path. Yet, whatever way the conversation with Jan and Derek went, she would be left feeling unsatisfied. If they walked away, yes, her other issues would go away, but she would feel guilty. It would be her fault for driving them away, and possibly keeping them from finding something that could eventually bring some relief and joy. If they didn't walk away, she would have to decide to keep moving forward and reject Dad's advice, possibly driving an even larger wedge between them.

But Cleo was right—the only way to know which way to proceed would be to call and apologize to Jan.

They paid for their meal and exited the restaurant.

"You're still letting people come by Friday evening to set up, right?"

"Yeah."

Cleo nodded. "Since I don't have a booth, I'll stop by for moral support. You can catch me up on what happens with your phone call, and I'll see if I can find some studies linking some brain science stuff to helping kids with FASD."

"Thank you." She gave Cleo a hug. "That would be amazing. And thanks for letting me talk your ear off, and for showing me the path through the forest."

Cleo chucked her lightly on the chin. "That's what I'm here for, girl."

Back in her truck, she dialed the Rodenbaums' number and got their voice mail. "Hi, it's Heather. I'd like to see if we can meet up sometime this week and talk. Give me a call. Thanks."

Chapter 16

Tuesday morning, Heather grabbed some apples, cut them into slices, and put them in her treat pouch. After tying the pouch around her waist, she grabbed a brush and her hoof kit and headed out back to work with Littlefoot. In a couple of hours she would head to town for lunch with the Rodenbaums. Until then, to try and expend some of her nervous energy, she would train her horses.

Setting the hoof kit and brush on the ground by the fence, she climbed over, took an apple slice from her pouch, and waited to see if Littlefoot would come to her.

He stood on the opposite side of the ring, watching her. When he saw the apple, his ears perked up and he took a few steps toward her but stopped.

"What's wrong, Littlefoot? Come get your treat." She took a couple of steps toward the middle and stopped again. After about a minute of watching her, Littlefoot closed the distance between them and accepted his treat. Heather lightly patted the side of his face. "Good boy."

He'd continued to make progress, and she could now touch his face and ears for an extended time. Today, she planned to push him a little.

She gave him another apple slice, then ran her hand down his side, walking backward so she could watch his body language. When she reached his tail, she ran her fingers through the long strands of hair. He flinched at the touch and disassociated. She returned to stand near his head, and when he became alert again, she ran her hand over his chest and down the other side. No more twitching, no disassociation this time. A little wariness, but he was learning to trust her. She smiled and fed him another apple slice. Until he allowed the same interaction without being sedated, she couldn't fully trust his progress. But it was something, and that pleased her.

Retrieving the brush from where she'd left it, she let Littlefoot smell it before running the bristles over his chest. He snorted and backed away. Heather fished an apple slice from her bag and held it out. He came forward again. When she gave him the apple, she simultaneously stroked his chest with the brush. This time the skin on his chest flinched, but he seemed to accept it.

Slowly and lightly she brushed him from head to tail, the first brushing he'd had since arriving here three weeks ago. As she brushed, she thought about Xavier and the conversation she would have with his parents in a little more than an hour. What did Xavier think about the situation? Would it matter to him at all if he no longer came here? Would he eventually forget? Or would he feel rejected?

After the brushing was done, Heather grabbed the hoof kit. She wanted to clean Littlefoot's hooves if she could. This would be a real test, because this was the most touch he'd had in who knows how long. It also meant he had to trust her enough to lift each leg and hold it for an extended period. Today she would try to lift each leg for a few seconds. If he allowed that, she would attempt to clean them.

Setting the hoof kit on the ground nearby, she stood as close to his front leg as she could and ran her hand down it until she reached the fetlock. Lightly pulling on the hair there, she waited. After a few seconds, Littlefoot lifted his leg, and she grasped it in both hands, running her fingers over the hoof before setting it down again. He could do with a good nail trimming, too. But that would have to come later.

She repeated the process with his other front leg, which also went smoothly. Moving to the back legs, she started the same routine, but this time Littlefoot snorted, attempted a half-hearted kick, and moved away. She corrected him and tried again. Again he tried to kick and moved away from her. She tried the other back leg, with the same result.

"Okay, bud, let's try one more thing."

She lightly pushed on his rump to direct him toward the fence. He walked, and she waved her arms to keep him from trotting past her. He resisted a little but went where she wanted him to go.

When he was next to the fence, she stood next to his back leg, leaning against him so that his rear was pinned between the fence and herself. She ran her hand down his back leg and tugged on the fetlock. He tried to kick and then rear, and she moved out of the way. She'd found his limits there. But at least she'd gotten a good look at his hooves and could relax knowing he hadn't injured himself the day he'd arrived.

"Okay, Littlefoot. We're done." She held out an apple slice to entice him back toward her. It took more than a minute for him to make the choice to approach her, but eventually he did. She rubbed his neck while he munched. "Good job. I know you were pinned in that trailer, and pinning you next to the fence was a risk, but I had to try."

She gave him another piece of apple, then picked up her things and headed back to the barn.

She met the Rodenbaums in front of Pablo's, a popular pizza joint in downtown Ogden.

"I'd like to pay today," said Heather.

Derek and Jan looked at each other. "That's really not necessary," Derek said.

"I know, but I'd still like to make this my treat." They both looked tired today, and maybe a little annoyed.

"Thank you," said Derek, and they headed inside to place their order and find a seat among the busy lunch crowd. Heather paid for their food as promised and joined them at a table nestled in the corner by the front windows.

A server joined them as Heather settled into her seat and verified their drink order while he placed a stack of napkins, two trivets for their pizzas, and a pile of forks for the salad Jan had ordered for everyone to share.

"Thank you for letting me take you all out to lunch," said Heather.

"You're welcome," said Xavier.

Heather chuckled.

"I think we're the ones who are supposed to be thanking you," said Derek.

"Yes, you're paying, after all," said Jan, as she unfolded the coloring page the server had given Xavier and set it in front of him.

"Our conversation didn't go well on Friday," Heather said, jumping to the point, "which is why I wanted to talk to you both."

Derek and Jan glanced at each other, then back to Heather.

"Yeah, sorry. We should have called before now, but things have been rough," said Derek, glancing at Xavier.

Heather shook her head. "No, I didn't communicate very clearly. I never meant to imply I wanted to fix him. I feel awful about that."

Derek looked at Jan, who hung her head but didn't respond.

"I understand if you want to back out, but I'd at least like to explain what I meant to say on Friday."

Jan looked up, a pained expression on her face. "Please, it's not your fault. I know you've been trying really hard with Xavier. We've been through a lot of resources—some helpful, some not so helpful—but everyone gives us advice, and new things to try, and I'm a little sensitive about it because a lot of suggestions come from people who won't or can't help us, so they tell us about some resource they heard about. Plus, the back-to-school behaviors are rearing their ugly head and … I just wasn't in a good place on Friday."

Heather was almost speechless. The expression on Jan's face was genuine and raw. This was the first time Jan had appeared as something more than a shell of herself.

"Heather, I meant what I said on Friday. You have a business to run, and our situation is a complicated one. I don't want our family to be a burden to you," Jan continued.

Derek nodded. "I wanted this to work out because of the articles I'd read, but it's not fair to ask you to continue when it seems more and more likely it won't succeed."

Here it was: her opportunity to walk away. Dad would be happy; the gap between them would close. She looked at Jan's and Derek's exhausted faces and remembered the desperate enthusiasm in Derek's voice when he first called her. She thought about the information she'd learned from Pastor Barker's messages, the books he'd loaned her, and his encouragement to reach out to Xavier. And the way Derek had made sure she was okay, even in the middle of their own crisis. She glanced at Xavier who sat silently beside her, coloring. Cleo's words filtered through all of it: *What do you want to do?*

She realized that no matter what she decided about Xavier, she wanted to keep learning about brain science. It intrigued her and made her think about her own relationships and what she could do to strengthen them. She hadn't been able to help this family when Xavier had his meltdown at the park because she had no idea what she could do or what would be best. And now, looking at Jan's and Derek's tired faces, she felt that helplessness again. She wanted so much to help them, but how?

"I appreciate you offering me a graceful way out." She paused. "My family has expressed concern about these lessons, so I'm feeling a little stuck as to whether I should continue or not. But from the beginning, you said you wanted to find somewhere for Xavier to go so you could have a break. I know I don't know what I'm doing, but I'm learning. I might not be the perfect choice for that reason, but, like I said, I've learned some things since last Friday that have made me look at his lessons differently. I'd like to share what I've learned and see how you feel about the direction I'm considering before I make a final decision."

Jan and Derek nodded.

The server returned with their pizzas and salad, and two pitchers, one filled with water, the other with Coke. After he placed their food and beverages on the table and everyone filled their plates, Heather resumed.

"I've been getting a lot of advice from people too, not all of it helpful. I'm sure not to the degree you've experienced, but it does make it difficult to decide what the right thing to do is when you have so many voices in your head. So I can understand being sensitive to that. But I have hope that some of what I've been learning will work for anyone." She glanced at Xavier, then stabbed a piece of lettuce with her fork and stuck it into her mouth, giving herself a moment to gather her thoughts. Cleo hadn't found any helpful articles yet related directly to Xavier's problems, but the more Heather read, the more convinced she was that what scientists were learning about the brain's capacity to grow new connections would help.

"I hope I've learned enough about this subject to explain it correctly, because it's really interesting. And because you've done a lot of your own research about FASD, you may know some of this already, which is one of the things I want to find out. If you already know about this stuff, I guess I want to find out if you think it's really helpful or not."

Derek and Jan nodded, and she continued. "Our brains are divided into two hemispheres. The right side regulates our emotions and helps us in our relationships. And it works kind of like an elevator. We receive input—everything we experience through our senses—and that input goes up the different levels in our brain, each making decisions about how to respond to that input as it goes along.

"The goal is for that input to reach the prefrontal cortex." She pointed at her forehead. "That's kind of like the top floor; it's the part of our brain that is supposed to have executive control over the other levels. But the input can get stuck at any of the lower levels, which can cause unique problems depending on where it stops." She wiped her mouth with her napkin and sipped her soda.

"So, level one is what they call the attachment center. It's where we form attachments with other people, and it's the first area of our brains to develop when we're born. When we don't form healthy attachments to other people, starting when we're babies, then it becomes easier for us to attach to objects or get into addictive behaviors.

"The second level is the assessment center, based in the amygdala. Its job is basically to determine if the input is good, bad, or scary. It does this by consulting our memories. If input gets stuck on this level, it can lead to PTSD-type responses. While the amygdala is fully formed at birth, it can take in new experiences and quickly decide if they are scary or not. An overactive amygdala can cause us to react and make poor choices when we perceive and react to things as threats, even though they aren't true threats.

"Then there's the attunement center. This level lets us look at the people around us to see if they relate to our experience or not. When input gets stuck here, it can cause social awkwardness, misreading social cues, being unable to read body language. A lot of the issues you're trying to help Xavier with.

"The last level is the prefrontal cortex. It's the last to develop as we grow up, and it doesn't stop developing until we're well into our twenties. It's where we develop our identity, and it's also the area of our brain that can exercise control over the rest. If the input reaches the prefrontal cortex, it can tell the other three levels what to do with the information they've received. For example, if the amygdala perceives something as scary—like being on top of Queenie, for example—the prefrontal cortex can calm the amygdala down and let it know everything is safe. Does that make sense so far?"

Derek and Jan nodded.

"It's much more involved than that, obviously. But the point is that psychologists and neuroscientists have discovered ways to help the brain get unstuck so that the input can reach the prefrontal cortex. We all react differently to various levels of stimuli, depending on how strong our brain's connections are to each emotion. The neurons in our brains create pathways to and from every emotion, but those pathways have to be traveled a lot to make strong connections. The stronger the connection, the less likely we'll be able to get overwhelmed by a certain emotion. But for extreme emotions, it requires outside influences—the people around us—to recognize when we're stuck and encourage us to use the exercises these neuroscientists have come up with. Over time, if we use the exercises while we're experiencing those negative emotions, it will take less time for us to recover and calm down, because our brains will begin forming a new pathway out of that negative emotion. The more that pathway is traveled, the stronger it gets and the less those negative emotions trip us up.

"There are a lot of reasons the brain can get stuck, like I mentioned, but, in what I've been reading, the experts explain that when input gets stuck, it results in our brain being overwhelmed and shutting down. And when a brain is overwhelmed, it can look like hyperactivity, meltdowns, withdrawing into ourselves… which is why I wondered if it might be useful to look into those exercises for Xavier, even though nothing I've read so far has specifically mentioned special-needs children. But they do say the brain has an amazing ability to rewire itself, even if areas of the brain are damaged."

Heather stopped and took a bite of her pizza.

"What kinds of exercises do they recommend?" asked Derek, who appeared intrigued.

Jan, on the other hand, seemed closed off again. Heather hoped she hadn't offended her all over again.

"Well, I've only learned one or two so far, but from what I can gather, most of them have to do with doing different breathing exercises, or tapping on different parts of your body, or finding things to be grateful for. I'm not sure how the exercises relate to the different levels yet, but they all seem simple enough."

"Xavier's therapist has talked to us about breathing and tapping exercises, but we haven't really tried them," said Jan. "We could ask him if he's getting that from this brain science stuff when we see him later this week."

A tickle of hope twisted in Heather's stomach. Jan was willing to look into it more. That was a good sign.

"Yeah, it sounds fascinating. I wouldn't mind looking into it a little more myself," said Derek. "We know FASD affects the prefrontal cortex as well as the hippocampus, which is important for learning and memory. It's one of the reasons we have to be so diligent about having a routine and structure. The idea is that the skills we're teaching him will eventually become habit. Learned behavior. A way to circumvent the damaged hippocampus so he can learn. So it's easy for me to see how the brain could rewire itself in other areas."

Heather beamed. "I'm borrowing the books I have from someone else, but I can email you the names so you can look them up," offered Heather.

"That would be great," Derek replied.

"I have an aunt who works in the public school system. She's given me some insight to how things work with special-needs kids, and I think it would be useful to stop focusing so much on Xavier riding the horse right away and instead focus on the social and emotional skills he can learn just by being around horses."

"How would that work?" asked Derek.

"I'm still figuring it out, but I think we can start with our five senses. Paying attention to how we feel when we see, touch, smell, and hear different things. Learning how to care for the horse, what chores are involved, how to feed and groom them, that kind of thing."

Derek nodded and looked at Jan.

"I've also been thinking about getting in touch with some of the therapy ranches and asking if I can get a tour, which will give me even more ideas," Heather said, looking hopefully at each of them. "So what do you think? Are these ideas worth pursuing?"

"I think it all sounds great," said Derek.

They both looked at Jan.

"I'm still worried we're asking too much of you," Jan said. "I mean, all of this sounds good, and it means a lot that you've put in so much time and effort to look into this, but you aren't a therapist. I don't want you to think you have to incorporate therapy techniques into his lessons."

Heather nodded. "I understand, but I don't see it that way. Everyone approaches horses differently. Some love them and show up ready to ride, confident to get started. Others are fearful but want to learn not to be. In every situation, I, as the trainer, have to look at the needs of the student and decide the best way to get them comfortable with the horse so they keep wanting to ride. So in a way, I've been doing this all along. Riding is a two-way relationship between horse and rider. The act of learning to ride takes trust on both sides. And I've been learning so much about human relationships in this process, and the correlations between brain science, Xavier, and the work I do with horses are astounding. I have never given up on a horse before, and I'm learning that in our human relationships, we need to have the same kind of determination to do life with each other through all our hard stuff. If I have to learn a few new things in order to teach Xavier to ride, then I just view that as part of my job.

"My aunt told me I needed to decide if I was going to teach Xavier how to ride a horse, or if I was going to teach Xavier, the child with special needs. That really stuck with me, and I understand what she meant. But I don't think those are necessarily two different things. I just have to learn how to read Xavier and understand him better; then I can teach him how to be comfortable around horses, and at the same time he'll learn a lot about patience, confidence, and a lot of other things."

Jan blew out a slow breath and glanced at Derek. "Well, if you're sure you want to keep going, then I'm okay with it. But I hope you don't feel obligated, and if it ever becomes too much, I hope you'll tell us."

She thought for a moment, remembering Cleo telling her she had a tendency to be a people pleaser. But she didn't think that was the case here.

She remembered Jan's demeanor at the last lesson.

"I do have one concern. After the last lesson, I realized I probably should have given Xavier extra time to feel comfortable with each step of getting on the horse. Jan, you seemed upset and I didn't want to bother you with a lot of questions. I'm going to need help as I learn how best to help Xavier. I think it might be wise to take things slow. If you've had a bad day at home, could you let me know so I can adjust and expect less?"

Jan nodded. "That was a pretty rough day, and I probably should have canceled. I will do better at communicating with you."

"Then let's keep going," Heather said, smiling but feeling her heart racing with a mixture of excitement and fear.

Jan and Derek both grinned. Real, genuine smiles.

She didn't know how she was going to break this news to Dad, but she would jump that hurdle when she came to it. This felt *right*.

"Xavier, what are you drawing?" she asked, somewhat amazed at how quiet he'd been through this long conversation. She noticed his one slice of pizza had hardly been touched, and the salad Jan had piled on his plate had been pushed around but looked mostly uneaten as well.

He shrugged and didn't answer.

"He gets overstimulated in crowds," said Jan. "He loves coming here and loves the food, but it's hard for him to actually eat the food here."

Heather nodded and glanced around at the crowded restaurant, wondering how the things she'd been learning about brain science would help in this situation. That was a question she should ask at the therapy ranches. How did they deal with easily overstimulated kids?

"I'll get some to-go boxes," said Derek. "Xavier will only eat one or two pieces, so you can take the rest home, Heather."

"Oh," she waved her hand. "Please, take it all. There are too many people at my house for the little that's left."

"Okay."

"Thanks so much for lunch today," said Jan.

"You're welcome. I'm glad we got to talk."

As they gathered their things, Heather thought about the busy weekend ahead: Friday's lesson with Xavier, followed by a team meeting and the start of setup for the fundraiser; the actual fundraiser on Saturday; and family dinner on Sunday. Plus all the tasks she still had to complete before then. She remembered her promise to Grandpa to bring Xavier by to meet him. Maybe Grandpa would mention meeting Xavier to Dad. It would give him time to accept the idea before telling her, again, how much of a mistake this was.

"Do you want to take your drawing with you?" Derek asked Xavier as he returned with two boxes and placed them on the table. Jan started packing the food into them. Xavier shook his head.

"All right, well, it's time to head home. Do you want to say bye to Heather?"

Xavier looked at her thoughtfully for a moment, then stood and moved to stand beside his dad. He watched his mom close the food containers, then looked at Heather. "Bye," he said and started walking toward the door.

Heather smiled. "I'll see you guys later."

Chapter 17

By Friday afternoon, Heather was glad she'd decided to make Xavier's lesson a bit slower paced. She'd been working nonstop on finalizing details for the fundraiser, dropping into bed near midnight and getting up at her usual wake-up time of six o'clock. She was exhausted. Tonight, she told herself, no matter what was left on her to-do list, she was going to bed early.

Jan pulled up in their van, and Xavier jumped out. "Can I give Queenie a treat?"

"Sure." Heather smiled. "But after, I want you to meet someone."

"Who?" asked Xavier.

"My grandpa. He lives in that house over there. He's been watching your lessons and wants to meet you."

"Oh, Okay." Xavier didn't waste any more time and ran into the barn.

Heather followed him, cut up an apple, and handed him two slices. "Are you sure about this? Last time you didn't like how her lips felt on your hand."

He nodded and ran back outside.

"Hey, what's the rule about running?" she shouted after him.

He slowed to a fast walk.

They reached Queenie, and Heather reminded him to hold his hand flat. He did so and let Queenie scoop the apple slices from his hand. His face contorted at the touch, and when the apple slices were gone, he shook his hands and wiped them on his jeans.

"Come on, let's go say hello to my grandpa, and then we'll get started with your lesson."

They headed toward the house, and Heather knocked loudly on the door before opening it. Leading the way inside, she found Grandpa shuffling down the hallway toward the living room. "Hi, Grandpa. I brought Xavier over to meet you."

"I saw you coming. I always watch from the window in my room," he said, lowering himself onto the couch. "Parker's around here somewhere, too."

"Right here, Grandpa. I made you some tea," he said, joining them from the kitchen.

Xavier stood beside her, twisting his fingers together. "Who's that?"

"That's my little brother, Parker. Grandpa, this is Xavier's mom, Jan." She invited Jan to take a seat and rested a hand on Xavier's shoulder.

Parker set the mug of tea on the table next to the couch and went back to the kitchen.

"Very nice to meet you," Grandpa said. "I hear you have an exceptional child."

Jan's eyes softened, making the smile she gave appear almost genuine. "That I do."

"What does *ceptional* mean?" asked Xavier.

"It means wonderful," said Grandpa, motioning Xavier over and patting his shirt pocket. "Do you like lollipops?"

Xavier nodded and stepped forward.

"Why don't you ask your mama if you can have one?"

Xavier glanced at his mother but said nothing. Jan nodded, and Xavier looked back at Grandpa and stuck his hand out.

Grandpa looked up at Jan, having not seen her nod.

"He can have one," said Jan.

Grandpa nodded, reached into his pocket, and pulled out a sucker. After handing it to Xavier, he tweaked the boy's nose with his fingers. "You like your teacher here?" he asked, nodding toward Heather.

Xavier was busy unwrapping his treat, but nodded.

Parker returned, holding a glass of soda. He leaned on the door frame between the kitchen and living room.

"She's pretty smart, isn't she?" Grandpa said.

Xavier freed the sucker from its wrapping and popped it in his mouth. "Yep."

Grandpa chuckled and watched Xavier enjoying his treat for a moment before looking up at Jan. "I want you to know, my granddaughter here—" He reached up and patted Heather's arm. "You can trust her. She'll get the job done, no matter what."

Heather blushed and swallowed the lump forming in her throat. She didn't know how much Grandpa had seen of her lessons with Xavier, but he'd probably seen more than anyone else in her family. She hadn't told him about her struggles or the conversations she'd had with Dad or Michelle, yet he had faith she could teach Xavier based on what he'd seen out his window. She wondered what her lessons with Xavier looked like from his perspective.

She glanced at Jan. She had a smile on her face, but her eyes held sadness in them. "It sounds like she has a wonderful family to support her, too."

"Oh yes. We're pretty close around here," said Grandpa.

A pang went through Heather. They weren't all as close these days, and part of that was her fault. Would Grandpa still support her efforts if he knew the whole story? She glanced at Parker, who frowned at her. Was he aware of the growing rift between her and Dad? Or was he thinking, again, about the difficulty of moving away from them all?

They spent another five minutes with Grandpa before Xavier got bored and started asking to go outside. They said their goodbyes, and Grandpa said he hoped he'd be able to go outside and watch their lesson sometime. This prompted Parker to offer to take him out, and he agreed happily.

Outside, Xavier stomped the ground as they walked, fascinated by the poofs of dust that rose every time his shoe connected with the dry ground.

"Ready for your lesson?" asked Heather.

Xavier nodded and ran ahead to where Queenie was waiting in the ring.

"Okay, okay, okay, what are we learning? Huh? Huh? Hurry! We have to hurry and learn everything!" Xavier exclaimed, holding on to a bar of the fence and jumping up and down.

"I'm coming, I'm coming." She joined him at the fence. "I know you like to touch things and find out how they feel, so today we're going to explore how different parts of Queenie's body feel. Come on." She climbed through the fence, and Xavier followed. She had researched sensory techniques for kids with special needs last night and had planned their entire lesson today around getting as many of Xavier's senses involved in learning about Queenie as she could.

She heard the purr of Grandpa's golf cart behind them and glanced over her shoulder. Parker had stopped the cart near Jan and was staring at his phone. Grandpa looked delighted to be involved. She smiled at him.

"Let's start with her head." She put a finger on Queenie's nose and traced each nostril. "Can you tell me what you feel on this part of her nose?"

Xavier followed her example and traced a finger around each nostril. "Kind of soft, but pokey with these long hair things."

"Right. The soft part is tiny hairs, and the pokey ones are whiskers."

"Like a cat?"

"Exactly. The whiskers help them feel things. Can you hear that noise she's making and feel the warmth of her breath?"

"Yeah."

"Those short puffs of air actually mean she's smelling us right now."

Xavier stepped back. "Stop, horse, don't smell me."

Heather heard Grandpa's chuckle behind them. She motioned for Xavier to step forward again, pleased with how attentive and engaged he was today. "Now, we don't want to put our fingers in her mouth, but you can touch her lip right here." Heather demonstrated by running a finger over Queenie's lip. Mostly, Queenie stood still for them and didn't open her mouth much.

Xavier leaned toward her but didn't step forward. He reached out a hand, running a finger over the horse's lip like Heather had shown him.

"What do you think?"

"It's weird. Kind of bumpy and squishy."

"That's right. Let's move on to her neck." Heather enticed Queenie with a treat to lower her head so Xavier could reach, then she ran a hand down Queenie's neck and Xavier did the same. "That's a big muscle right there."

Xavier nodded.

Heather moved her hand over Queenie's shoulder, and Xavier matched her movements, standing on tiptoe to reach up as high as he could. "This is her shoulder. It's not as round as our shoulders, but it does the same thing our shoulders do. Now let's look at her ears."

Xavier looked up at Queenie's ears, which were pointed toward them. Heather took a few steps back, gently pulling on Xavier's arm as she did so. He looked back at her, but she pointed back to Queenie's ears. He watched the ears twist around a little more.

"She's listening to us and trying to figure out what we're doing," Heather said.

"Cool! I wish I could move my ears!" He grabbed his lobes and wiggled them.

Heather laughed. This was going so well. Finally!

Xavier walked back and forth, keeping one hand on Queenie's side, watching her ears.

"Ready to move on to the tail?" asked Heather.

"Uh-huh." Xavier faced her again.

"Do you remember what rule we have about being near a horse's hind end?"

He cocked his head to one side. "Hind?"

"The back end."

He giggled. "You mean her butt?"

"Yes, her butt. What is the rule. Do you remember?"

He giggled again, shaking his head. "Butt, butt, butt."

Heather shook her head. "We don't stand behind the horse."

"Oh, yeah. I remember that," said Xavier, sobering again and moving to stand next to her. He peered around her and tried to reach for Queenie's tail but couldn't reach.

"Here, I'll show you and then move so you can touch it." She reached out and cupped the horse's tail in her hand and let the long hair fall through her fingers as she moved her arm downward. Then she stepped back and let Xavier take her spot. Xavier took the tail in his hands and rubbed it against his face. "It's kind of rough, like a rope, but I like it. Can I swing on it like a rope?" He grabbed the tail like he would try, and Heather grabbed him under his arms as he let his legs go limp.

"No, no, no," she said, keeping pressure on his arms until she was certain he would stand on his own weight.

"Why?" he asked, looking up at her.

"Because that would hurt the horse. Look, she's already nervous. See how she's moving around and making that noise?"

Xavier stood still and observed for a moment, then reached out and ran his fingers through her tail, watching her head at the same time.

"Ready to move on?"

He nodded.

She moved Xavier to the side, and took his place next to Queenie's back leg. She lifted the leg and held it. "Come feel her toe."

"They're called hooves," he said matter-of-factly, approaching and running his hand over the smooth surface.

"They are called that, but they're like really thick toenails, and I have to trim them sometimes, just like we trim our nails sometimes."

"Cool! It feels hard, but smooth."

Heather smiled and released the leg.

"Can I feel the tail again?" Xavier asked.

"Sure, but then we're going to bring those steps over here so you can climb up and feel her ears."

He reached for the tail, tugging it slightly.

"Hey, remember that's a bad idea," Heather said.

He brought the tail to his face and rubbed the coarse hair across his cheek. Then he twirled it like a jump rope.

Queenie snorted.

"Let's move on." She reached over to grab the tail so he'd stop, but he twisted away from her and squatted on the ground, tugging the horse's tail as he went while watching the horse curiously.

Heather gasped and lunged forward, but a sharp pain in her thigh, just above her knee, sent her sprawling forward on top of Xavier. She hugged Xavier to her and rolled to the side, her eyes squeezed shut from the pain. She sucked in a breath as her whole right side throbbed and her leg burned where Queenie had kicked her.

Xavier was screaming. She released him and lay still for a moment, catching her breath. Forcing her eyes open, she looked around and saw Xavier up and running toward the fence, where Jan, Grandpa, and Parker stood, looking horror-stricken. At least Xavier didn't appear to be injured. Probably just scared. She gritted her teeth and sat up, noting where Queenie now stood, on the other side of the ring.

"Get in there, Parker," Grandpa said. "Help her get up, and make sure she's all right."

She shook her head and glanced at her leg. It wasn't at an odd angle, so that was good. "No, I'm okay." She held up her hand. "I'm okay. I just need a minute."

Gently, she probed the area. Nothing felt broken, but the pain was so severe, she wasn't sure she could stand without help. This wasn't her first horse kick, though. She really would be fine. She needed to assure the three of them of that.

Keeping the injured leg straight, she bent her left leg under her and moved to a squat. Parker was by her side now. The blood rushed from her head and the world spun. She grabbed her brother's arm to steady herself and squeezed her eyes shut before slowly straightening and coming to a stand on her left leg, with Parker's assistance. Once upright, she opened her eyes and gingerly tried putting weight on her right leg. Searing pain shot through her and she clenched her jaw.

Twisting around so she could see Jan and Xavier, she smiled and waved. "See, I'm okay." She dusted herself off as best she could.

"Bull," said Parker under his breath.

"Just help me get to the fence," she responded quietly.

The gate was about two yards away, not too far, but at the moment the task felt impossible. She didn't want Jan to worry or feel guilty. She could handle this. When she looked their way again, she saw Jan crouched down in front of Xavier, dusting him off and trying to comfort him.

"Come on." She wrapped an arm around Parker's neck, and together they closed the distance. She kept her head down and attempted to control her breathing. When she got to the gate, she was overcome with dizziness and had to stop, but she had made it.

"Are you sure you're all right?" asked Jan, standing again. "I feel awful."

"Oh, yeah. I've been kicked before. I'll have a nice bruise on my leg, but nothing is broken. Really, I'm fine. I've had much worse." She pasted a smile on her face and gripped the fence as another wave of nausea crashed over her. What she really wanted was for Jan to take Xavier home so she could see how bad her leg really was and try to convince Parker and Grandpa not to call Dad.

"Well, since you have family here, I guess I'll let them take care of you and I'll take Xavier home now. Are you sure I can't do something?"

A lump began forming in her throat and she swallowed hard. "I'll be okay. I'm just going to rest here for a minute, but really, I'll be fine. He didn't get injured, did he?" she asked, recalling that she'd landed on Xavier.

"No, it doesn't look like it. I think he was mostly scared."

"Good. Next week, then?"

Jan hesitated. "Maybe we should wait and see how you feel in a couple days."

Heather felt her bottom lip tremble and tears prick at the back of her eyes. Clearing her throat and forcing the biggest grin she could manage onto her face, she again promised she was fine. "If you come to the fundraiser tomorrow, you'll see, but I'll call in a few days, too."

Jan nodded and guided Xavier back to their car.

Heather watched them as they went, and neither she nor Parker spoke until Jan and Xavier were halfway down the driveway.

"You should get on the cart," said Parker.

"No, help me get to my office. I want to see the damage for myself."

"I've called your father," Grandpa shouted to them. "He's on his way."

Heather groaned.

"You didn't really think you would get out of going to urgent care, did you?" asked Parker, opening the gate.

"I can't go to urgent care. I have people showing up in a couple hours, and I need to be here to direct them. Besides, Dad already doesn't like that I teach Xavier." She took a sharp intake of breath as her leg spasmed.

"Gee, I can't imagine why. But you know Dad's rule. Every kick gets checked out." He wrapped his arm around her waist and put her arm around his neck again. "Come on. You can sit in the cart until Dad gets here."

"Your car is right there. Why don't you take me instead?" Since she obviously wasn't going to get out of going to urgent care, then maybe she could at least avoid Dad.

"I can't leave Grandpa out here. He needs help getting back inside. Even if I got him inside right now, Dad would be here before I was ready to go."

"At least take me to my office so I can see how bad it is for myself and get an ice pack."

Parker rolled his eyes as they hobbled toward the golf cart. "Fine."

He helped her onto the backseat of the cart and climbed behind the wheel.

"That was a good, solid kick that old mare got in," said Grandpa.

"Yeah." She winced as her leg spasmed again.

Parker drove into the barn and parked next to her office door.

"I'll be right back," she said, hoisting herself to her feet with the help of the bar that connected the roof to the cart.

She dug her keys from her pocket and unlocked the door. Inside, she closed the door then rested her hands on her desk as a wave of nausea passed over her. Once it was over, she unbuckled her jeans and gingerly slid them down her legs until she could see the injured area.

A dark bruise was already forming, and there was a slight, curved indent where Queenie's hoof had connected with her leg. Another spasm wracked her leg. She squeezed her eyes shut and groaned, holding her breath through the worst of it.

Once the spasm passed, she pulled her pants up and buckled them before grabbing an ice pack from her emergency kit, the kind you had to knead to mix the chemicals inside to make it cold.

The injury was bad enough to make her concerned about blood clots, maybe even a hairline fracture. Her knee seemed to be fine; nothing out of place there, thankfully.

Tears spilled from her eyes and she wiped them away, frustrated. Any second, Dad would arrive to drive her to the urgent care center in

town. She didn't want him to see her upset and in pain, didn't want to hear a lecture from him or, worse, complete silence. He could use this as proof of why she shouldn't teach Xavier. And right now she didn't know how to respond to that argument. It was valid. But still, she knew helping Xavier was the right thing to do.

Chapter 18

The drive to urgent care had been silent. Parker had agreed to direct vendors for the fundraiser until she could get back. She was grateful for her obsession with being organized. All she'd had to do was hand Parker her clipboard and give him a few instructions. She'd created a map, showing exactly where every booth would go, the location of the entertainment stage, the paddocks for the animals, the outhouses, and every other thing she could think of.

Now she sat in the small room at the urgent care center holding an ice pack against her leg, wearing a hospital gown and waiting for the doctor to come in. She was impatient to get this over with but dreading the twenty-minute drive home.

When Dad arrived at her barn, he'd asked her questions about the injury, then helped her to his truck. On the drive down he'd clearly been upset but said nothing. She almost wished he'd lectured her instead of being silent. But she expected that the drive, and now sitting in the waiting room, would give him plenty of time to figure out what he wanted to say. If only she could prepare herself for that storm.

Thirty minutes passed after the nurse took her vitals and noted the details of her injury before the doctor entered.

"Sounds like you had an eventful afternoon," said the doctor, looking over his notes.

"Yeah." Her leg still throbbed, but the spasms had stopped since she'd been there.

"All right, let's take a look."

She lifted the gown to reveal the darkening bruise on her right thigh. The doctor sucked in a breath before gently pressing on the area. Heather groaned.

"Sorry, I just want to see if I can feel any tears in the muscle." A few more seconds and he stopped pressing on the spot, which now felt like it was on fire. "It's definitely a contusion, and there is probably some damage to the muscle fibers, but I didn't feel any tearing, so I think some anti-inflammatories, pain meds, ice, and rest are all you need."

"So you don't think the bone is broken?"

He shook his head. "We can get an X-ray if you'd like, but if we do see a hairline fracture, we can't do much to treat it. It would still be rest and pain management."

She nodded.

"I'll write you a prescription for the anti-inflammatory, but you should be fine on Advil or Tylenol for pain management. You can alternate them if the pain is bad enough for the first few days. You can get dressed, and I'll be back with that prescription."

"Thank you."

The doctor left and she began the arduous task of dressing herself. As she buttoned her shirt, the nurse knocked on the door, entered, and handed her a small piece of paper with the prescription on it. She thanked her and hobbled out to the waiting room.

"All good?" asked Dad.

She nodded. "They gave me this." She handed him the paper.

He took it and sighed. "We'll stop on the way home."

She nodded again.

"I'll go get the truck and meet you out front."

"Okay." She rested a moment, leaning against the wall. Her leg still felt hot, and the pain was beginning to radiate along her whole side. She hadn't taken anything for the pain yet and wished she had.

Taking a deep breath, she pushed herself off the wall and made her way out the door. Dad pulled the truck to a stop just as she stepped outside.

"Do you have painkillers in the truck?" she asked when they were both inside.

"Yeah, how much have you had already?"

She shook her head. "None."

He opened a compartment in the center console and pulled out a bottle of Tylenol. "Trying to tough it out?"

She squeezed her eyes shut as they filled with tears.

He nudged her hand, and she opened her eyes. He dropped two pills into it, then gave her a bottle of water. "Water's warm. Sorry."

"Thanks." She downed the pills, screwed the cap back on the lid, and rested her head against the seat.

They drove in silence to the nearest drugstore. Dad climbed out, leaving her alone. She wished she knew what to say to him. "Sorry" didn't seem to cut it.

Even after this, she still wanted to teach Xavier. It was her fault, she told herself. She'd been tired, not fully attentive. In the doctor's office she'd had plenty of time to reflect, and she could clearly see the signs she'd missed in Xavier's behavior. He'd kept wanting to return to Queenie's tail, fixated on the idea of finding out what would happen. The small tug he gave was testing the boundaries.

Dad returned and placed a small paper bag in her lap. She opened it and looked at the directions before taking a pill from the bottle and swallowing it.

Back on the road, the silence that stretched between them became unbearable.

"Dad," she started, still unsure of what to say but needing to fill the silence.

"Hmm?"

"I'm sorry I—" Tears choked out the words.

Dad reached over, taking her hand in his. "We don't need to worry about that right now. You're okay. That's all that matters."

She nodded. "But—"

"Heather, we'll talk about it later, when you're more rested." His tone was firm.

She turned her head toward the window, feeling the weight of their unspoken words and the warm gentleness of her hand cradled in his.

Back at her parents' house, she washed her face. Her tears had dried up halfway home and the medication was doing its job, but walking the half-mile to her barn and then all over the field to tell people where to set up was out of the question. Instead, she borrowed one of Grandpa's golf carts.

Pulling up to her barn, she found Parker inside. He looked relieved to see her. "You okay?"

"Yeah, just a big, bad bruise."

He nodded and handed her the clipboard.

"Thanks for supervising this for me," she said.

"Uh-huh. I don't ever want to do this again, though."

She smiled. "Noted."

"Cleo showed up thirty minutes ago. I think she's over by the stage."

"Thanks," she said, looking toward the spot where a handful of people were erecting a temporary stage. Seeing her friend, she drove over.

"Oh my gosh, Parker told me what happened. Are you all right?" Cleo asked, climbing into the seat next to her.

"Yeah, just bruised."

"I take it you decided to keep teaching that kid?"

She nodded.

Cleo's eyes got wide. "What did your dad say?"

She shook her head. "Nothing."

"Nothing at all?"

"Nope. I didn't talk to him about it after my conversation with Xavier's parents and today, on the drive to town, silence. He stayed in the waiting room while I saw the doctor. On the way to the drugstore he was silent. I tried to talk about it after that, but he stopped me and said we could talk later."

"Well, maybe that's a good thing."

"How?"

"He probably realizes making sure you're okay is more important than whatever his problem is with you teaching Xavier."

"I doubt it. Xavier's the reason I got kicked. He's probably building a case to convince me I should quit."

"Well, everything seems to be going smooth here, at least."

"Yeah. Thanks for coming up to help. I should probably check in with everyone, see what they need."

Cleo nodded. "I'll stay with you. Ain't no way you're doing any lifting or walking with that leg today."

Heather smiled, grateful her friend was here to keep her from stressing too much about Dad.

Chapter 19

Tucking her clipboard under her arm, Heather left the barn and limped out to the golf cart. Her leg was tender, but the pain meds were helping. She just needed to be careful and not overdo it. The fundraiser would officially start in thirty minutes, and she needed to do a final check-in with everyone before the attendees started arriving.

This year, all the vendor booths were arranged in a semicircle spanning the length of the three-acre field: food on one side, items for sale in the middle, and services offered on the opposite side. In the middle were the attractions including horse rides, a bounce house, a tractor train, the entertainment stage where three local bands would play, and the two horses she'd finished rehabilitating that were ready to find new homes. As she drove the cart to the first booth, she glanced around at all the people setting up and her stomach knotted. This year's fundraiser was so much bigger than last year's. How was it possible she was in charge of all this?

The vendors who weren't able to make it yesterday were still assembling their booths.

"Hi, Heather. Everything looks so great this year!" said a booth owner who was offering five-minute neck massages and a discount coupon to everyone who scheduled an appointment with her during the fundraiser.

"Thanks. Are you good here?" she asked, stopping the cart to wait for the woman's reply.

"All set." She gave Heather a thumbs-up.

Heather smiled, made a check on her clipboard next to the

vendor's name, and continued on her way, asking the same question of each vendor and mostly getting the same response. A few people had questions about where to find certain supplies, like trash bags, that they'd forgotten. Heather directed them to the barn, where she'd stockpiled all kinds of supplies for just that reason.

About halfway around the circle of booths, she found Zeke tending to the small petting zoo of farm animals their neighbor brought each year, hoping to sell whatever babies they'd determined they didn't want to keep.

"Hey, have you seen Scott?" she asked him. She hadn't seen him yet, and her worry over whether he would show up had grown as the minutes passed. In the chaos that followed her injury, she'd forgotten about her brother, but seeing Queenie in her ring this morning brought it all back.

"Yeah, I saw him head into the barn a few minutes ago," Zeke said.

She breathed a sigh of relief. "Thanks!"

She turned the cart toward the barn, wanting to check in with him and make sure, for her own peace of mind, that he knew where he was supposed to be and would be there on time. At the last second, she decided to divert around the back of the barn to check on Littlefoot and see how he was doing with the increasing noise. She'd been worried about leaving him outside during the fundraiser, but he still wasn't ready to go back inside the barn. She'd decided to take her chances with an extra dose of sedative.

When she reached the back of the barn, she could see Littlefoot standing in the corner, far from her and close to the barn door. She climbed out of the cart and limped closer to him, concerned that the cart might frighten him. He seemed okay so far. Littlefoot watched her approach, a little wary, but she thought she saw some curiosity in his eyes.

"Hey, big guy. You doing all right?" she asked, rubbing his nose. "You look like you're doing all right. I'm sorry about all the noise today, but I promise it's only temporary." She gave him one last pat on his neck and headed into the barn to find Scott.

Upon entering, she heard a noise in her office. "Scott?" she asked as she turned the corner and entered the office. Scott was standing next to her desk, but at the sound of her voice, he'd quickly twisted his body so his back was toward her. He didn't do it fast enough, though: she saw the needle sticking out of his arm.

"What are you doing?" she hissed, stepping quickly inside and closing the door behind her.

"Nothing," he said, turning toward her and smiling, keeping his hands behind his back. "I was just looking for something."

"You're seriously going to stand there and lie to me? I saw the needle." She swiped at a bottle on her desk and looked at the label. "DEPO-Testosterone. What the hell is this, Scott?"

"It's nothing, really. It's just something I've been taking to help me with energy."

"Energy? This is a steroid. Where are you getting it?"

"A doctor, of course," he said, glancing away from her. "Don't you have a thing to run that starts any second now?"

She thought back quickly about his behavior during the past couple of months: the anger, the hyperactivity, the canceled plans, and avoiding family. It all made sense now. "How long have you been using this stuff?" she asked, holding up the bottle.

"God, you're freaking out about nothing. This isn't a big deal, really."

"Oh? Well then, I guess you won't mind when I tell Mom and Dad about this. Or how about the race committee? Do they know about this?"

The color drained from Scott's face. "Come on, Heather. Don't do that."

"Why not? I thought it wasn't a big deal."

"Heather, please. I'm being careful."

She shook her head in disgust. "Go home, Scott."

"But what about the horse rides?"

"Are you kidding me? You can't give kids rides when you're on drugs. What the hell are you thinking? Get out of here. Now. We will talk about this later." Turning, she opened the door of her office and marched out, then stopped and retraced her steps. "And make sure you take your dirty needle with you. I don't want it anywhere near my barn, my horses, or my fundraiser."

She glanced toward the front of the barn, where she'd set up folding tables of extra supplies. A couple of vendors were there, looking through things, and she watched them for a moment, wondering if they'd heard her yelling at her brother. They didn't show any sign of alarm if they had.

Wiping the back of her hand across her forehead, she tried to collect herself. She had a fundraiser to run and a replacement to find. There was no time to let her brother's idiotic actions distract her from the tasks at hand. Walking out back, she got back in the golf cart and drove around to the front, glancing toward the ring where Queenie waited. Cars were lining up in the field next to Grandpa's house, reserved for that purpose.

She headed to the booth she'd left off at and continued checking in with the vendors. By the time she reached Harry and Lisa's food stand, she'd managed to get back in the flow of the event and felt able to interact with her brother and sister-in-law without raising suspicions. The fundraiser had officially started five minutes ago, and she was feeling desperate. But she couldn't very well ask Harry Jr. for suggestions on a replacement without answering a bunch of questions. She had twenty minutes before she had to make the first announcement of the day, and several parents were already lined up in front of Queenie's ring.

While checking in with Harry Jr., she saw Uncle William and got an idea. Heading his way, she called out and waved.

"This is quite the event," said William. "I don't remember it being so big last year."

"Yeah, it's definitely grown," she said. "I actually have a bit of a situation. One of my volunteers can't stay. I was wondering if I could have you give rides to kids on Queenie instead of showing Brazen Fire and Lady?" She knew Cleo was more than capable of showing both horses herself. She pointed toward the ring where Queenie stood.

William shrugged. "Sure. But I thought Scott was doing that."

She hesitated. "Yeah, he bailed on me," she said finally. It wasn't exactly a lie; his actions had made it impossible for her to allow him to help out.

William furrowed his brows. "That's not like him."

"I know. He's been a little off lately. Thank you. You're a lifesaver." She gave him a few additional instructions, then sent him off, wanting to avoid further questioning.

"Heather, Heather!"

Heather turned toward the voice calling her name and saw a vendor waving frantically at her. She drove over.

"Heather, this young person just scraped her knee pretty good, and I've lost my map and can't remember where the first-aid station is," said the woman at the booth.

Heather pulled another map from her clipboard and handed it to the woman. "It's right in the middle, over there." She pointed and offered to take the child and her parents there on the golf cart.

"And we're off," she whispered to herself as the family climbed aboard.

After bringing the family to the first-aid station, she headed back toward the stage. She would need to make an announcement soon. This was the first year there would be live music, all local artists. After welcoming everyone to the event and explaining how funds were raised and collected, she needed to introduce the first band, and at the moment she couldn't for the life of her remember what their name was.

She flipped through the pages on her clipboard and found the schedule for the stage and read the name, then approached the sound guy and asked him if everything was ready to go. He said it was, but the band was still setting up and wouldn't be ready for another five minutes.

Taking the opportunity to rest a moment, she stood nearby and watched as the musicians plugged cords into instruments, tuned guitars, and pressed pedals. She had no idea what any of the equipment did, other than the instruments themselves, but it was fascinating to watch. As she waited, she took deep breaths to calm her nerves. Having to make introductions, announcements, and anything else that required her to stand in front of a microphone and talk to a crowd of people was not her favorite part of this event. And it didn't help that her confrontation with Scott had left her feeling frazzled.

Finally, the band gave her the signal, and she stepped onto the stage, trying not to limp. Glancing back at the sound guy and pointing at the microphone, she received a thumbs-up and cleared her throat.

"Welcome everyone! I'm Heather Fletcher, the organizer of this event and owner of Fletcher Horse Rescue, and I'd like to welcome you all to our third annual fundraiser."

The crowd, which seemed to double before her eyes, clapped. She could see that people milling about the booths could hear her, which was exactly what she'd wanted when she'd decided on the layout. She waited until the sound died down before continuing.

"Here at Fletcher Horse Rescue we take in and rehabilitate horses. You can read information about each of the horses we have here on the posters hanging on the side of the barn and find out the history of each one, as well as some of the things I'm doing to rehabilitate them.

"Because we're a nonprofit, this event helps us raise money to care for the horses and keep this place up and running. At noon today, I'll be doing a demonstration with the two horses in the center paddock. Both of these horses have been fully rehabilitated and are ready to find new homes, so if you've been thinking about getting a horse, make your way over there and check out Brazen Fire and Lady.

"As you know, it's free to get into this event, so how do we raise funds? Well, there are several ways. Over by the barn there is an information booth where you can find a list of our most-needed items. You can donate money at that booth, or take a list, purchase the items, and drop them off here.

"Our amazing vendors also had a choice of either donating a portion of their proceeds to the ranch, or donating items to go into a raffle. Raffle tickets can be purchased at the same information booth over by the barn. The items you can win in this raffle are located over here, to the left of the stage.

"We will draw names at two different times today. The first will be at eleven o'clock, so in two hours. The second will be at one o'clock, an hour before we close things down. You don't have to be here to win the prize. As long as you include your information on your raffle ticket and we can get ahold of you, we'll hold the prize and get in touch with you next week. And if you haven't joined us for this event before, we have our vendors tally up how much we've raised about fifteen to twenty minutes before we end, so right when this event ends, we can let you know an estimate of how much we've raised.

"And, last but not least, I want to announce a new feature at this event. We have live music!"

A round of applause broke out, and several whooping noises drew her gaze to a couple in the middle of the crowd. Her parents. Both were smiling. Of course they were. They might be opposed to her decision about Xavier, but they still supported her. Her stomach knotted. It would devastate them to learn about Scott's drug use.

She glanced at her notes, reminding herself what she was doing: announcing the band. "Yeah, it's pretty exciting!" She hoped the grin pasted on her face was enough to keep the grief and anger she felt hidden. "All the artists and bands are local to Mylin Valley or Ogden. So without further delay, let's welcome our first band: The Sidewinders!" She waved her hand toward the band and walked off the stage, wondering how and when Scott's news should be made known to her parents.

Forty-five minutes left. She'd just wrapped up the second raffle. The booths would announce last sales in thirty minutes. Her parents had offered to collect the sales data and tally the estimated amount they had raised so she could make the announcement right at two.

She'd seen the Rodenbaum family in the crowd when she announced the raffle winners but hadn't had a chance to talk to them.

"Hey, girl." Cleo knocked her shoulder lightly against Heather's. "I'm surprised you have time to just stand here."

Heather smiled at her friend. "Me too."

"How's the leg?"

"It hurts a little more since my demonstration with the horses, but it's not too bad."

Cleo nodded. "Wishing you'd taken me up on my offer to do the demo for you?"

Heather shook her head. "No way, it's my favorite part."

Cleo laughed. "So listen, Brazen Fire might have a buyer."

"Really? That's great!"

"Yeah, it is. He watched your demonstration and he's stopped by two or three times to look him over, and I keep encouraging him to come back often."

Heather laughed. "So he's cute?"

"Very. He filled out a form, and because this is the first time I've seen you not running around like a chicken with its head cut off, I'm here to give it to you." She handed Heather a piece of paper.

"Thank you," she said, slipping the paper under the metal clip of the clipboard in her hand.

"So how's it going?" asked Cleo, waving a hand around to indicate she meant the fundraiser.

Heather shrugged. "Seems to be going well. No major issues."

"What was going on this morning?"

"When?"

"When you zoomed out here on that cart looking mad as hell, just before everything started."

She sighed, unsure how much detail to give. "Scott's being an idiot."

Her eyebrows shot up. "More than usual?"

Heather chuckled and nodded. "I'll fill you in on the details later."

"I'm gonna hold you to that."

Heather smiled.

"All right, I better get back. Don't want to miss out on another visit from Brazen Fire's future daddy."

Heather grinned and checked her watch.

Chapter 20

Booths would announce last sales in the next few minutes. Her parents would be calculating numbers. She should probably make another round in case anyone needed anything from her. But the brief break had given her body enough time to protest more movement, and her leg throbbed. She opened the glove compartment of the golf cart and took out a few painkillers. Other than this morning, after she first woke up, she hadn't taken anything for the pain. Now, as she approached her last speech of the day, she needed to dull the growing ache.

As she made her final rounds, she saw Xavier getting his face painted. He sat stock-still, as if he were afraid to even breathe in case it messed up the design being painted. She smiled and shook her head.

"There you are," said Mom, jogging up to the cart.

"Hi, Mom."

"Your dad and I are tallying numbers, and I know you said a few of the food booths were donating a portion of their profits, but I can't remember which ones, besides Harry and Lisa's."

"Oh." She glanced down at the seat and picked up the clipboard. She flipped through the pages, took out the sheet of paper with the names of the booths, and handed it to Mom.

"Thanks. How are you doing? How's your leg? You look tired."

Heather sighed. "Leg hurts a little, but not bad. I am tired, suddenly."

"Well, it's almost over and you'll be able to rest," Mom said, rubbing her arm quickly as if she were trying to transfer some energy into her. "I'll finish getting those numbers for you."

"Thanks." She drove the cart to the stage and waited, rehearsing her final speech in her head.

When the band stopped playing, she jerked her head toward the stage. She had this one last thing she had to do, and then her only responsibility for the rest of the day was to be available to the vendors as they packed up.

The singer for the band wrapped up his speech, thanking everyone for letting them play. Heather stood and made her way onto the stage, glancing around for her parents and not seeing them. She would need to buy some time.

Pasting a smile on her face, she stepped in front of the microphone. "I hope you've all enjoyed the events we've had here today." A round of applause came from the crowd that grew around the stage.

"Thank you for coming out today to support our fundraiser event." She searched the crowd for her parents and saw Mom working her way to the front. She breathed a sigh of relief. "I want to remind you that the money we've raised today will help bring in, care for, and rehabilitate more horses as well as care for the current horses here. Our tally is just about complete, so we can announce our estimated number to you as we get ready to end today's event."

"Here, I've got it here," Mom called, waving to her from the side of the stage.

Heather left the microphone and went to her mother, who held out a slip of paper. "This is the estimated amount, rounded up from what we had, because there were a few sales still being completed," Mom said.

"Thanks," she said, and glanced at the number on the slip of paper. Her mouth fell open, and she looked at Mom. "Are you sure this is right?"

Mom beamed and nodded. "Congratulations, honey. You did a great thing here today."

She nodded and made her way back to the microphone, her mouth suddenly dry. Clearing her throat, she leaned into the microphone, but paused. She didn't want her voice to crack when she spoke. "I have the number here." She paused and cleared her throat again. The sound guy handed her a bottle of water and she thanked him, took a quick swallow, and leaned into the microphone. "It appears we've more than doubled the amount raised from last year." Applause and cheers broke out, and she waited for them to die down.

"This year we've raised twenty thousand dollars," she said, unable to keep the grin from her face now. The cheers grew louder, and she scanned the faces in the crowd, seeing her parents, Parker, Harry Jr., Lisa, the Rodenbaums, people from her church, and several of her aunts, uncles, and cousins. The only face missing in the crowd was Scott's.

"Thank you, everyone, for coming and supporting these horses and the work we do here. Thanks to our vendors, our volunteers, and all my family who showed up and helped today. Enjoy the rest of your Saturday!"

She waved and walked off the stage to where her parents were waiting. They hugged her and congratulated her, and she thanked them in return for all their help.

"Heather!" Derek's frantic voice cut through the noise around her, and she turned toward his voice. "Have you seen Xavier? We can't find him anywhere."

"No. Have you checked the barn?" she asked.

Derek shook his head. "We weren't sure if we could go in there."

"I'll go with you," she said, stepping out from the group around her.

"Do you need help?" asked Mom.

"Just keep your eye out for him," she called over her shoulder as she jogged toward the barn, almost forgetting the pain in the midst of her rising anxiety.

Jan met them there, and they searched every inch of the barn but didn't find him.

"Wait, I think I hear him," said Jan.

They all stopped and listened, and sure enough, his giggles were coming from out back.

Dread filled Heather as she jogged in that direction, still ignoring the pain shooting through her thigh. Jan and Derek were close behind.

Xavier was inside Littlefoot's ring, standing on his toes so he could hug Littlefoot's neck.

Heather's eyes darted to Littlefoot's.

"Xavier, there you are. I told you not to run off," said Jan.

"I wanted to see the horses," said Xavier.

Heather shook her head, trying to take in the scene in front of her.

"Is he safe in there?" asked Derek.

"I ... I ..." she glanced at Derek, then back at the horse, who was sniffing Xavier with interest and curiosity, like a perfectly normal, untraumatized horse. "I don't know."

"What do you mean?" asked Jan worriedly. "Xavier, come over here, please. It's time to go."

"I don't want to go," said Xavier.

"Um ... well, if you'd asked me that question before we came out here, I would have said he wasn't safe in there, but ..." Heather trailed off, watching as Littlefoot nuzzled Xavier.

"It tickles, horse," Xavier said, giggling as Littlefoot tried to nibble on the collar of his shirt.

Parker and Dad came up and joined them watching this scene. *Great*, she thought.

Heather climbed into the ring and noticed Littlefoot's gaze lock onto hers. He stepped back, watching warily. She stayed by the fence. Apparently Littlefoot's trauma didn't extend to children, only adults.

"Xavier, honey, come on out of there," said Jan.

"I don't want to. I want to stay with the horse."

"Heather," said Dad, in a warning tone that told her he wasn't happy at finding her in this situation. She held a hand up to stop him from saying more.

"Xavier, that horse is named Littlefoot," she said.

"Littlefoot?" Xavier looked at the horse's hooves. "Are his feet smaller than other horses?"

Heather swallowed. "No. I'm not sure why his name is Littlefoot. But Littlefoot was in a really terrible car accident last fall, and he gets scared really easily."

"He doesn't look scared to me," said Xavier.

"You're right. He doesn't look scared right now."

How could she explain this to him? She thought about the incident at the park and wondered if it was appropriate for her to bring that up to Xavier or if saying anything about his meltdowns was a bad idea. She glanced over her shoulder at Jan and Derek. She'd have to risk it.

With her leg injured, she wouldn't be able to pull him from harm's way if either Littlefoot or Xavier acted up.

"Xavier, do you remember at the park when you got mad because the other little boy wouldn't let you finish crossing the monkey bars before you were done?"

"Yeah." He scowled at her.

"Do you think you got mad a little at a time or all at once?"

He reached up to rub Littlefoot's nose. "All at once."

"Right, well, Littlefoot is the same way. He can get scared all at once, and no one will see it coming, but a horse can be pretty dangerous when they're scared, which is why it's not a good idea for you to be in here right now."

Xavier looked up at Littlefoot, considering this information. "If he gets dangerous, will you call the police on him?" he asked. Then he slowly left Littlefoot's side and came to stand next to Heather.

She bent over so she was more on his level and rested her hands on his shoulders. Did this little eight-year-old boy really think of himself as dangerous?

"No. We don't call the police on horses. Besides, I've been working with horses for a really long time, since I was your age. And I know what to do with a dangerous horse to help them calm down."

Xavier grabbed the end of her braid and twirled it around his finger. "Can I ride Littlefoot at my next lesson?"

"No, Xavier. No one can ride Littlefoot right now, not even me."

He glanced back at Littlefoot. "But can I visit him?"

"If you promise me you won't visit him by yourself anymore, then yes, we can say hello when you're here."

He nodded.

Heather straightened, and they climbed out of the ring.

"Thank you," said Jan.

Heather nodded.

"How's your leg?"

"It's bruised and sore, but no major damage."

"Good."

"We should get going," said Derek.

Heather watched them as they disappeared inside the barn, wishing she could go with them and avoid what was coming.

Dad stood nearby, arms folded, his jaw working back and forth. "Dad."

He held up a hand. "When you started this rescue, I knew there would be an element of danger. But horses have always been your passion. You studied them, you studied other trainers, and you know what you're doing. I trusted you to be careful. But this past month, I've seen you put yourself in more unnecessarily dangerous situations in the name of helping that boy ride." He pointed at Littlefoot. "This could have been really bad. With all these people still here, what if he'd been injured? What if he'd gotten upset in there with Littlefoot? You put yourself in danger with that boy around. What are you thinking, Heather? Your insurance doesn't cover stuff like this. One injury. That boy only has to be injured once, and you could lose everything. The horses, the business, your reputation … have you considered that? All these people are trusting you to use those twenty thousand dollars wisely with these troubled horses. What happens if they find out you're taking all these risks? You could lose all of it." He waved his hand around. "Your grandfather passed this land down to me and me to you. Maybe I made a mistake, trusting you with this land that's so important to our family."

She stared at the ground. He was right. Her insurance covered injuries if a student fell from a horse during a training session. Her contract with the parents of her students covered her in other ways, but neither would protect her or her business if Xavier were injured because of his own impulsiveness. She had no argument, and the accusation that she was not thinking of her family stung.

She heard him blow out a breath. "I'm glad no one was hurt today."

She looked up at him, but he'd turned and was disappearing into the barn. Parker followed closely behind.

Chapter 21

The blaring alarm clock next to Heather's bed woke her from a deep sleep. Reaching over to turn it off, she stared at the window that revealed the predawn light. She flung the covers off and gingerly moved her injured leg. It was stiff, and the movement made her take a sharp intake of breath.

As a teen, she'd learned not to stay in bed in the morning. No matter how dark, how cold, how tired, or how much pain she felt, if she let herself think about any of those things, she would go back to sleep. But she'd never been this exhausted and sore. And the thought of doing chores with Dad, either in awkward silence or hearing more about how angry he was with her, wasn't appealing. But she still had chores to do. The horses wouldn't be happy if she were late with their breakfast.

It was her turn to make coffee, which meant taking care of the cattle first. She climbed out of bed, hobbled to the bathroom, downed some painkillers, braided her hair, and dressed. By the time she finished, she was woefully late.

Downstairs, Mom stood in front of the coffee maker in her bathrobe, drumming her fingers on the counter. She looked at Heather as she came in. "Morning."

Heather nodded. "Morning."

"Your dad filled his thermos already. He figured you wouldn't be up for all the chores this morning after your busy weekend."

"Is he still angry?"

Mom sighed. "Yes, but he'll get over it. He's more upset that you didn't tell us you were going to keep teaching Xavier than anything."

"He thinks I'm going to lose my reputation in the community—and the family land."

Mom folded her arms. "Helping Xavier is a risk, especially because you have no experience working with kids like him, but if for some reason your business does fail, we would take those ten acres back. It wouldn't be lost or sold to someone else."

"So you made a backup plan in case I failed?" She knew it was practical of her parents to do so, but at the moment it felt like a slap in the face. They weren't as confident in her abilities as they had always claimed.

"Honey, we never expect any of our kids to fail, you know that. But it's a fact of life that failure happens, and we didn't want any of you kids to feel like you didn't have a net to fall into if you did fail at something. That's how we raised all four of you. Let you do all the things you wanted to do, but made sure you had that net in case things didn't work out."

Heather nodded. Even though she hadn't relished the idea of working alongside Dad this morning, his starting without her felt more like a punishment than showing concern. Like he didn't really want to be around her, either. She took a deep breath and grabbed a coffee thermos from the cabinet. Punishment or concern, she could take care of the chores in her own barn.

Mom poured a cup for herself, then filled Heather's waiting thermos.

"Thanks," said Heather, screwing the lid on.

"Sweetheart ..."

Heather shook her head and stopped at the kitchen door. "I won't be going to church today. I want to rest."

Mom sighed and nodded.

Heather headed out to the barn as tears slid down her cheeks. Not even seven o'clock in the morning, and already the day sucked. It was true she wanted to rest this morning, but she also needed to talk to Scott.

Out in the barn, she unlocked her office, wiped her face, and checked in with the horses in the barn. She always did a visual checkup on each horse every morning before she released them out to the field. If they weren't acting normal, she'd know it immediately.

Littlefoot stood in his ring near the back door of the barn, making her checkup easy. All was well. When she headed out to fill water troughs for the field animals, she'd check on her horses that stayed outside.

Back inside, she started mucking stalls. When that was done, she rolled the wheelbarrow she used to carry out the old hay and manure to the compost pile and returned it to the back of the barn, where she kept her tools and equipment, while a hose filled the last water trough. Once the chores were all done, Heather headed inside to clean up. Mom wasn't there. When Heather came back downstairs and saw Mom still hadn't appeared, she started making breakfast.

She remembered that Parker was living with Grandpa during his school break and placed extra strips of bacon on the baking sheet and put them in the oven. Then she started cracking eggs into a bowl for scrambled eggs.

While she waited for the bacon to cook, she ran a frozen container of orange juice under hot tap water until she could squeeze the concentrated mush out into a pitcher. She filled the pitcher with cool water and stirred until the large chunks broke up into smaller chunks and dissolved. Then she took out a loaf of bread and cut five slices, placing two in the toaster at a time and buttering them as soon as they popped up.

Checking on the bacon and seeing it was almost done, she turned the stove on and buttered a pan for the eggs. As she poured the eggs into the pan, Mom entered, dressed in dirty overalls, strands of hair sticking out around her face.

"Oh, sweetheart, thank you for making breakfast. The Johnsons' cow went into labor and the calf was stuck."

"No problem," she said, pushing the eggs around the pan.

Mom paused in the doorway. "Are you okay, Heather?"

"Fine." She didn't look up from the pan, but she could feel Mom watching her.

Finally, Mom sighed. "I'm going to go clean up. Don't wait for me if I'm not here when everyone's ready to eat."

"Okay."

A few minutes later, she turned the stove off, sprinkled shredded cheese on top of the eggs, and pulled the bacon out of the oven. As she grabbed plates from the cabinet, Parker and Grandpa entered the house. And a moment later, Dad came in, too.

"I see you took care of the chores in your barn."

She nodded, glancing at him, but quickly focused her attention back on the food.

"You didn't have to do that. I'm sure your leg is pretty sore."

Parker took the plates from her and set the table while she carried the pans of food out.

"Moving around keeps it from getting too stiff. Sorry I was too late to help you. Mom said not to wait for her," said Heather, taking a seat across from Parker, who had picked up on the tension between her and their dad and was watching both of them.

"Go ahead without me. I'm going to clean up first," Dad said as he walked through the room.

"All right then. Parker, pray over our food," said Grandpa.

Parker said a quick prayer, and they helped themselves. Before they started digging in, Mom joined them.

Other than an update on Parker's schooling, a summary of Mom's emergency vet call, and some conversation about the fundraiser, the breakfast was a quiet one.

"I can clean up," said Heather as they finished their meal.

"Nonsense," said Mom. "You're resting today, and you cooked. Besides, your dad still needs to eat. Parker and I can clean up."

Parker rolled his eyes but stood and gathered plates.

"Well, then, I'm going to head to the barn to do a few things on my computer. I'll see you all later today." She bent down and kissed Grandpa on the cheek and headed out.

In the barn, she checked her watch. She still had an hour before the family left for church, which meant she couldn't leave to talk to Scott until then. She sat at her desk and opened one of the brain science books she'd left there, wanting some distraction from the pain of her leg and her parents' disapproval.

After finishing a chapter, she got online to do research on confronting a drug-using family member. She started researching rehab centers and, thirty minutes into her search, found herself looking instead for horse therapy ranches in northern Utah. There was only a handful. All private businesses. None listed prices, but each had a section on their website about where financial help could be obtained. She thought again about taking a tour of one of these places but reminded herself she was supposed to be finding a way to help her brother.

Sighing, she opened a new tab on her browser and started her search again. The articles on spotting an addict showed her that all the slightly "off" things she'd noticed about Scott were signs, ones she had not known to look for. She glanced at the clock. Her family should have left for church by now.

On impulse, she switched back to a tab she'd left open on the website of a therapy ranch and sent them a quick message asking about tours and explaining why she wanted one. Before sending it, she copied her request, then found four other therapy ranch websites and sent the same request to them as well. There was no telling what would come of the emails, but she had to find out what she was doing wrong with Xavier.

She might not have the words yet to explain things to her angry dad, but she couldn't walk away from the Rodenbaums.

Shutting down her computer, she locked up the barn and climbed into her truck. It was time to find out what was going on with Scott. She didn't want to keep his secret, but she needed more information to know what to do. If Scott was having trouble with something, he should have come to his family, not tried to solve his problems with drugs.

This summer, he'd been living in a yurt as a maintenance man and groundskeeper for one of the yurt rental companies up by the ski resort. Scott was always moving from place to place, depending on the season and what sports happened that time of year. In the winter, he worked for the ski resort and scored himself a free ski pass, and he usually roomed with a couple of other guys who also lived Scott's nomadic lifestyle. He'd built up a reputation in the community as an honest, hard worker willing to do all kinds of odd jobs no one else wanted to do, for just enough money to cover the rent wherever he was staying plus free or cheap access to the sports and recreational activities he loved. What would happen if people found out about his drug use?

Since everyone in the family had noticed his odd behavior as of late, it seemed likely others had as well. His employer, perhaps? People he'd been racing against this summer? If they had, surely they would know what signs to look for in a drug user.

Twenty minutes after leaving the barn, she parked in front of her brother's yurt and climbed out of the truck. Knocking on his door, she listened and heard movement inside. A moment later, Scott answered the door, shirtless and wearing sweatpants. He scratched his lean, well-toned torso and yawned.

She pushed past him and entered the small, round hut and looked around. A thin mattress with no sheets on it lay in the middle of the floor, a rumpled blanket on top of it. Clothes were scattered around the space and hung out of a cardboard box near a wall that jutted out about three feet. She realized there was a small bathroom behind it. A green folding camp chair sat beside the bed, and next to it was a large cooler. Other than his bike, which leaned against the wall near the door, there was nothing else to see.

She turned to him, crossing her arms.

"Don't start," said Scott.

She shook her head. "How long have you been using drugs?"

Scott sighed and sat down in the camp chair but didn't respond. Instead, he opened the cooler and pulled out a coffee mug, a jar of instant coffee, and a spoon. He scooped two spoonful's of coffee grounds into the mug, placed the jar back into the cooler, then stood and went into the bathroom, where he turned on the faucet and waited for several seconds before filling the mug with hot water. He returned, resumed his seat in the camp chair, and stirred his coffee.

"Scott, how long have you been on drugs?"

He took a sip of his beverage and glanced up at her. "You sound like a cheesy D.A.R.E. commercial. This really isn't a big deal. It's a small dose of testosterone, perfectly safe, little sister."

"Really? Where do you get it? Do you have a prescription? Show me the prescription and I'll leave you alone."

He didn't answer, just sipped his coffee.

"You know, I looked up the effects of performance drugs: increased aggressiveness, depression, nervousness, irritability—not to mention what they could do to your health. And you've had all those things. You couldn't sit still at family dinner last month, you've been unreliable, canceling on the fundraiser and then changing your mind, and you looked unwell when you picked up those barrels. This isn't like you, Scott, and it needs to stop. How long have you been on these drugs?"

"Heather, stop. I'm using a safe amount. I'm not using more than the recommended dose. You're freaking out over nothing."

Heather sighed. "I can't keep this a secret. I came here to talk some sense into you and make a plan, but if you're just going to sit here and deny it, then I'll have to tell Mom and Dad."

"Make a plan? Tell Mom and Dad?" he scoffed. "What kind of plan? And you know we're adults now, right? Mom and Dad can't ground me anymore."

"No, but like I said, I won't keep your secret. It's not good what you're doing, and eventually they'll find out. I'd rather get it out in the open now, rather than try to hide it."

Scott gave a frustrated groan and rubbed a hand over his stubbled face. "This isn't any of your business."

"And I suppose it's not the race committee's business either, right? You know they have people who look for signs of drug use. You yourself have talked about how strict the committee is about this kind of thing." She stopped, a realization dawning on her. "That's why you changed your mind about helping at the fundraiser, isn't it? You knew you wouldn't be able to pass the drug test for the race."

He eyed her, and his jaw worked back and forth, just like Dad's did when he was irritated, but he said nothing.

"Everyone at home knows you're acting strange and they're worried, but they don't know what's wrong. They will figure it out, eventually. So will the race committee, your boss, everyone."

Scott blew out a breath, set his coffee mug on top of the cooler, and stood up. "I don't need you coming here and trying to boss me around. I know what I'm doing, and you're sticking your nose where it doesn't belong. Tell everyone whatever you want. I won't be at dinner tonight. Now get out." He pointed to the door, but Heather didn't budge.

"Let's remember how I discovered your little secret here, shall we? You were sticking a needle in your arm in MY office, in MY barn. And I'd really like to know how many times you've done that, because if a kid like Zeke or the kids I give riding lessons to were to find one of your dirty needles, my business would be ruined."

"I only used your office one time. Just mind your own business and stop worrying about me."

"You need help, Scott."

He rolled his eyes. "Oh, please."

"Hey. Instead of being a jerk, maybe you should listen to what I came to say. After all, I know what you're up to. I could share your little secret with several people who would make life suck big-time for you."

She folded her arms and waited.

Scott glared at her for a moment, then ran a hand through his hair. "Well, Miss High and Mighty, let's hear your blackmail strategy."

Heather shook her head. She couldn't believe how ugly he'd become in such a short time. "Do you hear yourself? You don't even sound like the same person. You don't want to come to family dinner, fine. If you skip it, I'm telling Mom and Dad what I saw yesterday. If you show up, I'll give you a week to figure out how you're going to get sober and stay sober. I don't currently see any reason to tell your boss or the race committee. I think they'll figure it out on their own before long, but I will not keep your secret. I have my own problems to deal with."

He rolled his eyes.

"You haven't been around much, Scott, so you don't know what's been going on, which really sucks. I could have used your advice." She walked toward the door to leave.

"You don't understand," he said through gritted teeth.

She stopped and faced him again. "What?"

He hung his head. "You're doing what you love, taking care of those horses, and you get to do that forever. But the older I get, the more irrelevant I get." His eyes pleaded for her to understand. "I can't compete like I used to. I get injured easier. No matter how healthy I am, how much sleep I get, how well I eat and take care of myself, younger people pass me by. I'm only twenty-six, and I can't keep up like I used to, and the older I get, the worse it will get. You don't have to worry about that. None of you do."

Heather considered his words for a moment. She thought about

Pastor Barker's teaching about needing to belong to a people. Somehow her brother felt that his family no longer understood him, but the people who raced, those were his people, and he didn't want to lose that. She thought about the question Aunt Michelle had challenged her with. Either teach about horses or teach the special-needs kid; you can't do both. And Dad's stinging rebuke.

"You're wrong. The horses I work with are dangerous. If I were to get injured—which I was, recently, in case you haven't noticed my limp—I wouldn't be able to continue doing what I do. I could be crippled with one bad kick from a horse or being thrown off a horse's back. There are a lot of unknowns in what I do. The same goes for all of us. The economy could turn, Harry and Lisa could lose their restaurant. We're not guaranteed anything."

"No, of course not. But all those things you listed are possibilities. They may or may not happen. I don't have that choice. I *am* getting older, and it's a fact that I won't always be able to compete like I do now."

"So you're going to destroy your life, your relationships with family and friends, for one more race? What will you have left when you've lost the ability to compete?"

Scott rubbed the back of his neck, staring at the floor.

She shook her head and walked out, slamming the door of the yurt behind her.

Weariness overcame Heather as she made her way home. The past few days had been a roller coaster of emotions and activity. She wasn't sure what she'd expected from her encounter with Scott, but the hopelessness she'd heard in his voice took all the anger out of her and left her wondering if her ultimatum was the right thing to do.

Hot tears trickled down her face. She hated this. Hated feeling like every choice she'd made recently was the wrong one and not knowing whom to talk to or where to turn so she could make the right choices. Everyone had a different opinion about what she should do. Dad was mad at her and avoiding her. She had no idea what the right thing to do was. It felt like it all was spiraling out of control.

Chapter 22

The cool water ran over her hands, washing away the dirt and grime from her afternoon of training the horses as best she could with her still-hurting leg. She sighed, sat down at her desk, and rubbed her leg where she'd been kicked. If she sat for too long, it ached. So even though she was tired, she needed to move.

Her family would arrive at any moment for their monthly family dinner, and the closer the time came to head back to the house, the more anxious she felt. Besides Parker and Mom, no one else knew how upset Dad was with her. It wouldn't take long for them all to figure it out. And on top of everything, if Scott didn't show up, she had to figure out how to tell her parents why she sent him home yesterday.

Why had she given Scott that ultimatum? Yes, his snide remark about not coming to family dinner had irritated her, but was it more than that? Had she simply wanted to find a way to get all this negative attention off herself? She shook her head, remembering his comment from that morning about how she didn't understand what it meant to be faced with losing everything. He had no idea. And she still had no idea what the right thing to do was.

This wasn't something a conversation with Cleo would make clear, either. She had to make things right with Dad, but it seemed the only way to do that was to quit teaching Xavier. And she didn't want to do that.

The Rodenbaums needed a people; they needed to belong, like Pastor Barker talked about. She'd seen small signs of Jan coming back to life, and what if that was the purpose of teaching Xavier?

More than teaching him about horses, or how to ride, or even social skills, what if the only benefit to come from her time with them was that Jan was able to relax, unwind, and find some joy?

Locking her office door, she headed outside. Parker and Grandpa passed her in the golf cart but stopped just in front of her and offered her a ride. She declined, choosing to walk the half mile to the house to keep her leg muscle loose and delay the inevitable.

Fifteen minutes later, she entered the kitchen. Mom was busy preparing food.

"What can I do to help?" she asked, glancing around.

"Peel those potatoes, please. I decided last minute to do mashed potatoes and haven't gotten to them yet."

Heather nodded and got to work.

"I saw you out working the horses earlier. Have you been doing that all afternoon?" asked Mom, sounding a little frustrated.

"Yeah."

"I thought you were resting today."

"I did, but my leg hurts if I sit too long."

She nodded. "How is Littlefoot?"

"I didn't train with him today, but he seems good."

"Are you seeing progress with him on the sedative?"

"Yeah, a little."

Mom sighed and leaned on the counter beside her. "Have you decided what you're going to do about Xavier?"

Heather stopped peeling and glanced at Mom, unsure how to answer. There was no question in her mind about stopping his lessons. She would need ... she wasn't sure, exactly, but something to convince her she was the absolute wrong person for Xavier. The battle in her mind was how to get Dad, and apparently Mom, too, to understand why she didn't want to quit. But there was no point getting into all that right now, so she simply responded, "No."

Mom nodded and went back to cooking.

Heather finished her task, rinsed her hands, and went to the living room, where Parker and Grandpa were. Lisa and Harry entered the house a moment later and joined them.

"Where's Dad?" asked Harry Jr.

"Mom said he's out in the garage," said Parker, glancing at

Heather.

"Weird."

Heather ignored Parker's look. It was weird. Other than chores, Dad never worked on Sunday. More proof he was avoiding her.

"Food's ready," Mom called from the kitchen, and Parker left to help her set food on the table as everyone took their seats. As they did, Dad entered the house and headed upstairs to wash up.

Scott still hadn't shown up.

Mom stood at the head of the table, her hands on her hips, as she surveyed her family. "Has anyone heard from Scott?" she asked.

Everyone responded in the negative.

Mom sighed, returned to the kitchen, and picked up the phone. Heather's anxiety increased. She glanced around and saw most everyone else at the table had noticed Mom was on edge. She didn't want to think how awkward things would get after Dad returned.

The phone slammed in the cradle and Mom rejoined them at the table as Dad entered the room. "Is everything okay?" he asked.

"Have you heard from Scott?" Mom asked.

He shook his head and took his seat.

"Well, I guess we'll get started, then," said Mom. "Who wants to pray?"

"I will," said Parker. They all bowed their heads.

Parker's prayer was brief and to the point. Little conversation took place as food was passed and plates were filled. The uncomfortable silence continued as everyone ate.

Mom cleared her throat, drawing everyone's attention. At that moment, the front door opened and Scott entered.

"Sorry I'm late," he said.

Heather breathed a sigh of relief and let herself relax a little. But only a little.

Scott took his seat, and everyone passed food to him. Once he had his food and started eating, Mom spoke up.

"Now that we're all here, I would like to remind you, the reason we have this monthly family dinner is so we don't drift apart. You're adults now, and you're living your own lives, and all I ask is that we keep the close bond we've always had by having dinner together once a month and catching up on what is happening in one another's lives."

Heather's stomach knotted.

"I've seen a trend this past month that I don't like. Scott, you haven't been coming to church, you've been dismissive to all of us, and I don't know what happened yesterday, but I was very disappointed when I didn't see you at Heather's fundraiser and heard from my brother, William, that you bailed on your sister. I was under the impression you promised to help."

Heather and Scott looked at each other. She'd told him everyone had noticed his strange behavior, but she hadn't expected this. Scott hung his head and didn't lift it again until Mom changed focus.

"The withdrawal I've seen in you, Scott, has been going on for months, gradually increasing."

By this time everyone had stopped eating and looked uncomfortable.

"Heather, you haven't been communicating well lately and you were injured on Friday, kicked by a horse. The last time that happened, you were in high school. There is an increasing wedge between you and your father, and I know it's not entirely your fault." She glanced at her husband, who looked annoyed by the accusation.

"I can't fix these issues, but I expect you all to stop avoiding each other and start talking." She picked up her fork, stabbed a green bean, and stuck it in her mouth. No one else moved, and for a solid minute the only sound was the scraping of Mom's fork against her plate.

"What is this about a rift between Heather and Harry?" asked Grandpa.

Mom looked at Heather and then her husband, apparently expecting one of them to explain.

Heather glanced at Dad. "Dad thinks it's too dangerous for me to teach Xavier," she said finally. "That I'm putting myself and others at risk. And he's worried I'm going to ruin my business and lose the family land with it."

"Oh, poppycock!" Grandpa hit the table with the flat of his hand, making the dishes rattle. Everyone looked at him in surprise.

"Dad," said Harry Sr.

"He's right," Heather said at the same time.

Dad looked at her in surprise.

"He's right, Grandpa. Xavier is impulsive. He runs and doesn't see the danger, yells, screams, and he can get out of control in a matter of seconds. I got kicked because Xavier pulled on Queenie's tail. You were there. You saw it. It didn't matter that I'd told him it was a bad idea. He did it anyway. I don't know how to handle Xavier or keep him safe without putting myself in harm's way."

She stared at her plate, unable to say more, unable to find the words to explain why she didn't want to quit teaching Xavier, despite the risk.

"There's always a risk when you mix humans and horses," said Grandpa. "No matter the age or issue of the person, no matter the temperament of the horses. Son, have you watched Heather teach that boy?"

"No, I've only seen how the lessons end," Dad said.

Grandpa hit the table again. "I've watched every dadgum lesson, and bless it if it don't take me back to when I taught you."

Heather looked up then, first at Grandpa, then Dad.

"This is different," said Dad.

Grandpa waved a hand at his son and scowled. "No, it ain't. He might be a little more hyper and stubborn, but just because some doctor gave him a diagnosis don't make him any more dangerous than any other kid. You think your mom and I knew what the hell we were doing with you?"

"Dad," said Harry Sr.

"No. Now, you listen to me. I'm proud to be your dad. Mom and I were happy to adopt you after your daddy, my little brother, died, but we didn't know what to do with you. We had given up having kids of our own, and suddenly we had a toddler to raise. We didn't have all these fancy gadgets to entertain kids back then, and you were underfoot, demanding our attention, all day and most of the night.

"It took you a good year to overcome your grief of losing your dad. Never took your eyes off either of us the whole time and cried if we got out of sight for a second. Then, once you got over that, we had to keep our eyes on you. If we didn't, you were out the door, usually half naked, runnin' around in the fields with all those cattle. Near gave us a heart attack several times, and no matter how many times we spanked your bottom, or put you in time-out, the second we weren't looking, you were back out there. And now look at you—

you're still chasing after those cattle and doing a damn fine job of it. Made this business more successful than I ever did."

"I can't quite imagine Dad ever being that wild," said Harry Jr., smirking. And everyone, except Dad and Heather, chuckled.

"Oh, he was, and it didn't stop until he got chased and nearly run through by one of the bulls."

"That explains why you always got so mad at us when we goofed off around the cattle," said Parker.

The joke seemed to relieve some of the tension in the room, and everyone but Heather had resumed eating again. She knew Grandpa's story didn't change anything. She wasn't the little kid in this scenario; she was an adult, with her own business, and in Dad's eyes, she'd made poor choices in her personal and professional life. There was no comparison for that. Grandpa certainly didn't think he and Grandma adopting Dad or handing the family business over to him had been a poor choice, but Dad had made it clear he thought he'd made a mistake trusting her with the ten acres he'd given her.

"I've had more than one hazy run-in with bulls to make me want everyone to be cautious, but I get your point," Dad said.

"Good. Because our Heather has a natural talent with that boy. Rescuing horses is an admirable profession, but helping out kids who have no one else is a far greater purpose in life. It ain't an easy one but if that's what Heather decides to do, we should support her in that. I'm sure I don't have to remind you how Heather ran around the horses when she was a little girl."

"Yeah, I'm pretty sure she was half naked most of the time, too," said Harry Jr.

Heather couldn't help but grin at this. But her lip trembled and tears threatened, so she didn't say anything.

"I know Heather knows horses better than anyone. I trust her to know what she's doing whenever horses are involved," said Dad.

Grandpa nodded. "Good. I don't want to hear any more about anyone at this table being in a rift. We're family. We work these things out and love one another, no matter what."

Heather glanced at Dad. He sat hunched over his plate, not looking at anyone. They would have to talk later. She knew nothing was settled yet. Conversation waned again, and silence filled the room.

"Lisa and I have some news to share," said Harry Jr., clearing his throat. His cheerful tone suggested a big change of subject.

Everyone looked their way.

"As you know," said Lisa, "we've been holding off on having kids until our restaurant was firmly established."

"We've decided we're at that point," said Harry.

"So, we're officially trying to get pregnant." Lisa beamed.

Mom clapped. "Oh, I can't wait to have grandbabies!"

While everyone congratulated the couple, Heather glanced up at Scott. He'd remained quiet all through dinner. The expression on his face told her he was in the midst of an internal battle.

As dinner wrapped up and the table was being cleared, Scott stayed in his seat. Everyone noticed.

"Scott?" asked Mom.

He looked up.

"Something on your mind?"

"I was at the fundraiser, but Heather made me leave."

"What?" Mom glanced at her.

"She ..." He wiped a hand across his face. "She caught me ..." Tears streamed down his face now.

Mom set the stack of plates she was holding back down on the table and sat in the chair next to Scott.

"Do you want me to explain, Scott?" Heather asked, her voice trembling.

He shook his head. "I've been using performance drugs, and Heather caught me the morning of the fundraiser and told me to leave." Scott sobbed in his seat, and Mom held him.

He'd done it. The relief Heather felt was immense, and she wiped tears from her face with her napkin.

Dad reached out and grasped Scott's arm. "I know it wasn't easy for you to tell us about this, son."

Heather looked at him, noting the mixture of emotions playing over his face. She suspected he was angry but knew it was important to be supportive at this moment.

"Scott stopped by our booth when he arrived at the fundraiser, so when I didn't see him again, I figured something was up. I just couldn't figure out what it was," Harry Jr. said. "If you need any help looking into any of those rehab centers, or want someone to go with you, I will help. If that's your plan."

Scott had calmed down and was no longer crying. He nodded. "Thanks, man."

Mom kissed the top of his head and picked up the plates. "Well, this has been an interesting dinner, but I hope you all see that we are here for one another, even if we don't agree or don't make the best decisions. I love you all, I'm proud of you all, and Scott, we're all here to help in whatever way we can."

Scott nodded.

As cleanup got underway again, Heather saw Dad slip out back. Scott's revelation and Grandpa's lecture were a lot to handle. She wondered if she should let him be for tonight or try to talk to him. As everyone said their goodbyes, Heather went out back. She could at least try to explain, try to repair some of the damage and lessen the pain she and Scott had inflicted.

A light in the garage told her he was probably there. Slipping in through the side door, she saw him at his workbench, putting tools away.

"Hey."

He looked up at her but didn't stop what he was doing.

Heather took a seat on a stool near the door.

"I know Grandpa's storytelling didn't change how you feel about me teaching Xavier. And I'm sorry you're disappointed in me and the decisions I've made lately."

He paused in his task. "Heather."

"I wish I could explain why I don't want to give up on his lessons, but all I can say is, it feels like it's the right thing to do. I'm not ignoring your advice or concern, though. I hope you can see that."

A pained expression crossed his face.

"I meant what I said in there. You are right: it is dangerous; it is a risk. But Xavier needs and deserves all the love and support he can get, and I have a way to help give him that. Isn't that what Pastor Barker has been teaching us? That relationships matter most to people, and when those relationships aren't good, aren't loving, aren't available to us, then we have issues?

"I've been extremely blessed to be in a family who loves me, supports me, and encourages me. All I want to do is show other people the same love you and Mom provided to us kids."

Dad buried his face in his hands.

Tears choked her, but she continued, desperate for him to hear her. "I'm really sorry I keep disappointing you. I want to make things right, but I don't know how." She got up from the stool. "I'm sorry." Her voice cracked, and she ran out the door and down the lane to her own barn until her leg throbbed so badly, she had to slow down.

Chapter 23

Tuesday morning, Heather dashed into her office to grab the notebook on her desk that contained the list of questions she'd compiled for her tour of the therapy ranch. Glancing at her watch as she locked her office door, she jogged outside to her truck. If traffic was bad, she would be late. Really late. If traffic was good, she'd only be a little late.

She tossed the notebook on the passenger seat, started up the truck, and called Mom. Putting the phone up to her ear, she put the truck in reverse and headed down the driveway to the main road.

"Hello?"

"Hey, Mom, would you have any time to check on Littlefoot today? He has diarrhea." She had noticed this vague sign of illness while doing her chores this morning and spent more time than she had to spare trying to see if she could discover anything wrong with him. That's why she was running late now.

"Any other symptoms?"

"No, I checked his temperature and a few other things, and everything looked normal, but if you could give him a once-over to be sure, I'd really appreciate it. Could it be the sedative?"

"Possibly," she said, her tone instantly transforming from Mom to Professional Veterinarian. "But we're giving him such a low dose that I would be surprised if it were the medication. I should have some time this morning, because my first appointment isn't until ten o'clock."

"Thanks, Mom."

"Sure. Where are you headed off to this morning?"

She hesitated. She hadn't told anyone about the tour, and mentioning it would probably be a slap in the face to Dad, even though the whole reason for the tour was to find out if she was heading in the right direction with Xavier or completely off base. "Uh, I'm touring a therapy ranch. Research for helping Xavier."

Mom sighed. "I see."

"Are you mad?"

"No. Has your dad spoken to you yet?"

"No."

Another sigh.

"I know Dad is still upset, and I know I don't entirely know what I'm doing," she admitted. "But that's why I'm taking this tour. I don't know how to explain it, but teaching Xavier feels right. I'm trying to find a way to confirm whether I'm on the right track, because right now it feels like I have to choose between Dad and Xavier. People will be hurt either way, it seems. So I want to get answers. I need to be able to explain why this is the right thing for me to do, in hopes that can alleviate some of Dad's concern. I'm not taking any of this lightly, and I'm trying not to be stubborn about it. I'm open to learning something today that will make me change my mind, but so far, the more I've learned, the more I want to help."

"I know, honey. I'm sure you'll figure it all out. I'll call you after I take a look at Littlefoot."

Forty-five minutes later, Heather pulled into a driveway that ended in a roundabout in front of a large building with stone and natural wood siding. Two other cars were parked in the roundabout, so she pulled off to one side of the driveway and parked. The place was impressive. As she climbed out, she glanced at the building's design. It looked like a large house, not quite a mansion, but almost. Large windows at least two stories high covered one corner of the building. Inside, she could see that the windows were part of a large common room. She headed up the stairs to a set of large wooden doors and pulled on the handle. The door gave way easily, and she entered.

A gas fireplace dominated one wall, with two leather couches facing each other on each side of the fireplace. A square coffee table made of natural logs and what looked to be some kind of animal hide stretched across it stood in the middle between the couches.

"Can I help you?"

Heather turned and found an older gentleman, spectacled, bald, and slightly hunched over, standing near the door of a glass-walled room filled with cubicles. "Yes, I have an appointment with ..." She patted her pockets and realized she had left her notebook in the truck. "I think it's Sara. I actually need to grab my notebook from my truck." She pointed her thumb behind her.

"Okay. You must be here for the tour."

"Yes, that's right."

The old man nodded. "I'm Alan, the director here at Wellness Therapy." He held his hand out to her.

"Heather Fletcher," she said, shaking his hand.

"Ah, yes. You're the young lady who wanted to know how we choose our horses for the clients."

Heather smiled. "That's me."

"Well, I'll let Sara know you're here. You can wait over there." He pointed to the couches.

"Thank you." Heather waited until he turned and went to the room full of cubicles before going to her truck to retrieve her notebook.

Back inside, she headed toward a couch to take a seat but was stopped by a woman's voice.

"Miss Fletcher?"

She whirled around and saw a woman about her own age, wearing jeans and a red-and-white plaid long-sleeved shirt, her blonde hair pulled back into a tight ponytail. "Yes."

The woman smiled and stretched her hand toward her.

Heather shook it.

"I'm Sara, and if you're ready, we can get started with the tour."

"Sounds great."

"When a child enters our program, they usually stay about three months, although they can stay longer." Sara led her out a back door in the room with the fireplace. They were on a large patio, with several plastic tables scattered along it, each surrounded by matching plastic chairs. A teenage boy sat at one of the tables, looking at a comic book. His baggy jeans were stained, his yellow T-shirt wrinkled, and his black hair greasy and tangled. It reminded her of Xavier's unkempt appearance. The boy looked out of place in these expensively furnished facilities.

Sara took her down the three steps of the patio into a garden lined with paths. "We offer two programs: a residential, where the children live here, and a day program. The kids in the day program arrive in the morning and leave around three o'clock. Our residential kids stay in one of two dorms." She pointed to two rectangular buildings on either side of the one they stood behind. The exteriors were built in the same style as the main building. "One is for boys, the other for girls."

"So the day-program kids aren't attending school?" asked Heather.

"No, we use an online school program for regular schooling. It includes tutors who are available to help with whatever they need."

Heather nodded.

"The great building we just came from is where our kids start each day. Breakfast for the residential kids starts at seven-thirty and ends at eight-thirty. Since our day-program kids arrive at eight, they're given the option of having breakfast here if they wish.

"After that, all the kids do schoolwork until lunchtime. We serve all the meals in the dorms, so the boys and girls eat separately. Once lunch is over, they're divided into their therapy groups. They'll spend about forty-five minutes in a discussion group, and the remaining therapy happens out at the barn." She pointed at a large building opposite the great building.

It was also built in the same style as the great house, and it looked almost as big as the house, too. Heather felt a pang of barn envy. She could rescue a lot of horses with a barn like that.

"None of our therapists can have more than six kids in their group, so things stay manageable."

"Do you divide the kids up by needs?"

"No, we think it's good for the children to interact with others of varying abilities and needs. We focus on accepting one another's differences, practice having patience and offering forgiveness, and it allows them to experience different people and situations. We're there to help them learn how to navigate those social situations."

Heather nodded. "How do you handle meltdowns?"

Sara stopped and turned to her. "We have staff on hand whom we call assistants. They monitor the dorms and the therapy sessions. If a child has a meltdown, an assistant and the therapist will restrain the child until they are calm. Meltdowns don't happen very often, though; we teach the kids to recognize how they're feeling and encourage them to take a break if they feel upset. There are several small rooms in every building. I'll show you one in the barn. We call them quiet rooms. The walls are made with thick foam so the kids can't hurt themselves if they're angry, and we provide pillows, blankets, and swings to help them calm down. These rooms are also monitored by our assistants."

"How do you teach them to recognize their emotions?"

Sara motioned for her to follow, and they headed toward the barn again. "In the group therapy sessions. The kids talk about situations they encountered here or at home, and they go through an exercise of identifying what their body felt like in that situation. Sometimes they assign a color to the emotion, so if they feel red, they know it's time to take a break and calm down, that kind of thing."

Heather nodded, wondering if that would work with Xavier. Somehow she doubted it.

"Besides the quiet rooms, there are three garden areas on site and a full-sized gym on the second floor of the great building. If any of our kids are having a rough time in therapy, they are allowed to go to any of these areas to calm themselves, or they can use the gym to work out some of their frustrations if needed. Our residential kids also have free time in the evening, depending on what level they're on, and they can spend their time in any of these areas as well."

They reached the barn and entered. Heather's mouth dropped open. Three rows of stalls, each with ... she counted the stalls in the first row: ten stalls. And each one appeared big enough to hold two horses comfortably.

"This is our barn, and where most of our therapy work happens. Over there is one of the quiet rooms I mentioned." She pointed to a small metal box. The door, also metal, had a large sliding lever lock on it and a round porthole window.

Heather stepped over to it and glanced into a small, padded room. She imagined Xavier inside, and it unsettled her. "You don't lock the kids in there, do you?"

Sara chuckled. "No, some kids like, and request, the door to be closed, but we have never had to use the lock. We would use the lock only if a child couldn't be restrained by staff and became a danger to themselves and others and we needed to call an ambulance to take them to the hospital."

Heather turned her back on the small room and rejoined Sara.

"Some of our therapists keep their own horses and board them here, but the majority of the animals are owned by the ranch. Back there"—Sara pointed to a door at the end of the row—"there is another space, not quite as large as this one, but almost. It's divided up with fencing, so each therapist has their own indoor ring to work in. That way, if the weather turns bad, we can still have our sessions."

"Do the horses have any special training to become a therapy horse?"

"Yes, and no. We work our horses just like any other horse so they don't scare, bolt, or have aggressive behaviors. We do require our horses to pass a list of requirements that are pretty strict, though, so we don't take just any horse. But there is also an element of letting the bond between these kids and horses form as well. The horses naturally seem to understand that many of these kids can't keep their emotions or bodies in control all the time. But there isn't a horse out there that will tolerate too much abuse without reacting. That's one of the reasons horse therapy is so great. The kids get to earn the trust of a large animal, and in turn, the kids themselves learn to trust, gain confidence, learn boundaries, and overall do much better in other areas of their life."

"Have you ever had a child injured by a horse?"

"On occasion. We do everything we can to avoid it, of course, but parents sign papers so we aren't liable for those injuries and everyone is made aware of the risks up front. We also have cameras all over the barn to ensure staff are doing what they're supposed to and to document any incidents."

"How long does it typically take before a child is allowed to get on a horse and ride it?"

"Oh, well, most of our students never learn to ride a horse. Most of our sessions focus on learning and understanding body language, working the horses, grooming and feeding them. Learning to read and care for a horse or other animal is often an easier way for these children to learn how to read human body language and develop communication skills and trust. A few express an interest in learning to ride, but they have to meet certain requirements of the program to do that."

"What kind of requirements?" asked Heather, thinking about her Aunt Michelle's advice on teaching riding or teaching the special-needs child.

"It's a level system. There are five levels, and every child who enters the program starts on level two. The child is required to stay on a particular level for a certain amount of time before they can move up. If they reach level five and can stay there for two weeks, then they are given the option of learning to ride. But that is a special privilege and takes place outside of therapy hours. Kind of like an after-school program."

"What happens if they drop a level after they start riding lessons?"

"Then the privilege is taken away until they can earn it back."

"Doesn't that interfere with their progress? Demotivate them?"

Sara shrugged. "Our focus is that they learn to cope in healthy ways and learn to be a productive member of society. If they really want to ride, they have to learn the social and emotional skills. If they drop a level, it's because they've demonstrated they don't have the ability to use those skills for a sustained length of time."

"What about children who don't respond well to level systems? Do you have anything in place for them?"

Sara shook her head. "No, we find that with most children, the level system works really well, because they can see their goals in a tangible way. We do occasionally have students who never make progress in the level system, but as long as they want to keep working with the horses, and they keep trying, they can stay in the program. We try not to make the level system a competitive thing. Our therapists meet with each child in their group individually at the end of each day and update them on their progress. We encourage the kids not to share their status with the others, but of course they do. We use it as an opportunity to teach them about boasting and comparing ourselves with others."

Heather understood the logic behind the program, but something about it bothered her. They continued on through the barn, into the back where the rings were set up. Heather leaned against one of the fence panels.

"How many students do you typically have in a month?" She'd calculated that the barn could comfortably hold at least thirty horses, more if each stall really could fit two horses, but at least half the stalls were empty. If they were feeding and caring for thirty horses, the feed bill alone would be high, not to mention a therapist's pay. She calculated that if each therapist had access to two or three horses for each session, and only had a group of six kids, they could provide services for at least sixty kids at a time. Three thousand dollars a month per kid was way more than enough to pay for upkeep, salary, and feed.

"We typically have fifteen to twenty kids a month. There is a waiting list, but this line of therapy has a high staff turnover rate, so although we can take more horses and more students, we don't always have the staff to accommodate."

"Why the high turnover rate?" She was pretty sure she knew the answer already.

"We work with high-risk kids, meaning they can be violent and get into a lot of legal trouble. So it's a stressful job, and many therapists want to work here straight out of college, with the mindset that they're doing a great thing, helping people who both need it and want it. And then they get here and discover it's not as easy as they thought to teach these kids the skills they learned to teach them, and they burn out or get overwhelmed."

"Do you have anything in place for your staff to prevent that from happening?"

"Yes, we offer lots of training. We remind them to use the skills they're teaching on themselves, and we require them to use all of their earned vacation time every year. No one is allowed to take work home with them or contact clients outside office hours. We do our best to encourage our staff to take care of themselves, just as much as they desire to care for and teach our clients."

Heather considered this for a moment. "Are any of your students diagnosed with FASD?"

"Oh, yes. Probably a third of the kids who come in here have that diagnosis, or their parents suspect that's the case but can't get a definitive diagnosis."

"And you've seen those students improve and succeed?"

"To a degree. They can be very resistant to change. But because the program offers a level of consistency, we often see their behavior improve over time. When they're in a good place mentally and physically, that's when we see the program benefit them the most. It's getting them to that good place that's the hardest. Many parents will pull them out of the program before we reach that point, because they can't afford to keep paying for the program or because they lose hope that anything will ever change. Unfortunately, a lot of them learn things the hard way, or not at all, and some, depending on how severe their condition is, never learn and end up spending their lives in and out of jail for petty crimes.

"I'll take you around and show you the rest of the facilities and answer any more questions you have."

Heather followed Sara out of the barn. She couldn't imagine that all the hard work Derek and Jan were doing to help Xavier could result in him growing up to become a petty criminal, in and out of jail. He was still young. Surely, helping him at this stage could prevent that.

At the end of the tour, Sara walked her back to the main house. "If you think of any other questions, give me a call." She handed Heather a business card.

"Thank you. Actually, I do have another question. These facilities are very nice and well maintained, and the barn is incredible. It looks like it's temp-controlled and everything is state of the art. But why?"

Sara smiled. "I'm not sure I understand."

"You mentioned the turnover rate. That couldn't have been an unknown factor when this place was built, so why not start smaller scale, knowing it would be hard to maintain staff? Why all the bells and whistles instead of a basic setup?"

"Many of the parents who bring their children here expect the best."

"That's it?"

"A well-built institution that can provide for every need is more appealing than a rundown building with few accommodations."

"Right, but the cost of upkeep must be insanely expensive."

"Parents are willing to pay more for better facilities. I take it you haven't seen any of the state-run facilities?"

"No."

"Since they rely on state or federal income, the buildings are often the last thing to get attention; they're small, rundown, and overcrowded."

"But parents don't typically pay for state services, right? Insurance covers it?"

"Yes, but they still have the same staffing issues we do, and they can't choose what methods they use to help their residents. That's all decided by the government. And they don't have therapy animals unless an outside program brings them in on occasion or a staff member happens to have a trained therapy animal."

Heather nodded.

"If things don't work out for you to keep helping the little boy you mentioned, have his parents call us. We have options to help with the financial side of things, and we'd be happy to discuss those with the family if needed."

Heather smiled, knowing she would never recommend this place to the Rodenbaums. She knew what bugged her about the place now. Kids didn't need a gas fireplace worth thousands of dollars or fancy leather couches to sit on. They needed people who cared about them. This place catered to the parents, especially parents with money. Their therapy methods might work, but this was an area that still needed a lot of research. A fancy building or barn wasn't the answer. And the whole idea of taking away a reward, giving it back, and taking it away again in order to teach a set of skills didn't sit well with her. It hadn't set well with her since Aunt Michelle had mentioned it.

Of course, there could be other, better facilities that didn't operate this way, but if it was true that the options were an overcrowded, rundown state facility or an overpriced private one, the system needed some work.

She thanked Sara for the tour, exited the building, and climbed into her truck, her mind buzzing. She checked her phone and found a message from Mom. She hit the speaker button before pressing play, then put the truck in gear as she listened.

"Littlefoot looks great. I did a parasite check and a thorough exam, and he appears perfectly healthy. It could have been something he ate, but I didn't see anything when I looked around. By the way, fantastic job, sweetheart! Littlefoot has made some amazing progress since I saw him last. I'd even suggest you think about taking him off the sedative, to see how he does. Looks like I was wrong about this one! Have a great day. See you later tonight. Love you."

Heather bit her lip. She was grateful for Mom's praise. It appeared Littlefoot was officially off the euthanasia list. But it further complicated a thought she'd considered since she'd learned how the therapy ranches used the horses with the kids. Littlefoot just might make the perfect therapy horse one day.

Chapter 24

"You're going to do great in competition next year," said Heather as Zeke brought One With Wind to a stop near her.

"As long as Mom still lets me," Zeke said.

"She will." Heather patted One With Wind's neck, a twinge of doubt flickering at the back of her mind. She'd intended to put in a good word for Zeke and assure her aunt he was ready for something more challenging. But knowing how Michelle felt about kids with special needs, she wasn't entirely sure her aunt would think much of her advice, given that she was still teaching Xavier. Michelle might agree with Dad and believe Heather was a little too willing to put her son in a dangerous situation, because she was obviously willing to put volatile kids around horses. The last thing she'd wanted, or expected, was for her decision to affect her family. But now she worried that she couldn't escape it.

Almost an entire week had passed since the family dinner, and still she and Dad weren't speaking to each other. Mom assured her he wasn't, in fact, mad or disappointed, but the longer he froze her out, the harder it was to believe.

"How is Littlefoot doing?" asked Zeke, hopping down from One With Wind.

"I took him off the sedative on Wednesday. He seems a little on edge, but he's still showing progress, so that's good."

"Will he ever be able to find a new home or heal completely? Or will he be a permanent resident here?"

Heather shrugged. "Littlefoot has a long road in front of him, and he may never get totally better, but I'm convinced he can learn to cope, learn to trust, and be a good horse for someone, eventually. After all, no horse is perfect, and just like with any horse, normal or traumatized, it's about building a trusting relationship with the horse. Understanding each other and being willing to work with each other. As long as Littlefoot has someone who refuses to give up on him, he has a chance."

Just like Xavier. It was remarkable how many similarities she had found between training horses and helping Xavier over the past month. If only she could help other people see that too. Maybe that's what she needed to tell Dad. Explain the correlation she saw.

"I better grab Queenie and get her in the ring. Xavier should be here any minute, and I promised to bring Grandpa out so he could watch today."

Zeke nodded and started brushing One With Wind.

Inside the barn, she attached a harness and lead to Queenie and stroked her nose. "Could you please not kick me today?" she asked and gave Queenie a kiss before leading her out of her stall.

Jan's van drove up as Heather released Queenie into the ring and closed the fence panel.

Xavier climbed out, looking tired and grumpy. Heather's shoulders tensed, and she looked to Jan for an explanation.

"Sorry, he started back to school on Wednesday, and he's been exhausted every day. He only has a half day on Friday, and he took a nap as soon as he got home. I had to wake him up to come here, and he slept the whole way."

Heather frowned. "Would it help if we changed our lessons to Saturday?"

Jan nodded. "It might."

"Let's plan on that for next weekend, then. I promised my grandpa I'd bring him outside today, so I'll go get him and come right back."

Jan nodded.

Heather jogged to Grandpa's house. Her leg still had a bruise, but it wasn't as deep or as painful and she no longer had to take pain meds. But the tightness in her leg brought a twinge of guilt to her mind. Every lesson was beginning to feel like another door slamming between her and Dad. She knocked and let herself in. Grandpa sat on the couch with his cane between his legs. He looked at her expectantly when she entered. "Ready to go?" she asked.

He smiled and slowly got to his feet.

She took his arm and helped him into his wheelchair, which he only used to get in and out of the house. Dad had built a ramp off the back stairs, so she rolled him outside and helped him into the golf cart they kept parked there.

She drove him around front, where Jan and Xavier waited. Xavier sat cross-legged in the dirt, his chin resting on his hand. Climbing out of the golf cart, she knelt in front of Xavier. "Since you're kind of tired, what do you want to do today?"

"Can I see Littlefoot?" There was a slight whine in his voice.

"Sure, we can go say hello to Littlefoot."

Xavier perked up a little, and Heather motioned for him to go ahead. He got to his feet and hurried toward the barn. Heather stood, got back in the golf cart, invited Jan to take a seat on the back, which she did, and followed Xavier.

On the other side of the barn, Heather noticed Dad on horseback in the field. He headed their way at a slow pace. Her stomach twisted in knots as she turned off the golf cart and stepped out. She turned her back toward the field to give her full attention to Xavier, who was climbing through the fence.

She joined him, wishing he'd waited for her first. "Hey, if I say we have to leave, you need to listen, okay? Remember, this horse gets scared easily. And I don't want either of us to get hurt."

Xavier nodded. He walked confidently up to Littlefoot, stood on his toes, and wrapped his arms the best he could around Littlefoot's neck. He simply stood there.

Heather smiled as she watched. Littlefoot stood still, his neck bent over the boy's body as if returning the hug.

She shook her head, amazed again at the way Littlefoot changed with Xavier, even without the sedative.

Behind her, Jan made a noise. Heather looked at her and saw she had a huge grin on her face. Behind her she saw Dad near the fence, still on his horse, watching them. She tried to ignore the butterflies in her stomach and returned her attention to Jan.

"That is the most adorable thing I've ever seen," she whispered.

Heather grinned and nodded.

Jan pulled her cell phone out of her pocket and crept toward the fence to snap pictures.

Heather folded her arms and watched. The deep knowledge that somehow this was the right thing to do was overcoming any lingering guilt, despite Dad's presence. If nothing else came from it, if Xavier never learned to ride a horse, or never improved in impulse control or behavior, this moment was worth it. Because, as insignificant as it seemed, she knew this moment was huge. She wondered if Jan had noticed the change in herself, the way she'd opened herself up and relaxed a little.

Now if only she could fix things with Dad. She wanted him to see what she saw, to understand why it was worth it to her to face a difficult journey with this boy. *Give me the words, Lord.*

After several minutes, Xavier released his hold on the horse and climbed back through the fence. "When I try to ride a horse again, I only want it to be on Littlefoot," he said, looking up at her.

Heather crouched down so that she was on his level again and looked him in the eye. "That sounds like a great goal to work on. I still have a lot of work to do with Littlefoot, and you might be ready to ride again before Littlefoot is ready to have a rider, but I'll do my best to get him ready for when you're ready. Deal?"

He nodded.

Standing, she took a step or two away from him.

"He looks pretty tuckered," said Grandpa.

Jan nodded. "We'll probably have to keep this lesson short. He is so tired."

"That's fine. It's enough to let him visit with his new friend," Heather said, indicating Littlefoot.

Jan nodded.

"You've done good with that horse," said Grandpa. "I can see it in his eyes."

"Thanks." She smiled and kissed his cheek.

A tug on the bottom of her shirt made her look down. Xavier stared up at her with a serious look on his face. "Yes?" she said.

"Can I help get Littlefoot ready?"

Heather grinned. "As long as your parents say it's okay and Littlefoot keeps doing well."

Xavier looked at Jan, his eyes pleading.

"I think Heather has proved she knows what she's doing. If she's okay with it, so am I."

The little boy's eyes grew wide, and a slow smile spread over his face. He nodded, hugged Heather, then turned to his mom and hugged her too. "I get to train Littlefoot!" he shouted.

Jan smiled. "Next week, we'll move your lesson to Saturday so you'll have more energy, okay?"

He nodded again and clung to Jan. "Can we go home now?"

"Yes, we can." Jan looked up at her. "Thank you. Sorry we're cutting things short."

Heather smiled back. "It's okay."

"Hey, young man, do I get one of those hugs too?" asked Grandpa.

Xavier grinned and obliged him. "Do you have any suckers?" he whispered.

"What's that? You'll have to speak up. These old ears don't work so good anymore."

Xavier repeated his request much louder, and Grandpa chuckled. "I might. Let's see here." He dug around in his shirt pocket and pulled out a sucker, handing it to Xavier.

Xavier tore the wrapper off, thrust the trash into Jan's hand, and popped the sugary treat in his mouth.

"What do you say, Xavier?" asked Jan.

"Thank you."

Grandpa chuckled again. "You're welcome."

"Do you want to head back or stay here for a minute while I walk them to their car?" Heather asked Grandpa.

"Oh, I'll stay here and have a look at this horse."

She walked Jan and Xavier to their van and watched as they headed down the driveway to the road, before turning to retrieve Queenie from the ring she'd put her in and take her back to her stall.

Inside the barn, she gave Queenie a handful of oats as a treat and closed her stall door before heading out back to join Grandpa again. Dad stood near the golf cart, watching her, thumbs stuck in the belt loops of his jeans.

She stopped near the door of the barn and waited for him.

"Your mother has been talking to me a great deal this past week," he said. "Lecturing, actually."

Heather smiled.

"I came out today to see your lesson. The whole thing this time." He glanced at Grandpa, who nodded. "And I've been watching you with this horse, too." He nodded at Littlefoot.

He cleared his throat. "Baby Girl, I never want you to think I'm disappointed in you or don't support you." His voice cracked a little, and he wiped a hand over his face.

A lump formed in Heather's throat. He had only ever called her Baby Girl when he'd been afraid or she'd been hurt, like the time she'd been thrown from a horse during a competition. He had run out to the field along with the paramedics and said, "Baby Girl, can you hear me?" Or the time in high school when a boy had broken her heart. "Baby Girl, you're gonna be all right," he'd said as she cried in his arms.

"I watched you with that little boy today, and I can't say I understand, but I can see the passion inside you to help him. I still think it's dangerous to work with that boy, but I know what you're wanting to do with Xavier is a good thing, and I've given a lot of thought to what you said to me about it last Sunday, about it feeling like the right thing to do." He took a few steps toward her. "I'm not disappointed in you. I just want you to be happy and safe, and I've seen you struggle so much this past month. I hate seeing my kids struggle."

She nodded, unable to speak past the lump in her throat.

He took a few more steps toward her and now stood only a few feet away. "I'm sorry I made you feel I wasn't in your corner. This week, not speaking to each other." He shook his head. "It's been awful."

Heather laughed, nodded, and tears spilled down her cheeks. She reached toward him, and he closed the gap between them, wrapping his arms around her in a tight hug.

They stood there for several minutes, both of them crying.

When she was calm again, she drew away from him, looking up into his face. His eyes were red. "I'm sorry too, Dad."

"What for?" he asked in a hoarse whisper.

"For not being more open or explaining more what I was thinking and doing when it came to Xavier."

He nodded. "Most of what I felt last Sunday was directed toward Scott, not you. When you came to the garage, I was overwhelmed with Scott's confession. That's why I didn't say anything. And Grandpa's story did have an effect on me."

She nodded. "I have to tell you something, Dad." She had to tell him everything. All the things she'd kept to herself since touring the therapy ranch. Ideas had sprouted in her mind, things she wanted to do, but she'd stuffed them down, unwilling to acknowledge them further until she knew things would be all right between her and Dad. Even though helping Xavier was important to her and felt like the right thing to do, she couldn't bring herself to consider anything else that might cause an even greater wedge between them.

But Dad came today. He came to try and understand, met her halfway. She had to tell him the rest.

"What?"

"I toured a therapy ranch on Tuesday. I thought it would help me, either by giving me words to explain why teaching Xavier felt like the right thing or by convincing me I was in over my head."

"And what was the result?"

"Neither. It made me realize there are no easy solutions when it comes to helping families like the Rodenbaums. No one really has it figured out, even the professionals. And ..." She stuffed her hands in her pockets. "I kind of want to go to school and get a degree in psychology and become a licensed therapist, and possibly turn the ranch into a hybrid horse rescue and therapy ranch for kids like Xavier" She stared at the ground.

Dad let out a long, slow breath. "In that case, I have something to tell you."

She looked up at him, her eyebrows knitted together, and waited.

He ran a hand through his hair and over his face, making several strands of his graying, thin, wispy hair stick out at different angles from his head. "First of all, I never should have said what I did about you losing the land. There's no risk of that. I was just angry."

She nodded. "Mom told me about your backup plan."

He nodded. "After several attempts to get you to change your mind about helping this family, I saw your resistance. As much as I didn't like the idea, I had a feeling you were making big plans, because you've *never* made small plans. Any time an idea passes through that pretty little head of yours, it has to be well worth doing—which means a lot of thought, research, and planning goes into it. I'll be honest: the idea that you might be making big plans involving anything to do with that boy scared me. It still does." He stuck his thumbs back into his belt loops.

"But, so far, all your ideas have been successful. A few days ago, I asked your mother if she thought you were going to give up helping this boy, and she said you probably wouldn't. We didn't know what you were planning, and I still hoped you'd give it up, but we decided we would help you fund … whatever it was."

"What?" Her mouth dropped open in shock. Her idea to take classes or go to college and get certified to help other kids like Xavier was so new to her, she wasn't even sure her plan was a solid one. Yet somehow her parents had known she would do *something*.

He held a hand up. "Now, I know you thought the ten acres of land we gave you to start the horse rescue was an exchange for the college money your mom and I had saved up for each of you kids. We've always been upfront with you and your brothers about the fact we'd saved some money to help each of you get through college, if you went that route. Harry declined our help. Scott has shown no interest in college—yet." He sighed and shook his head. "Which means Parker is the only one who has accepted our offer to pay for school. The ten acres wasn't an exchange, Heather. None of your brothers want to take over the cattle business, which means one day all of this land will go to you, anyway. There's still money set aside for you for schooling." He smiled at her. "Your mother has been insisting all week that I be the one to tell you that."

Heather laughed. "I bet she has. Thank you, Dad. I have no idea where this will lead, but knowing I don't have to worry about how to pay for school makes figuring it out a little easier."

They embraced again. "I do think we should talk to a lawyer and update the contracts you give to parents, just to be safe. And you'll have to lend me some of those books you've been reading," he said, releasing her. "I think if I understand the situation better, like you have, I might not hate the idea so much."

Heather grinned. "You'll have to ask Pastor Barker. I borrowed the books from him and returned them earlier this week."

A confused look crossed his face. "Pastor Barker? I thought you were reading about FAFS ... FARU ... whatever the letters are."

She laughed. "It's FASD, and no, the books were all about what Pastor Barker has been teaching in church. So really, you can blame him for all these crazy new ideas I have."

He grinned and shook his head. "Well, all right then. I'll ask him about it on Sunday."

"Are you two done blubbering? I'm feeling left out over here," said Grandpa.

Heather and Dad laughed and rejoined Grandpa.

Chapter 25: Epilogue

Through the windows of The Gathering Place, Heather could see green and blue streamers hanging from the ceiling. The color of the land and sky, Grandpa's favorite colors. Turning off her truck, she climbed out, stuffing her hands into the pockets of her jacket. The chill October evening smelled of coming snow.

Reaching the door, she pulled the handle, only to find it locked. She bounced on her toes, trying to keep warm, and knocked on the door. Lisa saw her, waved, and came to let her in.

"Sorry, we didn't want anyone coming in thinking we were open tonight," said Lisa.

"That's okay," said Heather. "Sorry I'm late."

"You're not late. We haven't started anything yet."

"Hey, look who's finally here," said Scott, joining them and wrapping an arm around each of them. "How's school?"

"It's hard," she said, laughing. "But it's interesting." She'd enrolled in an online program to start her bachelor's degree in psychology. Most of her professors had certain times they'd get online to do a video lecture, and she liked to watch it live if possible so she could ask questions if she had any, instead of emailing and having to wait for a response, which is exactly why she'd been late to Grandpa's party.

Lisa removed herself from their group to help Harry Jr. finish setting up the food.

"How are you doing, Scott?" Heather asked in a low voice.

Mom, who was in conversation with Parker, Grandpa, and Dad, waved at her. Several others in the group did as well, and she waved back.

He gave her a wry grin. "I'm doing all right. Sticking with the program. I had a rough couple of days last week, and my sponsor gave me a great idea that's helped me a lot."

"Oh, what's that?"

"He suggested that because racing and taking part in all the various competitions is proving to be too tempting for me, that I should consider becoming a trainer or a mentor and teach kids the sports."

"That's a great idea."

Scott shook his head and chuckled. "Yeah, I can't believe I never thought of it myself. By the way, how's that kid you've been teaching?"

"Xavier?" She shook her head and smiled. "He's still a handful. His parents and I finally decided to see how he'd do at lessons without either of them there. It's only been two lessons, but so far it's going pretty well. Sometimes it feels like I'm running in circles trying to teach him something and making no progress whatsoever, but he and Littlefoot seem to have an understanding. I don't understand it at all, but when they're together, they're both better—calmer, more trusting. Neither of them are ready to ride yet, but that doesn't matter. They're perfectly content standing near one another, communicating without words.

"Littlefoot keeps making progress, and sometimes I wonder if he's motivated to improve because of Xavier. There's so much for me to learn still, and watching those two makes me eager to learn as much as I can, as quickly as I can. On the hard days, they're my incentive to stick with the program."

"That's awesome, little sis. If you decide to teach kids like him full-time, maybe I could help somehow. After all, you're the reason I'm sober."

She rolled her eyes. "Yeah, right."

Scott had entered a thirty-day drug rehab program on the first of September and moved in with Grandpa two weeks ago, when he was released from the program.

"I'm serious. I had no intention of confessing at that family dinner back in August."

"What?" She drew back in surprise.

"I came because I knew it would buy me a week to come up with a new plan. I didn't know anything about Xavier, and when Mom started in, I thought you'd already told them. But then your whole ordeal came out, and I remembered what you said to me earlier that day about how nothing was guaranteed and your job was dangerous. I thought you were just making a point, but you were in the middle of something difficult."

"Yeah, I was."

"Confessing was the hardest part. I figured if you could face hard things, so could I. All those things you pointed out about me ... I knew. I saw the changes and I didn't like them, but it was a vicious cycle and I couldn't get out of it."

He squeezed her shoulder.

"The hardest part about it now, though, is going to be my living situation. I really enjoyed being a nomad, but now I have to set down roots, find some stability." He made a face.

Heather laughed. "Poor guy." She shook her head and smiled.

"What?" he asked.

"I'm glad you're back. Not just from rehab, but I'm glad you're back to being you."

"Stop," he groaned, wrapping his arms around her and picking her up in a bear hug. "I can't stand all this sentimentality from everyone."

Heather giggled. "Put me down, you goof."

He set her down and released her.

"Since I'm your sister, I get to be sentimental sometimes. But I promise not to do it too often."

He grinned. "Thanks."

She walked over to where Grandpa sat, squeezed his shoulders in a hug, and kissed his cheek. "Happy birthday, Grandpa."

He patted her hand. "Thank you, granddaughter."

"Food is ready," announced Harry Jr.

"It smells amazing," said Mom. "Honey, would you say the prayer?" she asked her husband.

Dad nodded, and everyone bowed their heads. "Lord, thank you for another year with our beloved Sam. Thank you for this evening that we get to spend together as a family. I pray you'll bless this time, protect us when we all head to our homes, and bless the hands that made the food and made this evening possible. Amen."

Everyone headed toward the food table and started piling food on plates. Parker filled one for Grandpa before getting his own. Once everyone had their plate of food, they sat down around two tables that had been pushed together, with Grandpa at one end and Dad on the other, just like at home.

Conversation flowed easily as everyone chatted, laughed, and enjoyed one another's company. After the meal was over, Parker, Scott, and Harry set up a projection screen and they spent an hour looking at pictures of Grandpa's life and reminiscing. When that was done, Parker handed Grandpa a thumb drive.

"What's this?" asked Grandpa.

"Over the past few months, I've been asking you about your favorite music. I told you I wanted to explore all the different music through the decades and asked if you would like to help me. What I was actually doing was finding out all your favorite songs from over the years."

A look of surprise crossed Grandpa's face and his mouth gaped open.

Parker grinned. "I've compiled all of them on here so you can listen to them whenever you want. And I'll help you set it up so it's easy for you to play, too."

Grandpa held his arms open, and Parker bent over and stepped into his embrace. "Thank you, my dear boy. Whenever I'm missing you, I'm going to listen to these songs."

"Well, if it's time for presents, I think that means it's also time for cake," said Lisa, getting up and heading to the kitchen.

"Cake, too? I am a spoiled old man."

"And ice cream," said Harry Jr. "Your favorite, Neapolitan."

"I don't know what I did to deserve all of this attention."

"You're turning ninety-six. It's not every person who can make it to that age," said Mom.

Grandpa chuckled. "I get spoiled just for being an old fart."

Lisa brought out an impressive-looking two-tiered cake. The top was decorated to look like a barnyard, complete with small plastic farm animals. She set it on the table in front of Grandpa and added two number candles to the top.

Grandpa clapped his hands together in delight. "Oh, would you look at that? This is wonderful."

"Okay, everyone ready to sing?" asked Mom.

Lisa lit the candles, and they all sang "Happy Birthday." Once they were done, Harry and Lisa served up small plates of cake and ice cream, and when everyone had settled with their dessert, Dad presented Grandpa with a small wrapped box.

"When we were planning this gig," said Dad, "we decided all your gifts would be handmade: one from each of us. Here is mine."

Grandpa took the small package and carefully opened it. Inside was a small wooden case with a six-inch leather strap attached to it. He opened the lid, then looked up at his son for an explanation.

"It's for your pocketknife. I know you like to keep it in your pocket, and you've been having trouble getting at it. This box should be small enough to fit in your pocket, and the strap will help you fish it out when you need it."

"Thank you, son." He leaned to the side and tried to get the pocketknife from his pocket and nearly fell out of his chair. Dad scrambled to catch him and offered to retrieve the knife. Grandpa gratefully accepted, and after the knife was safely installed in the little box and returned to his pocket, the gift giving continued.

Mom gave Grandpa a photo album of all his grandkids over the years. Scott gave him a leather bracelet with small copper-wrapped stones and paper beads he'd made himself. Heather gave him a coupon book full of local scenic places he'd loved to visit when he could still drive himself around. He could turn in a coupon when he wanted her to take him for a drive. She promised that, no matter how busy she was, she would make the time to take him.

Harry and Lisa went last. "Grandpa, I'm afraid our gift is something we can't hand you yet. We were hoping to have pictures to give you, but it's too early for that," said Harry.

Grandpa's brows furrowed. "What is it?"

Lisa took Grandpa's hands in her own. "It's your first great-grandchild."

Mom screamed and covered her mouth, laughing as she did so.

Grandpa's eyes filled with tears, but he also laughed. "I hope I live long enough to see him or her born."

"Of course you will, Grandpa," said Harry, sounding a little choked up.

Heather watched her family as they celebrated the coming of new life while celebrating the life of one who'd seen so much, and she knew it was exactly how things were supposed to be. Three generations of people living life together. It was what she hoped to build on her ranch. A community of people loving one another. Each person unique, and facing their own challenges along the way, but still loved, valued, and supported every step of the way.

The End.

A Note From The Author

When I set out to write the Mylin Valley series, I didn't know I would write this book. In fact, book 2 in the series (Finding Home), was originally supposed to be book 1. But as I wrote that book, Heather's story came to me and I felt it needed to be told first.

There are elements in this story that are deeply personal to me. My husband and I have an adoptive son who may have FASD. As is mentioned throughout the book, FASD is difficult to diagnose and we spent years trying to get an accurate diagnosis for him, not so he would have to live with a label for the rest of his life, but so we could better understand how to help him.

The therapy ranch described in chapter 23 is not a real place. I had hoped to tour a real horse therapy ranch, but they were all closed down in 2020 for reasons I'm sure I don't have to explain. So, I had to do the best I could with the information I could find online.

The therapy ranch described in this book is an amalgamation of my experiences with over fifteen different organizations in a seven-year period, both private and state run, who assist families with special needs children. As Heather discovers, there are no easy solutions, when it comes to helping kids with special-needs. But more awareness of the issues these children and their families face is needed.

I have been Jan, exhausted and wishing someone would come along who understood what we were dealing with at home and offer to give us a break. I have been Heather, experiencing a sudden rush of adrenaline that comes with witnessing your first meltdown and not knowing what to do.

There were always people who offered sympathy, who prayed for us, but who, ultimately, didn't know how to help. This book is partly as a salute to the other parents who fight for their special-needs children day after day. And partly, it's for those who have maybe heard stories of special needs kids, but who haven't really experienced what it means to help them.

Autism has gained a lot of awareness, but other disabilities are still looming in the darkness, unnoticed and unseen. I'm not looking for more sympathy. My child is grown and living on his own now. But I'll never stop being a special-needs mom. I'll never stop advocating for more and better ways to help other families like mine.

I didn't set out to write a book just to create awareness around special-needs children, and that's not what the Mylin Valley series is about. It's actually about mental health and how important our relationships are to overcoming many of the mental health problems out there.

In his messages, Pastor Barker talks about bringing about a sense of belonging in his church and his community. I specifically wanted this message to start from the pulpit and work its way out into the community because as a long time Christian, I've been to a lot of churches and church events.

I've served in almost every church I've ever attended in one form or another. I've worked in children's ministry for over twenty years, worked with youth groups, led Bible studies, led classes, written and directed plays, and I've had my heart broken by church leadership. I've also seen the hearts of others broken, and I've seen people walk away from their belief in God because of how they were treated by a church. And for many years now my heart has longed for changed in the church without knowing what needed to change.

For the record, I am not mad at churches. I'm not mad at pastors. But just as there needs to be more awareness about special needs families and what they endure, there needs to be more authenticity in church. Like Pastor Barker says, "All of this I'm talking about, and will be talking about, has to start with me. And I'm making the effort to put into practice what I'm teaching you. I hope you'll each, in turn, catch the excitement for this process and will want to begin implementing this yourself in your relationships with others in our community."

For the past four years I've studied brain science in an effort to help my son manage his emotions. And while it did help as long as he was willing to participate, I found the things I was learning had a far greater impact on myself. To such a degree that I decided I wanted to write a series of books showing what these mental health issues looked like and how being in relationship with people who were willing to help us fight through our struggles, could lead to our healing.

I have made the effort to put mindfulness and authentic relationships into practice in my own life. And I suspect it will be a life-long journey of learning and growing.

I am making an attempt at writing a series of books that both bring a little bit of awareness to different situations in small doses so it doesn't overwhelm, and encouragement in a fun, easy to read story.

I am both a teacher and a storyteller, and I hope my books do just that – teach you something you didn't know before and intrigue you to keep turning the pages. Thank you for using some of your valuable time to read one of my stories. It's an honor to have my words in your hands.

Angela E. Powell

Acknowledgments

First and foremost I want to thank God. I can clearly see how the past decade of my life has been a journey, crafted by him, to bring me to a place of inner strength and healing, as well as a deeper love and understanding of who he is and what he has designed me to do. And this book series is just a small part of what has come from my own journey in the past ten years.

I want to thank my husband, Craig, who has been very patient with me as I talked his ears off about brain science and tried to get him to do brain science exercises with me. Also, for supporting me in my desire to write and publish my own books. I love you always and forever.

I also want to thank my mom who introduced me to the LifeModel by suggesting it might be helpful to our son, Israel, which kick started my obsession with all thing's brain related.

Thank you to my editors, Doreen Martens and Kelly Messier. Your knowledge, both of the themes in this book, and of grammar, made this book a thousand times better.

I'd also like to thank 100Covers for the amazing job they did on the cover design. I can't even express how much I love this cover.

And of course, I can't forget you, dear readers. Thank you for supporting my work. Your purchase of my books, your reviews, and your letters of encouragement mean the world to me.